GREAT
AMERICAN
GHOST
STORIES

An imprint of Globe Pequot

Distributed by NATIONAL BOOK NETWORK

Copyright © 2017 by Rowman & Littlefield

British Library Cataloguing in Publication Information Available

Library of Congress Cataloging-in-Publication Data

ISBN 978-1-4930-2935-8 (paperback)
ISBN 978-1-4930-2936-5 (e-book)

♾ The paper used in this publication meets the minimum requirements of American National Standard for Information Sciences—Permanence of Paper for Printed Library Materials, ANSI/NISO Z39.48-1992.

Printed in the United States of America

CONTENTS

INTRODUCTION

Let no ill dreams disturb my rest,
Nor powers of darkness me molest.

—from Thomas Ken's
"Evening Hymn," ca. 1674

Ghost stories are as ancient as humankind, and their appeal has never waned. Anthropologists tell us that all cultures worldwide have always believed in ghosts and supernatural beings. Fear of ghosts probably springs from the eternal mystery of death, and our nearly universal dread of the unknown. Perhaps it's also tied with grief over departed loved ones—or lingering terror of departed enemies—and the hope, or fear, that their spirits may somehow continue to touch our earthly existence.

No doubt the first ghost stories were told or sung around nighttime campfires whose flickering light helped to keep the cold and mysterious darkness at bay. With the advent of writing and, later, films and television, the means of telling supernatural tales has changed and improved. But the darkness and the fear remain.

Like other cultures around the world, America has fostered a rich tradition of ghost stories. But what exactly *is* a "ghost story," as opposed to a horror story or a mystery story? In choosing stories for a volume like this one, I wondered, must I limit the selection strictly to tales of disembodied spirits? To do so seemed arbitrary and needlessly restrictive. Edgar Allan Poe (represented here by his classic "The Tell-Tale Heart") called his stories "tales of mystery and imagination." So this is what I have attempted to assemble here: some of the finest tales of mystery and imagination, from the pens of some of America's greatest authors.

Most would agree that Mark Twain belongs in this "greatest authors" category, and I've included his "A Ghost Story." Less famous than some of his work, it is nonetheless brilliantly written and suffused with Twain's trademark sardonic wit.

Many other celebrated American writers are included here, even though ghost stories may not be among their most famous works: Washington Irving, Bret Harte, Nathaniel Hawthorne, Harriet Beecher Stowe, O. Henry, and Pulitzer Prize winners Edith Wharton and Willa Cather.

Another (posthumous) Pulitzer laureate was Amy Lowell, best known for her poetry. This is evident in "The Cross-Roads," which reads almost like a poem in prose.

Elia W. Peattie, Rebecca Harding Davis, and Ambrose Bierce are relatively little known today, though all were famous in their time. Peattie and Davis were pioneering female journalists and writers, and Bierce was renowned for his satire and his frighteningly realistic descriptions of his terrible battlefield experiences in the American Civil War. Henry van Dyke was well known as a foreign-service diplomat in the administration of President Woodrow Wilson, though few remember him today. Nonetheless, he was also a supremely talented writer, as you will see when you read "The Night Call."

Wilbur Daniel Steele, Mary E. Wilkins Freeman, and George Washington Cable were perhaps best known for their many supernatural stories, though they are little read today. Perhaps this modest volume will help to change that unfortunate situation! Gertrude Morton (possibly a pseudonym) is known for only a single ghostly short story, "Mistress Marian's Light," gladly added here.

Here, then, are a few of my favorite American tales of mystery and imagination. It is my hope that you will enjoy perusing them as much as I have enjoyed collecting them, and that they will provide you with many hours of reading enjoyment.

Did you hear a strange noise just now, from out there in the darkness?

—Bill Bowers
Somewhere in New England

Editor's note: Because the stories in this volume were written long ago, some spellings, word choices, typographical errors, and punctuation may seem odd or even offensive to modern readers. Nonetheless, every effort has been made to preserve the "flavor" of the originals. This, after all, is what makes them classics.

1

~

THE CRIME OF MICAH ROOD

BY ELIA W. PEATTIE

~~~~~~

Elia W. Peattie (1862–1935) was raised in Chicago, Illinois, as Elia Wilkinson. She became a well-known journalist, first in Chicago and later in Omaha, Nebraska. The author of more than a dozen novels, she also wrote countless popular short stories, most of which first appeared in magazines. She was the mother of renowned naturalist Donald Culross Peattie (1898–1964). "The Crime of Micah Rood" first appeared in 1888.

~~~~~~

In the early part of the last century there lived in eastern Connecticut a man named Micah Rood. He was a solitary soul, and occupied a low, tumble-down house, in which he had seen his sisters and his brothers, his father and his mother, die. The mice used the bare floors for a play-ground; the swallows filled up the unused chimneys; in the cellar the gophers frolicked, and in the attic a hundred bats made their home. Micah Rood disturbed no living creature, unless now and then he killed a hare for his day's dinner, or cast bait for a glistening trout in the Shetucket. For the most part his food came from the garden and the orchard, which his father had planted and nurtured years before.

Into whatever disrepair the house had fallen, the garden bloomed and flourished like a western Eden. The brambles, with their luscious burden, clambered up the stone walls, sentineled by trim rows of English currants. The strawberry nestled among its wayward creepers, and on the trellises hung grapes of varied hues. In seemly rows, down the sunny expanse of the garden spot, grew every vegetable indigenous to the western world, or transplanted by colonial industry. Everything here took seed, and bore fruit with a prodigal exuberance. Beyond the garden lay the orchard, a labyrinth of flowers in the springtime, a paradise of verdure in the summer, and in the season of fruition a miracle of plenty.

Often the master of the orchard stood by the gate in the crisp autumn mornings, with his hat filled with apples for the children as they passed to school. There was only one tree in the orchard of whose fruit he was chary. Consequently it was the bearings of this tree that the children most wanted.

"Prithee, Master Rood," they would say, "give us some of the gold apples?"

"I sell the gold apples for siller," he would say; "content ye with the red and green ones."

In all the region there grew no counterpart to this remarkable apple. Its skin was of the clearest amber, translucent and spotless, and the pulp was white as snow, mellow yet firm, and without a flaw from the glistening skin to the even brown seeds nestling like babies in their silken cradle. Its flavor was peculiar and piquant, with a suggestion of spiciness. The fame of Micah Rood's apple, as it was called, had extended far and wide, but all efforts to engraft it upon other trees failed utterly; and the envious farmers were fain to content themselves with the rare shoots.

If there dwelt any vanity in the heart of Micah Rood, it was in the possession of this apple tree, which took the prize at all the local fairs, and carried his name beyond the neighborhood where its owner lived. For the most part he was a modest man, averse to discussions of any sort, shrinking from men and their opinions. He talked more to his dog than to any human being. He fed his mind upon a few old books, and made Nature his religion. All things that made the woods their home were his friends. He possessed himself of their secrets, and insinuated himself into their confidences. But best of all he loved the children. When they told him their sorrows, the answering tears sprang to his eyes; when they told him of their delights, his laugh woke the echoes of the Shetucket as light and free as their own. He laughed frequently when with the children, throwing back his great head, while the tears of mirth ran from his merry blue eyes.

His teeth were like pearls, and constituted his chief charm. For the rest he was rugged and firmly knit. It seemed to the children, after a time, that some cloud was hanging over the serene spirit of their friend. After he had laughed he sighed, and they saw, as he walked down the green paths that led away from his place, that he would look lovingly back at the old homestead and shake his head again and again with a perplexed and melancholy air. The merchants, too, observed that he began to be closer in his bargains, and he barreled his apples so greedily that the birds and the children were quite robbed of their autumnal feast. A winter wore away and left Micah in this changed mood. He sat through the long, dull days brooding over his fire and smoking. He made his own simple meals of mush and bacon, kept his own counsels, and neither visited nor received the neighboring folk.

One day, in a heavy January rain, the boys noticed a strange man who rode rapidly through the village, and drew rein at Micah Rood's orchard gate. He passed through the leafless orchard, and up the muddy garden paths to the old dismantled house. The boys had time to learn by heart every good point of the chestnut mare fastened to the palings before the stranger emerged from the house. Micah followed him to the gate. The stranger swung himself upon the mare with a sort of jaunty flourish, while Micah stood heavily and moodily by, chewing the end of a straw.

"Well, Master Rood," the boys heard the stranger say, "thou'st till the first of next May, but not a day of grace more." He had a decisive, keen manner that took away the breath of the boys used to men of slow action and slow speech. "Mind ye," he snapped, like an angry cur, "not another day's grace." Micah said not a word, but stolidly chewed on his straw while the stranger cut his animal briskly with the whip, and mare and rider dashed away down the dreary road. The boys began to frisk about their old friend and pulled savagely at the tails of his coat, whooping and whistling to arouse him from his reverie. Micah looked up and roared:

"Off with ye! I'm in no mood for pranks."

As a pet dog slinks away in humiliation at a blow, so the boys, hurt and indignant, skulked down the road speechless at the cruelty of their old friend.

The April sunshine was bringing the dank odors from the earth when the village beauties were thrown into a flutter of excitement. Old Geoffry Peterkin, the peddler, came with such jewelry, such stuffs, and such laces as the maidens of Shetucket had never seen the like of before.

"You are getting rich, Geoffry," the men said to him.

"No, no!" and Geoffry shook his grizzled head with a flattered smile. "Not from your women-folk. There's no such bargain-drivers between here and Boston town."

"Thou'lt be a-setting up in Boston town, Geoffry," said another. "Thou'rt getting too fine to travel pack a-back amongst us simple country folk."

"Not a bit of it," protested Geoffry. "I couldn't let the pretty dears go without their beads and their ribbons. I come and go as reg'lar as the leaves, spring, summer, and autumn."

By twilight Geoffry had made his last visit, and with his pack somewhat lightened he tramped away in the raw dusk. He went straight down the road that led to the next village, until out of sight of the windows, then turned to his right and groped his way across the commons with his eye ever fixed on a deeper blackness in the gloom. This looming blackness was the orchard of Micah Rood. He found the gate, entered, and made his way to the dismantled house. A bat swept its wing against his face as he rapped his stick upon the door.

"What witchcraft's here?" he said, and pounded harder.

There were no cracks in the heavy oaken door through which a light might filter, and old Geoffry Peterkin was blinded like any owl when the door was flung open, and Micah Rood, with a forked candle-stick in his hands, appeared, recognized him, and bade him enter. The wind drove down the hallway, blew the flame an inch from the wicks, where it burned blue a moment, and then expired, leaving the men in darkness. Geoffry stepped in, and Micah threw his weight against the door, swung the bar into place, and led Geoffry into a large bare room lit up by a blazing hickory fire. When the candles were relit, Micah said:

"Hast thou supped this night, friend Peterkin?"

"That have I, and royally too, with Rogers the smith. No more for me."

Micah Rood stirred up the fire and produced a bottle of brandy from a cupboard. He filled a small glass and offered it to his guest. It was greedily quaffed by the peddler. Micah replaced the bottle, and took no liquor himself. Pipes were then lit. Micah smoked moodily and in silence. The peddler, too, was silent. He hugged his knee, puffed vigorously at his pipe, and stared at the blazing hickory. Micah spoke first.

"Thou hast prospered since thou sold milk-pans to my mother."

"I've made a fortune with that old pack," said the peddler, pointing to the corner where it lay. "Year after year I have trudged this road, and year after year has my pack been larger and my stops longer. My stuffs, too, have changed. I carry no more milk-pans. I leave that to others. I now have jewels and cloths. Why, man! There's a fortune even now in that old pack."

He arose and unstrapped the leathern bands that bound his burden. He drew from the pack a variety of jewel-cases and handed them to Micah. "I did not show these at the village," he continued, pointing over his shoulder. "I sell those in towns."

Micah clumsily opened one or two, and looked at their contents with restless eyes. There were rubies as red as a serpent's tongue; silver, carved as daintily as hoar-frost, gleaming with icy diamonds; pearls that nestled like precious eggs in fairy golden nests; turquois gleaming from beds of enamel, and bracelets of ebony capped with topaz balls.

"These," laughed Geoffry, dangling a translucent necklace of amber, "I keep to ward off ill-luck. She will be a witch indeed that gets me to sell these. But if thou'lt marry, good Master Rood, I'll give them to thy bride."

He chuckled, gasped, and gurgled mightily; but Micah checked his exuberance by looking up fiercely.

"There'll be never a bride for me," he said. "She'd be killed here with the rats and the damp rot. It takes gold to get a woman."

"Bah!" sneered Geoffry. "It takes youth, boy, blue eye, good laugh, and a strong leg. Why, if a bride could be had for gold, I've got that."

He unrolled a shimmering azure satin, and took from it two bags of soft, stout leather.

"There is where I keep my yellow boys shut up!" the old fellow cried in great glee; "and when I let them out, they'll bring me anything I want, Micah Rood, except a true heart. How have things prospered with thee?" he added, as he shot a shrewd glance at Micah from beneath his eyebrows.

"Bad," confessed Micah, "very bad. Everything has been against me of late."

"I say, boy," cried the peddler, suddenly, "I haven't been over this old house for years. Take the light and show us around."

"No," said Micah, shaking his head doggedly. "It is in bad shape and I would feel that I was showing a friend who was in rags."

"Nonsense!" cried the peddler, bursting into a hearty laugh. "Thou need'st not fear, I'll ne'er cut thy old friend."

He had replaced his stuffs, and now seized the branched candle-stick and waved his hand toward the door.

"Lead the way," he cried. "I want to see how things look," and Micah Rood sullenly obeyed.

From room to room they went in the miserable cold and the gloom. The candle threw a faint gleam through the unkept apartments, noxious with dust and decay. Not a flaw escaped the eye of the peddler. He ran his fingers into the cracks of the doors, he counted the panes of broken glass, he remarked the gaps in the plastering.

"The dry rot has got into the wainscoting," he said jauntily.

Micah Rood was burning with impotent anger. He tried to lead the peddler past one door, but the old man's keen eyes were too quick for him, and he kicked the door open with his foot.

"What have we here?" he cried.

It was the room where Micah and his brothers had slept when they were children. The little dismantled beds stood side by side. A workbench with some miniature tools was by the curtainless window. Everything that met his gaze brought with it a flood of early recollections.

"Here's a rare lot of old truck," Geoffry cried. "The first thing I should do would be to pitch this out of doors."

Micah caught him by the arm and pushed him from the room.

"It happens that it is not thine to pitch," he said.

Geoffry Peterkin began to laugh a low, irritating chuckle. He laughed all the way back to the room where the fire was. He laughed still as Micah showed him his room—the room where he was to pass the night; chuckled and guffawed, and clapped Micah on the back as they finally bade each other good-night. The master of the house went back and stood before the dying fire alone.

"What can he mean, in God's name?" he asked himself. "Does he know of the mortgage?"

Micah knew that the peddler, who was well off, frequently negotiated and dealt in the commercial paper of farmers. Pride and anger tore at his heart like wild beasts. What would the neighbors say when they saw his father's son driven from the house that had belonged to the family for generations? How could he endure their surprise and contempt? What would the children say when they found a stranger in possession of the famous apple-tree? "I've got no more to pay it with," he cried in helpless anguish, "than I had the day the cursed lawyer came here with his threats."

He determined to find out what Peterkin knew of the matter. He spread a bear's skin before the fire and threw himself upon it and fell into a feverish sleep, which ended long before the purple dawn broke.

He cooked a breakfast of bacon and corn cake, made a cup of coffee, and aroused his guest. The peddler, clean, keen, and alert, noted slyly the sullen heaviness of Micah. The meal was eaten in silence, and when it was finished, Geoffry put on his cloak, adjusted his pack, and prepared to leave. Micah put on his hat, took a pruning-knife from a shelf, remarking as he did so:

"I go early about my work in the orchard," and followed the peddler to the door. The trees in the orchard had begun to shimmer with young green. The perfume, so familiar to Micah, so suggestive of the place that he held dearer than all the rest of the world beside, wrought upon him till his curiosity got the better of his discretion.

"It is hard work for one man to keep up a place like this and make it pay," he remarked.

Geoffry smiled slyly, but said nothing.

"Bad luck has got the start of me of late," the master continued with an attempt at real candor.

The peddler knocked the tops off some gaunt, dead weeds that stood by the path.

"So I have heard," he said.

"What else didst thou hear?" cried Micah, quickly, his face burning, and shame and anger flashing from his blue eyes.

"Well," said the peddler, with a great show of caution, "I heard the mortgage was a good investment for any one who wanted to buy."

"Perhaps thou know'st more about it than that," sneered Micah.

Peterkin blew on his hands and rubbed them with a knowing air.

"Well," he said, "I know what I know."

"D— you," cried Micah, clinching his fist, "out with it!"

The peddler was getting heated. He thrust his hand into his breast and drew out a paper.

"When May comes about, Master Rood, I'll ask thee to look at the face of this document."

"Thou art a sneak!" foamed Micah. "A white-livered, cowardly sneak!"

"Rough words to call a man on his own property," said the peddler, with a malicious grin.

The insult was the deepest he could have offered to the man before him. A flood of ungovernable emotions rushed over Micah. The impulse latent in all angry animals to strike, to crush, to kill, came over him. He rushed forward madly, then the passion ebbed, and he saw the peddler on the ground. The pruning-knife in his own hand was red with blood. He gazed in cold horror, then tried in a weak, trembling way to heap leaves upon the body to hide it from his sight. He could gather only small hand-fuls, and they fluttered away in the wind.

The light was getting brighter. People would soon be passing down the road. He walked up and down aimlessly for a time, and then ran to the garden. He returned with a spade and began digging furiously. He made a trench between the dead man and the tree under which he had fallen; and when it was finished he pushed the body in with his foot, not daring to touch it with his hands.

Of the peddler's death there was no doubt. The rigid face and the blood-drenched garments over the heart attested the fact. So copiously had the blood gushed forth that all the soil, and the dead leaves about the body, and the exposed roots of the tree were stained with it. Involuntarily Micah looked up at the tree. He uttered an exclamation of dismay. It was the tree of the gold apples.

After a moment's silence he recommenced his work and tossed back the earth in mad haste. He smoothed the earth so carefully that when he had finished not even a mound appeared. He scattered dead leaves over the freshly turned earth, and then walked slowly back to the house.

For the first time the shadow that hung over it, the gloom deep as despair that looked from its vacant windows, struck him. The gloss of familiarity had hidden from his eyes what had long been patent to others—the decay, the ruin, the solitude. It swept over him as an icy breaker sweeps over a drowning man. The rats ran from him as he entered the hall. He held the arm on which the blood was rapidly drying far from him, as if he feared to let it touch his body with its confession of crime. The sleeve had stiffened to the arm, and inspired him with a nervous horror, as if a reptile was twined about it. He flung off his coat, and finally, trembling and sick, divested himself of a flannel undergarment, and still from fingertip to elbow there were blotches and smears on his arm. He realized at once the necessity of destroying the garments; and, naked to the waist, he stirred up the dying embers of the fire and threw the garments on. The heavy flannel of the coat refused to burn, and he threw it deeper and deeper in with a poker till he saw with dismay that he had quenched the fire.

"It is fate!" he cried. "I can not destroy them."

He lit a fire three times, but his haste and his confused horror made him throw on the heavy garments every time and strangle the infant blaze. At last he took them to the garret and locked them in an old chest. Starting at the shadows among the rafters, and the creaking of the boards, he crept back through the biting chill of the vacant rooms to the one that he occupied, and washed his arm again and again, until the deep glow on it seemed like another blood-stain.

After that for weeks he worked in his garden by day, and at night slept on the floor with the candles burning, and his hand on his flint-lock.

Meanwhile in the orchard the leaves budded and spread, and the perfumed blossoms came. The branches of the tree of the gold apples grew pink with swelling buds. Near that spot Micah never went. He felt as if his feet would be grasped by spectral hands.

One night a swelling wind arose, strong, steady, warm, seeming palpable to the touch like a fabric. In the morning the orchard had flung all its banners to the air. It dazzled Micah's eyes as he looked upon the tossing clouds of pink and white fragrance. But as his eye roamed about the waving splendor he caught sight of a thing that riveted him to the spot with awe.

The tree of the gold apples had blossomed blood-red.

That day he did no work. He sat from early morning till the light waned in the west, gazing at the tree flaunting its blossoms red as blood against the shifting sky. Few neighbors came that way; and as the tree stood in the heart of the orchard, fewer yet noticed its accursed beauty. To those that did, Micah stammeringly gave a hint of some ingenious ingrafting, the secret of which was to make his fortune. But though the rest of the world wondered and wagged its head and doubted not that it was some witchcraft, the children were enraptured. They stole into the orchard and pilfered handfuls of the roseate flowers, and bore them away to school; the girls fastened them in their braids or wore them above their innocent hearts, and the boys trimmed their hat-bands and danced away in glee like youthful Corydons.

Spring-time passed and its promises of plenty were fulfilled. In the garden there grew a luxury of greenness; in the orchard the boughs lagged low. Micah Rood toiled day and night. He visited no house, he sought no company. If a neighbor saw him in the field and came for a chat, before he had reached the spot Micah had hidden himself.

"He used to be as ready for the news as the rest of us," said they to themselves, "and he had a laugh like a horse. His sweetheart has jilted him, most like."

When the purple on the grapes began to grow through the amber, and the mellowed apples dropped from their stems, the children began to flock about the orchard gate like buzzards about a battle-field. But they found the gate padlocked and the board fence prickling with pointed sticks. Micah they saw but seldom, and his face, once so sunny, was as terrible to them as the angel's with the flaming sword that kept guard over the gates of Eden. So the sinless little Adams and Eves had no choice but to turn away with empty pockets.

However, one morning, accident took Micah to the bolted gate just as the children came trooping home in the early autumn sunset; for in those days they kept students of any age at work as many hours of the day as possible. A little fay, with curls as sunny as the tendrils of the grape, caught sight of him first. Her hat was wreathed with scarlet maple leaves; her dress was as ruddy as the cheeks of the apples. She seemed the sprite of autumn. She ran toward him, with arms outstretched, crying:

"Oh, Master Rood! Do come and play. Where hast thou been so long? We have wanted some apples, and the plaguy old gate was locked."

For the first time for months the pall of remembrance that hung over Micah's dead happiness was lifted, and the spirit of that time came back to him. He caught the little one in his brawny arms and threw her high, while she shrieked with terror and delight. After this the children gave no quarter. The breach begun, they sallied in and stormed the fortress. Like a dream of water to a man who is perishing of thirst, who knows while he yet dreams that he must wake and find his bliss an agony, this hour of innocence was to Micah. He ran, and leaped, and frolicked with the children in the shade of the trees till the orchard rang with their shouts, while the sky changed from daffodil to crimson, from crimson to gray, and sank into a deep autumn twilight. Micah stuffed their little pockets with fruit, and bade them run home. But they lingered dissatisfied.

"I wish he would give us of the golden apples," they whispered among themselves. At last one plucked up courage.

"Good Master Rood, give us of the gold apples, if thou please."

Micah shook his head sternly. They entreated him with eyes and tongues. They saw a chance for a frolic. They clung to him, climbed his back, and danced about him, shouting:

"The gold apples! The gold apples!"

A sudden change came over him; he marched to the tree with a look men wear when they go to battle.

"There is blood in them!" he cried hoarsely. "They are accursed—accursed!"

The children shrieked with delight at what they thought a jest.

"Blood in the apples! Ha! ha! ha!" and they rolled over one another on the grass, fighting for the windfalls.

"I tell ye 'tis so!" Micah continued. He took one of the apples and broke it into halves.

"Look," he cried, and in his eyes there came a look in which the light of reason was waning. The children pressed about him, peeping over each other at the apple. On the broken side of both halves, from the rind to the core, was a blood-red streak the width of a child's little finger. An amazed silence fell on the little group.

"Home with ye now!" he cried huskily. "Home with ye, and tell what ye have seen! Run, ye brats."

"Then let us take some of the apples with us," they persisted.

"Ha!" he cried, "ye tale-bearers! I know the trick ye'd play! Here then—"

He shook the tree like a giant. The apples rolled to the ground so fast that they looked like strands of amber beads. The children, laughing and shouting, gathered them as they fell. They began to compare the red spots. In some the drop of blood was found just under the skin, and a thin streak of carmine that penetrated to the core and colored the silvery pulp; in others it was an isolated clot, the size of a whortleberry, and on a few a narrow crescent of crimson reached half-way around the outside of the shining rind.

Suddenly a noise, not loud but agonizing, startled the little ones. They looked up at their friend. He had become horrible. His face was contorted until it was unrecognizable; his eyes were fixed on the ground as if he beheld a specter there. Shrieking, they ran from the orchard, nor cast one fearful glance behind.

The next day the smith, filled with curiosity by the tales of the children, found an odd hour in which to visit Micah Rood's house. He invited the tailor, a man thin with hunger for gossip, to go with him. The gate of the orchard stood open, flapping on its hinges as the children had left it. The visitors sauntered through, thinking to find Micah in the house, for it was the noon hour. They tasted of this fruit and that, tried a pear, now an apricot, now a pippin.

"The tree of the gold apples is right in the center," said the smith.

He pointed. The tailor looked; then his legs doubled under him as naturally as they ever did on the bench. The smith looked; his arm dropped by his side. After a time the two men went on, clinging to each other like children in the dark.

Micah Rood, with his sunny hair tangled in the branches, his tongue black and protruding, his face purple, and his clinched hands stained with dirt, hung from the tree of the golden apples. Beneath him, in a trench, from which the ground had been clawed by human hands, lay a shapeless, discolored bundle of clothes. A skull lay at one end of the trench, and beneath it a moldy pack was found with precious stones amid the decaying contents.

2

THE DEVIL AND TOM WALKER

BY WASHINGTON IRVING

Washington Irving (1783–1859) is the author of the world-famous stories "The Legend of Sleepy Hollow" and "Rip van Winkle," as well as biographies of George Washington, Muhammad, and others. Born in New York City (for which he coined the popular nickname "Gotham"), he was one of the first Americans to become an international best-selling author. Irving also served as U.S. ambassador to Spain under President John Tyler. "The Devil and Tom Walker" was first published in 1824.

A few miles from Boston, in Massachusetts, there is a deep inlet winding several miles into the interior of the country from Charles Bay, and terminating in a thickly wooded swamp, or morass.

On one side of this inlet is a beautiful dark grove; on the opposite side the land rises abruptly from the water's edge, into a high ridge on which grow a few scattered oaks of great age and immense size. Under one of these gigantic trees, according to old stories, there was a great amount of treasure buried by Kidd the pirate.

The inlet allowed a facility to bring the money in a boat secretly and at night to the very foot of the hill. The elevation of the place permitted a good look out to be kept that no one was at hand, while the remarkable trees formed good landmarks by which the place might easily be found again. The old stories add, moreover, that the devil presided at the hiding of the money, and took it under his guardianship; but this, it is well known, he always does with buried treasure, particularly when it has been ill gotten. Be that as it may, Kidd never returned to recover his wealth; being shortly after seized at Boston, sent out to England, and there hanged for a pirate.

About the year 1727, just at the time when earthquakes were prevalent in New England, and shook many tall sinners down upon their knees, there lived near this place a meagre miserly fellow of the name of Tom Walker.

He had a wife as miserly as himself; they were so miserly that they even conspired to cheat each other. Whatever the woman could lay hands on she hid away: a hen could not cackle but she was on the alert to secure the new-laid egg. Her husband was continually prying about to detect her secret hoards, and many and fierce were the conflicts that took place about what ought to have been common property.

They lived in a forlorn looking house, that stood alone and had an air of starvation. A few straggling savin trees, emblems of sterility, grew near it; no smoke ever curled from its chimney; no traveller stopped at its door. A miserable horse, whose ribs were as articulate as the bars of a gridiron, stalked about a field where a thin carpet of moss, scarcely covering the ragged beds of pudding stone, tantalized and balked his hunger; and sometimes he would lean his head over the fence, look piteously at the passer by, and seem to petition deliverance from this land of famine. The house and its inmates had altogether a bad name. Tom's wife was a tall termagant, fierce of temper, loud of tongue, and strong of arm. Her voice was often heard in wordy warfare with her husband; and his face sometimes showed signs that their conflicts were not confined to words. No one ventured, however, to interfere between them; the lonely wayfarer shrunk within himself at the horrid clamour and clapper clawing; eyed the den of discord askance, and hurried on his way, rejoicing, if a bachelor, in his celibacy.

One day that Tom Walker had been to a distant part of the neighbourhood, he took what he considered a short cut homewards through the swamp. Like most short cuts, it was an ill chosen route. The swamp was thickly grown with great gloomy pines and hemlocks, some of them ninety feet high; which made it dark at noonday, and a retreat for all the owls of the neighbourhood. It was full of pits and quagmires, partly covered with weeds and mosses; where the green surface often betrayed the traveller into a gulf of black smothering mud; there were also dark and stagnant pools, the abodes of the tadpole, the bull-frog, and the water snake, and where trunks of pines and hemlocks lay half drowned, half rotting, looking like alligators, sleeping in the mire.

Tom had long been picking his way cautiously through this treacherous forest; stepping from tuft to tuft of rushes and roots which afforded precarious footholds among deep sloughs; or pacing carefully, like a cat, along the prostrate trunks of trees; startled now and then by the sudden screaming of the bittern, or the quacking of a wild duck, rising on the wing from some solitary pool. At length he arrived at a piece of firm ground, which ran out like a peninsula into the deep bosom of the swamp. It had been one of the strong holds of the Indians during their wars with the first colonists. Here they had thrown up a kind of fort which they had looked upon as almost impregnable, and had used as a place of refuge for their squaws and children. Nothing remained of the Indian fort but a few embankments gradually sinking to the level of the surrounding earth, and already overgrown in part by oaks and other forest trees, the foliage of which formed a contrast to the dark pines and hemlocks of the swamp.

It was late in the dusk of evening that Tom Walker reached the old fort, and he paused there for a while to rest himself. Any one but he would have felt unwilling to linger in this lonely melancholy place, for the common people had a bad opinion of it from the stories handed down from the time of the Indian wars; when it was asserted that the savages held incantations here and made sacrifices to the evil spirit. Tom Walker, however, was not a man to be troubled with any fears of the kind.

He reposed himself for some time on the trunk of a fallen hemlock, listening to the boding cry of the tree toad, and delving with his walking staff into a mound of black mould at his feet. As he turned up the soil unconsciously, his staff struck against something hard. He raked it out of the vegetable mould, and lo! a cloven skull with an Indian tomahawk buried deep in it, lay before him. The rust on the weapon showed the time that had elapsed since this death blow had been given. It was a dreary memento of the fierce struggle that had taken place in this last foothold of the Indian warriors.

"Humph!" said Tom Walker, as he gave the skull a kick to shake the dirt from it.

"Let that skull alone!" said a gruff voice.

Tom lifted up his eyes and beheld a great black man, seated directly opposite him on the stump of a tree. He was exceedingly surprised, having neither seen nor heard any one approach, and he was still more perplexed on observing, as well as the gathering gloom would permit, that the stranger was neither negro nor Indian. It is true, he was dressed in a rude, half Indian garb, and had a red belt or sash swathed round his body, but his face was neither black nor copper colour, but swarthy and dingy and begrimed with soot, as if he had been accustomed to toil among fires and forges. He had a shock of coarse black hair, that stood out from his head in all directions; and bore an axe on his shoulder.

He scowled for a moment at Tom with a pair of great red eyes.

"What are you doing in my grounds?" said the black man, with a hoarse growling voice.

"Your grounds?" said Tom, with a sneer; "no more your grounds than mine: they belong to Deacon Peabody."

"Deacon Peabody be d—d," said the stranger, "as I flatter myself he will be, if he does not look more to his own sins and less to his neighbour's. Look yonder, and see how Deacon Peabody is faring."

Tom looked in the direction that the stranger pointed, and beheld one of the great trees, fair and flourishing without, but rotten at the core, and saw that it had been nearly hewn through, so that the first high wind was likely to blow it down. On the bark of the tree was scored the name of Deacon Peabody. He now looked round and found most of the tall trees marked with the name of some great men of the colony, and all more or less scored by the axe. The one on which he had been seated, and which had evidently just been hewn down, bore the name of Crowninshield; and he recollected a mighty rich man of that name, who made a vulgar display of wealth, which it was whispered he had acquired by buccaneering.

"He's just ready for burning!" said the black man, with a growl of triumph. "You see I am likely to have a good stock of firewood for winter."

"But what right have you," said Tom, "to cut down Deacon Peabody's timber?"

"The right of prior claim," said the other. "This woodland belonged to me long before one of your white faced race put foot upon the soil."

"And pray, who are you, if I may be so bold?" said Tom.

"Oh, I go by various names. I am the Wild Huntsman in some countries; the Black Miner in others. In this neighbourhood I am known by the name of the Black Woodsman. I am he to whom the red men devoted this spot, and now and then roasted a white man by way of sweet smelling sacrifice. Since the red men have been exterminated by you white savages, I amuse myself by presiding at the persecutions of quakers and anabaptists; I am the great patron and prompter of slave dealers, and the grand master of the Salem witches."

"The upshot of all which is, that, if I mistake not," said Tom, sturdily, "you are he commonly called Old Scratch."

"The same at your service!" replied the black man, with a half civil nod.

Such was the opening of this interview, according to the old story, though it has almost too familiar an air to be credited. One would think that to meet with such a singular personage in this wild lonely place, would have shaken any man's nerves: but Tom was a hard-minded fellow, not easily daunted, and he had lived so long with a termagant wife, that he did not even fear the devil.

It is said that after this commencement, they had a long and earnest conversation together, as Tom returned homewards. The black man told him of great sums of money which had been buried by Kidd the pirate, under the oak trees on the high ridge not far from the morass. All these were under his command and protected by his power, so that none could find them but such as propitiated his favour. These he offered to place within Tom Walker's reach, having conceived an especial kindness for him: but they were to be had only on certain conditions. What these conditions were, may easily be surmised, though Tom never disclosed them publicly. They must have been very hard, for he required time to think of them, and he was not a man to stick at trifles where money was in view. When they had reached the edge of the swamp the stranger paused.

"What proof have I that all you have been telling me is true?" said Tom.

"There is my signature," said the black man, pressing his finger on Tom's forehead. So saying, he turned off among the thickets of the swamp, and seemed, as Tom said, to go down, down, down, into the earth, until nothing but his head and shoulders could be seen, and so on until he totally disappeared.

When Tom reached home he found the black print of a finger burnt, as it were, into his forehead, which nothing could obliterate.

The first news his wife had to tell him was the sudden death of Absalom Crowninshield the rich buccaneer. It was announced in the papers with the usual flourish, that "a great man had fallen in Israel."

Tom recollected the tree which his black friend had just hewn down, and which was ready for burning. "Let the freebooter roast," said Tom, "who cares!" He now felt convinced that all he had heard and seen was no illusion.

He was not prone to let his wife into his confidence; but as this was an uneasy secret, he willingly shared it with her. All her avarice was awakened at the mention of hidden gold, and she urged her husband to comply with the black man's terms and secure what would make them wealthy for life. However Tom might have felt disposed to sell himself to the devil, he was determined not to do so to oblige his wife; so he flatly refused out of the mere spirit of contradiction. Many and bitter were the quarrels they had on the subject, but the more she talked the more resolute was Tom not to be damned to please her. At length she determined to drive the bargain on her own account, and if she succeeded, to keep all the gain to herself.

Being of the same fearless temper as her husband, she set off for the old Indian fort towards the close of a summer's day. She was many hours absent. When she came back she was reserved and sullen in her replies. She spoke something of a black man whom she had met about twilight, hewing at the root of a tall tree. He was sulky, however, and would not come to terms; she was to go again with a propitiatory offering, but what it was she forebore to say.

The next evening she set off again for the swamp, with her apron heavily laden. Tom waited and waited for her, but in vain: midnight came, but she did not make her appearance; morning, noon, night returned, but still she did not come. Tom now grew uneasy for her safety; especially as he found she had carried off in her apron the silver teapot and spoons and every portable article of value. Another night elapsed, another morning came; but no wife. In a word, she was never heard of more.

What was her real fate nobody knows, in consequence of so many pretending to know. It is one of those facts that have become confounded by a variety of historians. Some asserted that she lost her way among the tangled mazes of the swamp and sunk into some pit or slough; others, more uncharitable, hinted that she had eloped with the household booty, and made off to some other province; while others assert that the tempter had decoyed her into a dismal quagmire on top of which her hat was found lying. In confirmation of this, it was said a great black man with an axe on his shoulder was seen late that very evening coming out of the swamp, carrying a bundle tied in a check apron, with an air of surly triumph.

The most current and probable story, however, observes that Tom Walker grew so anxious about the fate of his wife and his property that he set out at length to seek them both at the Indian fort. During a long summer's afternoon he searched about the gloomy place, but no wife was to be seen. He called her name repeatedly, but she was no where to be heard. The bittern alone responded to his voice, as he flew screaming by; or the bull-frog croaked dolefully from a neighbouring pool. At length, it is said, just in the brown hour of twilight, when the owls began to hoot and the bats to flit about, his attention was attracted by the clamour of carrion crows that were hovering about a cypress tree. He looked and beheld a bundle tied in a check apron and hanging in the branches of the tree; with a great vulture perched hard by, as if keeping watch upon it. He leaped with joy, for he recognized his wife's apron, and supposed it to contain the household valuables.

"Let us get hold of the property," said he, consolingly to himself, "and we will endeavour to do without the woman."

As he scrambled up the tree the vulture spread its wide wings, and sailed off screaming into the deep shadows of the forest. Tom seized the check apron, but, woful sight! found nothing but a heart and liver tied up in it.

Such, according to the most authentic old story, was all that was to be found of Tom's wife. She had probably attempted to deal with the black man as she had been accustomed to deal with her husband; but though a female scold is generally considered a match for the devil, yet in this instance she appears to have had the worst of it. She must have died game however; for it is said Tom noticed many prints of cloven feet deeply stamped about the tree, and several handsful of hair, that looked as if they had been plucked from the coarse black shock of the woodsman. Tom knew his wife's prowess by experience. He shrugged his shoulders as he looked at the signs of a fierce clapper clawing.

"Egad," said he to himself, "Old Scratch must have had a tough time of it!"

Tom consoled himself for the loss of his property with the loss of his wife; for he was a man of fortitude. He even felt something like gratitude towards the black woodsman, who he considered had done him a kindness. He sought, therefore, to cultivate a farther acquaintance with him, but for some time without success; the old black legs played shy, for whatever people may think, he is not always to be had for calling for; he knows how to play his cards when pretty sure of his game.

At length, it is said, when delay had whetted Tom's eagerness to the quick, and prepared him to agree to any thing rather than not gain the promised treasure, he met the black man one evening in his usual woodsman dress, with his axe on his shoulder, sauntering along the edge of the swamp, and humming a tune. He affected to receive Tom's advance with great indifference, made brief replies, and went on humming his tune.

By degrees, however, Tom brought him to business, and they began to haggle about the terms on which the former was to have the pirate's treasure. There was one condition which need not be mentioned, being generally understood in all cases where the devil grants favours; but there were others about which, though of less importance, he was inflexibly obstinate. He insisted that the money found through his means should be employed in his service. He proposed, therefore, that Tom should employ it in the black traffick; that is to say, that he should fit out a slave ship. This, however, Tom resolutely refused; he was bad enough in all conscience; but the devil himself could not tempt him to turn slave dealer.

Finding Tom so squeamish on this point, he did not insist upon it, but proposed instead that he should turn usurer; the devil being extremely anxious for the increase of usurers, looking upon them as his peculiar people.

To this no objections were made, for it was just to Tom's taste.

"You shall open a broker's shop in Boston next month," said the black man.

"I'll do it to-morrow, if you wish," said Tom Walker.

"You shall lend money at two per cent. a month."

"Egad, I'll charge four!" replied Tom Walker.

"You shall extort bonds, foreclose mortgages, drive the merchant to bankruptcy-"

"I'll drive him to the d—l," cried Tom Walker, eagerly.

"You are the usurer for my money!" said the black legs, with delight. "When will you want the rhino?"

"This very night."

"Done!" said the devil.

"Done!" said Tom Walker. So they shook hands, and struck a bargain.

A few days' time saw Tom Walker seated behind his desk in a counting house in Boston. His reputation for a ready moneyed man, who would lend money out for a good consideration, soon spread abroad. Every body remembers the days of Governor Belcher, when money was particularly scarce. It was a time of paper credit. The country had been deluged with government bills; the famous Land Bank had been established; there had been a rage for speculating; the people had run mad with schemes for new settlements; for building cities in the wilderness; land jobbers went about with maps of grants, and townships, and Eldorados, lying nobody knew where, but which every body was ready to purchase. In a word, the great speculating fever which breaks out every now and then in the country, had raged to an alarming degree, and every body was dreaming of making sudden fortunes from nothing. As usual the fever had subsided; the dream had gone off, and the imaginary fortunes with it; the patients were left in doleful plight, and the whole country resounded with the consequent cry of "hard times."

At this propitious time of public distress did Tom Walker set up as a usurer in Boston. His door was soon thronged by customers. The needy and the adventurous; the gambling speculator; the dreaming land jobber; the thriftless tradesman; the merchant with cracked credit; in short, every one driven to raise money by desperate means and desperate sacrifices, hurried to Tom Walker.

Thus Tom was the universal friend of the needy, and he acted like a "friend in need"; that is to say, he always exacted good pay and good security. In proportion to the distress of the applicant was the hardness of his terms. He accumulated bonds and mortgages; gradually squeezed his customers closer and closer; and sent them at length, dry as a sponge, from his door.

In this way he made money hand over hand; became a rich and mighty man, and exalted his cocked hat upon change. He built himself, as usual, a vast house, out of ostentation; but left the greater part of it unfinished and unfurnished out of parsimony. He even set up a carriage in the fullness of his vain glory, though he nearly starved the horses which drew it; and as the ungreased wheels groaned and screeched on the axle trees, you would have thought you heard the souls of the poor debtors he was squeezing.

As Tom waxed old, however, he grew thoughtful. Having secured the good things of this world, he began to feel anxious about those of the next. He thought with regret on the bargain he had made with his black friend, and set his wits to work to cheat him out of the conditions. He became, therefore, all of a sudden, a violent church goer. He prayed loudly and strenuously as if heaven were to be taken by force of lungs. Indeed, one might always tell when he had sinned most during the week, by the clamour of his Sunday devotion. The quiet christians who had been modestly and steadfastly travelling Zionward, were struck with self reproach at seeing themselves so suddenly outstripped in their career by this new-made convert. Tom was as rigid in religious, as in money matters; he was a stern supervisor and censurer of his neighbours, and seemed to think every sin entered up to their account became a credit on his own side of the page. He even talked of the expediency of reviving the persecution of quakers and anabaptists. In a word, Tom's zeal became as notorious as his riches.

Still, in spite of all this strenuous attention to forms, Tom had a lurking dread that the devil, after all, would have his due. That he might not be taken unawares, therefore, it is said he always carried a small Bible in his coat pocket. He had also a great folio Bible on his counting house desk, and would frequently be found reading it when people called on business; on such occasions he would lay his green spectacles on the book, to mark the place, while he turned round to drive some usurious bargain.

Some say that Tom grew a little crack brained in his old days, and that fancying his end approaching, he had his horse new shod, saddled and bridled, and buried with his feet uppermost; because he supposed that at the last day the world would be turned upside down; in which case he should find his horse standing ready for mounting, and he was determined at the worst to give his old friend a run for it. This, however, is probably a mere old wives fable. If he really did take such a precaution it was totally superfluous; at least so says the authentic old legend which closes his story in the following manner.

On one hot afternoon in the dog days, just as a terrible black thundergust was coming up, Tom sat in his counting house in his white linen cap and India silk morning gown. He was on the point of foreclosing a mortgage, by which he would complete the ruin of an unlucky land speculator for whom he had professed the greatest friendship. The poor land jobber begged him to grant a few months indulgence. Tom had grown testy and irritated and refused another day.

"My family will be ruined and brought upon the parish," said the land jobber.

"Charity begins at home," replied Tom, "I must take care of myself in these hard times."

"You have made so much money out of me," said the speculator.

Tom lost his patience and his piety. "The devil take me," said he, "if I have made a farthing!"

Just then there were three loud knocks at the street door. He stepped out to see who was there. A black man was holding a black horse which neighed and stamped with impatience.

"Tom, you're come for!" said the black fellow, gruffly. Tom shrunk back, but too late. He had left his little Bible at the bottom of his coat pocket, and his big Bible on the desk buried under the mortgage he was about to foreclose: never was sinner taken more unawares. The black man whisked him like a child astride the horse and away he galloped in the midst of a thunder storm. The clerks stuck their pens behind their ears and stared after him from the windows. Away went Tom Walker, dashing down the streets; his white cap bobbing up and down; his morning gown fluttering in the wind, and his steed striking fire out of the pavement at every bound. When the clerks turned to look for the black man he had disappeared.

Tom Walker never returned to foreclose the mortgage. A countryman who lived on the borders of the swamp, reported that in the height of the thundergust he had heard a great clattering of hoofs and a howling along the road, and that when he ran to the window he just caught sight of a figure, such as I have described, on a horse that galloped like mad across the fields, over the hills and down into the black hemlock swamp towards the old Indian fort; and that shortly after a thunderbolt fell in that direction which seemed to set the whole forest in a blaze.

The good people of Boston shook their heads and shrugged their shoulders, but had been so much accustomed to witches and goblins and tricks of the devil in all kinds of shapes from the first settlement of the colony, that they were not so much horror struck as might have been expected. Trustees were appointed to take charge of Tom's effects. There was nothing, however, to administer upon. On searching his coffers all his bonds and mortgages were found reduced to cinders. In place of gold and silver his iron chest was filled with chips and shavings; two skeletons lay in his stable instead of his half starved horses, and the very next day his great house took fire and was burnt to the ground.

Such was the end of Tom Walker and his ill gotten wealth. Let all griping money brokers lay this story to heart. The truth of it is not to be doubted. The very hole under the oak trees, from whence he dug Kidd's money is to be seen to this day; and the neighbouring swamp and old Indian fort is often haunted on stormy nights by a figure on horseback, in a morning gown and white cap, which is doubtless the troubled spirit of the usurer. In fact, the story has resolved itself into a proverb, and is the origin of that popular saying, prevalent throughout New England, of "The Devil and Tom Walker."

3

AN OCCURRENCE AT OWL CREEK BRIDGE

BY AMBROSE BIERCE

Born in Ohio, Ambrose Bierce (1842–1914?) became a celebrated journalist and man of letters. At age nineteen, early in the American Civil War, he enlisted in the Union Army. Bierce's experience of terrible bloodshed at Shiloh, Antietam, Kennesaw Mountain, and other well-known battlefields inspired a dark view of life and humanity that infused his work. He wrote many stories of horror and the supernatural. At age seventy-one, in 1913, Bierce traveled to Mexico to cover the Mexican Revolution. He disappeared, and the circumstances and date of his death remain unknown. "An Occurrence at Owl Creek Bridge" appeared in 1890.

A man stood upon a railroad bridge in northern Alabama, looking down into the swift water twenty feet below. The man's hands were behind his back, the wrists bound with a cord. A rope closely encircled his neck. It was attached to a stout cross-timber above his head and the slack fell to the level of his knees. Some loose boards laid upon the sleepers supporting the metals of the railway supplied a footing for him and his executioners—two private soldiers of the Federal army, directed by a sergeant who in civil life may have been a deputy sheriff. At a short remove upon the same temporary platform was an officer in the uniform of his rank, armed. He was a captain. A sentinel at each end of the bridge stood with his rifle in the position known as "support," that is to say, vertical in front of the left shoulder, the hammer resting on the forearm thrown straight across the chest—a formal and unnatural position, enforcing an erect carriage of the body. It did not appear to be the duty of these two men to know what was occurring at the center of the bridge; they merely blockaded the two ends of the foot planking that traversed it.

Beyond one of the sentinels nobody was in sight; the railroad ran straight away into a forest for a hundred yards, then, curving, was lost to view. Doubtless there was an outpost farther along. The other bank of the stream was open ground—a gentle acclivity topped with a stockade of vertical tree trunks, loopholed for rifles, with a single embrasure through which protruded the muzzle of a brass cannon commanding the bridge. Midway of the slope between the bridge and fort were the spectators—a single company of infantry in line, at "parade rest," the butts of the rifles on the ground, the barrels inclining slightly backward against the right shoulder, the hands crossed upon the stock. A lieutenant stood at the right of the line, the point of his sword upon the ground, his left hand resting upon his right. Excepting the group of four at the center of the bridge, not a man moved. The company faced the bridge, staring stonily, motionless. The sentinels, facing the banks of the stream, might have been statues to adorn the bridge. The captain stood with folded arms, silent, observing the work of his subordinates, but making no sign. Death is a dignitary who when he comes announced is to be received with formal manifestations of respect, even by those most familiar with him. In the code of military etiquette silence and fixity are forms of deference.

The man who was engaged in being hanged was apparently about thirty-five years of age. He was a civilian, if one might judge from his habit, which was that of a planter. His features were good—a straight nose, firm mouth, broad forehead, from which his long, dark hair was combed straight back, falling behind his ears to the collar of his well-fitting frock coat. He wore a mustache and pointed beard, but no whiskers; his eyes were large and dark gray, and had a kindly expression which one would hardly have expected in one whose neck was in the hemp. Evidently this was no vulgar assassin. The liberal military code makes provision for hanging many kinds of persons, and gentlemen are not excluded.

The preparations being complete, the two private soldiers stepped aside and each drew away the plank upon which he had been standing. The sergeant turned to the captain, saluted and placed himself immediately behind that officer, who in turn moved apart one pace. These movements left the condemned man and the sergeant standing on the two ends of the same plank, which spanned three of the crossties of the bridge. The end upon which the civilian stood almost, but not quite, reached a fourth. This plank had been held in place by the weight of the captain; it was now held by that of the sergeant. At a signal from the former the latter would step aside, the plank would tilt and the condemned man go down between two ties. The arrangement commended itself to his judgment as simple and effective. His face had not been covered nor his eyes bandaged. He looked a moment at his "unsteadfast footing," then let his gaze wander to the swirling water of the stream racing madly beneath his feet. A piece of dancing drift-wood caught his attention and his eyes followed it down the current. How slowly it appeared to move, what a sluggish stream!

He closed his eyes in order to fix his last thoughts upon his wife and children. The water, touched to gold by the early sun, the brooding mists under the banks at some distance down the stream, the fort, the soldiers, the piece of drift—all had distracted him. And now he became conscious of a new disturbance. Striking through the thought of his dear ones was a sound which he could neither ignore nor understand, a sharp, distinct, metallic percussion like the stroke of a blacksmith's hammer upon the anvil; it had the same ringing quality. He wondered what it was, and whether immeasurably distant or near by—it seemed both. Its recurrence was regular, but as slow as the tolling of a death knell. He awaited each stroke with impatience and—he knew not why—apprehension. The intervals of silence grew progressively lon-ger, the delays became maddening. With their greater infrequency the sounds increased in strength and sharpness. They hurt his ear like the thrust of a knife; he feared he would shriek. What he heard was the ticking of his watch.

He unclosed his eyes and saw again the water below him. "If I could free my hands," he thought, "I might throw off the noose and spring into the stream. By diving I could evade the bullets and, swimming vigorously, reach the bank, take to the woods and get away home. My home, thank God, is as yet outside their lines; my wife and little ones are still beyond the invader's farthest advance."

As these thoughts, which have here to be set down in words, were flashed into the doomed man's brain rather than evolved from it the captain nodded to the sergeant. The sergeant stepped aside.

Peyton Farquhar was a well-to-do planter, of an old and highly respected Alabama family. Being a slave owner and like other slave owners a politician he was naturally an original secessionist and ardently devoted to the Southern cause. Circumstances of an imperious nature, which it is unnecessary to relate here, had prevented him from taking service with the gallant army that had fought the disastrous campaigns ending with the fall of Corinth, and he chafed under the inglorious restraint, longing for the release of his energies, the larger life of the soldier, the opportunity for distinction. That opportunity, he felt, would come, as it comes to all in war time. Meanwhile he did what he could. No service was too humble for him to perform in aid of the South, no adventure too perilous for him to undertake if consistent with the character of a civilian who was at heart a soldier, and who in good faith and without too much qualification assented to at least a part of the frankly villainous dictum that all is fair in love and war.

One evening while Farquhar and his wife were sitting on a rustic bench near the entrance to his grounds, a gray-clad soldier rode up to the gate and asked for a drink of water. Mrs. Farquhar was only too happy to serve him with her own white hands. While she was fetching the water her husband approached the dusty horseman and inquired eagerly for news from the front.

"The Yanks are repairing the railroads," said the man, "and are getting ready for another advance. They have reached the Owl Creek bridge, put it in order and built a stockade on the north bank. The commandant has issued an order, which is posted everywhere, declaring that any civilian caught interfering with the railroad, its bridges, tunnels or trains will be summarily hanged. I saw the order."

"How far is it to the Owl Creek bridge?" Farquhar asked.

"About thirty miles."

"Is there no force on this side the creek?"

"Only a picket post half a mile out, on the railroad, and a single sentinel at this end of the bridge."

"Suppose a man—a civilian and student of hanging—should elude the picket post and perhaps get the better of the sentinel," said Farquhar, smiling, "what could he accomplish?"

The soldier reflected. "I was there a month ago," he replied. "I observed that the flood of last winter had lodged a great quantity of driftwood against the wooden pier at this end of the bridge. It is now dry and would burn like tow."

The lady had now brought the water, which the soldier drank. He thanked her ceremoniously, bowed to her husband and rode away. An hour later, after nightfall, he repassed the plantation, going northward in the direction from which he had come. He was a Federal scout.

As Peyton Farquhar fell straight downward through the bridge he lost consciousness and was as one already dead. From this state he was awakened—ages later, it seemed to him—by the pain of a sharp pressure upon his throat, followed by a sense of suffocation. Keen, poignant agonies seemed to shoot from his neck downward through every fiber of his body and limbs. These pains appeared to flash along well-defined lines of ramification and to beat with an inconceivably rapid periodicity. They seemed like streams of pulsating fire heating him to an intolerable temperature. As to his head, he was conscious of nothing but a feeling of fullness—of congestion. These sensations were unaccompanied by thought. The intellectual part of his nature was already effaced; he had power only to feel, and feeling was torment. He was conscious of motion.

Encompassed in a luminous cloud, of which he was now merely the fiery heart, without material substance, he swung through unthinkable arcs of oscillation, like a vast pendulum. Then all at once, with terrible suddenness, the light about him shot upward with the noise of a loud splash; a frightful roaring was in his ears, and all was cold and dark. The power of thought was restored; he knew that the rope had broken and he had fallen into the stream. There was no additional strangulation; the noose about his neck was already suffocating him and kept the water from his lungs. To die of hanging at the bottom of a river!—the idea seemed to him ludicrous. He opened his eyes in the darkness and saw above him a gleam of light, but how distant, how inaccessible! He was still sinking, for the light became fainter and fainter until it was a mere glimmer. Then it began to grow and brighten, and he knew that he was rising toward the surface—knew it with reluctance, for he was now very comfortable. "To be hanged and drowned," he thought, "that is not so bad; but I do not wish to be shot. No; I will not be shot; that is not fair."

He was not conscious of an effort, but a sharp pain in his wrist apprised him that he was trying to free his hands. He gave the struggle his attention, as an idler might observe the feat of a juggler, without interest in the outcome. What splendid effort!—what magnificent, what superhuman strength! Ah, that was a fine endeavor! Bravo! The cord fell away; his arms parted and floated upward, the hands dimly seen on each side in the growing light. He watched them with a new interest as first one and then the other pounced upon the noose at his neck. They tore it away and thrust it fiercely aside, its undulations resembling those of a water snake. "Put it back, put it back!" He thought he shouted these words to his hands, for the undoing of the noose had been succeeded by the direst pang that he had yet experienced. His neck ached horribly; his brain was on fire; his heart, which had been fluttering faintly, gave a great leap, trying to force itself out at his mouth. His whole body was racked and wrenched with an insupportable anguish! But his disobedient hands gave no heed to the command. They beat the water vigorously with quick, downward strokes, forcing him to the surface. He felt his head emerge; his eyes were blinded by the sunlight; his chest expanded convulsively, and with a supreme and crowning agony his lungs engulfed a great draught of air, which instantly he expelled in a shriek!

He was now in full possession of his physical senses. They were, indeed, preternaturally keen and alert. Something in the awful disturbance of his organic system had so exalted and refined them that they made record of things never before perceived. He felt the ripples upon his face and heard their separate sounds as they struck. He looked at the forest on the bank of the stream, saw the individual trees, the leaves and the veining of each leaf—saw the very insects upon them: the locusts, the brilliant-bodied flies, the gray spiders stretching their webs from twig to twig. He noted the prismatic colors in all the dewdrops upon a million blades of grass. The humming of the gnats that danced above the eddies of the stream, the beating of the dragon flies' wings, the strokes of the water-spiders' legs, like oars which had lifted their boat—all these made audible music. A fish slid along beneath his eyes and he heard the rush of its body parting the water.

He had come to the surface facing down the stream; in a moment the visible world seemed to wheel slowly round, himself the pivotal point, and he saw the bridge, the fort, the soldiers upon the bridge, the captain, the sergeant, the two privates, his executioners. They were in silhouette against the blue sky. They shouted and gesticulated, pointing at him. The captain had drawn his pistol, but did not fire; the others were unarmed. Their movements were grotesque and horrible, their forms gigantic.

Suddenly he heard a sharp report and something struck the water smartly within a few inches of his head, spattering his face with spray. He heard a second report, and saw one of the sentinels with his rifle at his shoulder, a light cloud of blue smoke rising from the muzzle. The man in the water saw the eye of the man on the bridge gazing into his own through the sights of the rifle. He observed that it was a gray eye and remembered having read that gray eyes were keenest, and that all famous marksmen had them. Nevertheless, this one had missed.

A counter-swirl had caught Farquhar and turned him half round; he was again looking into the forest on the bank opposite the fort. The sound of a clear, high voice in a monotonous singsong now rang out behind him and came across the water with a distinctness that pierced and subdued all other sounds, even the beating of the ripples in his ears. Although no soldier, he had frequented camps enough to know the dread significance of that deliberate, drawling, aspirated chant; the lieutenant on shore was taking a part in the morning's work. How coldly and pitilessly—with what an even, calm intonation, presaging, and enforcing tranquillity in the men—with what accurately measured intervals fell those cruel words:

"Attention, company! . . . Shoulder arms! . . . Ready! . . . Aim! . . . Fire!"

Farquhar dived—dived as deeply as he could. The water roared in his ears like the voice of Niagara, yet he heard the dulled thunder of the volley and, rising again toward the surface, met shining bits of metal, singularly flattened, oscillating slowly downward. Some of them touched him on the face and hands, then fell away, continuing their descent. One lodged between his collar and neck; it was uncomfortably warm and he snatched it out.

As he rose to the surface, gasping for breath, he saw that he had been a long time under water; he was perceptibly farther down stream nearer to safety. The soldiers had almost finished reloading; the metal ramrods flashed all at once in the sunshine as they were drawn from the barrels, turned in the air, and thrust into their sockets. The two sentinels fired again, independently and ineffectually.

The hunted man saw all this over his shoulder; he was now swimming vigorously with the current. His brain was as energetic as his arms and legs; he thought with the rapidity of lightning.

"The officer," he reasoned, "will not make that martinet's error a second time. It is as easy to dodge a volley as a single shot. He has probably already given the command to fire at will. God help me, I cannot dodge them all!"

An appalling plash within two yards of him was followed by a loud, rushing sound, *diminuendo*, which seemed to travel back through the air to the fort and died in an explosion which stirred the very river to its deeps!

A rising sheet of water curved over him, fell down upon him, blinded him, strangled him! The cannon had taken a hand in the game. As he shook his head free from the commotion of the smitten water he heard the deflected shot humming through the air ahead, and in an instant it was cracking and smashing the branches in the forest beyond.

"They will not do that again," he thought; "the next time they will use a charge of grape. I must keep my eye upon the gun; the smoke will apprise me—the report arrives too late; it lags behind the missile. That is a good gun."

Suddenly he felt himself whirled round and round—spinning like a top. The water, the banks, the forests, the now distant bridge, fort and men—all were commingled and blurred. Objects were represented by their colors only; circular horizontal streaks of color—that was all he saw. He had been caught in a vortex and was being whirled on with a velocity of advance and gyration that made him giddy and sick. In a few moments he was flung upon the gravel at the foot of the left bank of the stream—the southern bank—and behind a projecting point which concealed him from his enemies. The sudden arrest of his motion, the abrasion of one of his hands on the gravel, restored him, and he wept with delight. He dug his fingers into the sand, threw it over himself in handfuls and audibly blessed it. It looked like diamonds, rubies, emeralds; he could think of nothing beautiful which it did not resemble. The trees upon the bank were giant garden plants; he noted a definite order in their arrangement, inhaled the fragrance of their blooms. A strange, roseate light shone through the spaces among their trunks and the wind made in their branches the music of Æolian harps. He had no wish to perfect his escape—was content to remain in that enchanting spot until retaken.

A whiz and rattle of grapeshot among the branches high above his head roused him from his dream. The baffled cannoneer had fired him a random farewell. He sprang to his feet, rushed up the sloping bank, and plunged into the forest.

All that day he traveled, laying his course by the rounding sun. The forest seemed interminable; nowhere did he discover a break in it, not even a woodman's road. He had not known that he lived in so wild a region. There was something uncanny in the revelation.

By nightfall he was fatigued, footsore, famishing. The thought of his wife and children urged him on. At last he found a road which led him in what he knew to be the right direction. It was as wide and straight as a city street, yet it seemed untraveled. No fields bordered it, no dwelling anywhere. Not so much as the barking of a dog suggested human habitation. The black bodies of the trees formed a straight wall on both sides, terminating on the horizon in a point, like a diagram in a lesson in perspective. Overhead, as he looked up through this rift in the wood, shone great garden stars looking unfamiliar and grouped in strange constellations. He was sure they were arranged in some order which had a secret and malign significance. The wood on either side was full of singular noises, among which—once, twice, and again—he distinctly heard whispers in an unknown tongue.

His neck was in pain and lifting his hand to it found it horribly swollen. He knew that it had a circle of black where the rope had bruised it. His eyes felt congested; he could no longer close them. His tongue was swollen with thirst; he relieved its fever by thrusting it forward from between his teeth into the cold air. How softly the turf had carpeted the untraveled avenue—he could no longer feel the roadway beneath his feet!

Doubtless, despite his suffering, he had fallen asleep while walking, for now he sees another scene—perhaps he has merely recovered from a delirium. He stands at the gate of his own home. All is as he left it, and all bright and beautiful in the morning sunshine. He must have traveled the entire night. As he pushes open the gate and passes up the wide white walk, he sees a flutter of female garments; his wife, looking fresh and cool and sweet, steps down from the veranda to meet him. At the bottom of the steps she stands waiting, with a smile of ineffable joy, an attitude of matchless grace and dignity. Ah, how beautiful she is! He springs forward with extended arms. As he is about to clasp her he feels a stunning blow upon the back of the neck; a blinding white light blazes all about him with a sound like the shock of a cannon—then all is darkness and silence!

Peyton Farquhar was dead; his body, with a broken neck, swung gently from side to side beneath the timbers of the Owl Creek bridge.

4

THE SNOW-IMAGE: A CHILDISH MIRACLE

BY NATHANIEL HAWTHORNE

Nathaniel Hawthorne (1804–1864), is best known for his popular nov-els The Scarlet Letter *and* The House of the Seven Gables. *Born in Salem, Massachusetts, Hawthorne came to know many of the artis-tic and political elites of his time, including Edgar Allan Poe, Herman Melville, and Ralph Waldo Emerson, as well as U.S. presidents Frank-lin Pierce (a close friend) and Abraham Lincoln. Hawthorne's writing is known for its atmospheric darkness and psychological complexity. "The Snow-Image: A Childish Miracle" was published in 1852.*

One afternoon of a cold winter's day, when the sun shone forth with chilly brightness, after a long storm, two children asked leave of their mother to run out and play in the new-fallen snow. The elder child was a little girl, whom, because she was of a tender and modest disposition, and was thought to be very beautiful, her parents, and other people who were familiar with her, used to call Violet. But her brother was known by the style and title of Peony, on account of the ruddiness of his broad and round little phiz, which made everybody think of sunshine and great scarlet flowers. The father of these two children, a certain Mr. Lindsey, it is important to say, was an excellent but exceedingly matter of fact sort of man, a dealer in hardware, and was sturdily accustomed to take what is called the common-sense view of all matters that came under his consideration. With a heart about as tender as other people's, he had a head as hard and impenetrable, and therefore, perhaps, as empty, as one of the iron pots which it was a part of his business to sell. The mother's character, on the other hand, had a strain of poetry in it, a trait of unworldly beauty,—a delicate and dewy flower, as it were, that had survived out of her imaginative youth, and still kept itself alive amid the dusty realities of matrimony and motherhood.

So, Violet and Peony, as I began with saying, besought their mother to let them run out and play in the new snow; for, though it had looked so dreary and dismal, drifting downward out of the gray sky, it had a very cheerful aspect, now that the sun was shining on it. The children dwelt in a city, and had no wider play-place than a little garden before the house, divided by a white fence from the street, and with a pear-tree and two or three plum-trees overshadowing it, and some rose-bushes just in front of the parlor windows. The trees and shrubs, however, were now leafless, and their twigs were enveloped in the light snow, which thus made a kind of wintry foliage, with here and there a pendent icicle for the fruit.

"Yes, Violet,—yes, my little Peony," said their kind mother, "you may go out and play in the new snow."

Accordingly, the good lady bundled up her darlings in woollen jackets and wadded sacks, and put comforters round their necks, and a pair of striped gaiters on each little pair of legs, and worsted mittens on their hands, and gave them a kiss apiece, by way of a spell to keep away Jack Frost. Forth sallied the two children, with a hop-skip-and-jump, that carried them at once into the very heart of a huge snow-drift, whence Violet emerged like a snow-bunting, while little Peony floundered out with his round face in full bloom. Then what a merry time had they! To look at them, frolicking in the wintry garden, you would have thought that the dark and pitiless storm had been sent for no other purpose but to provide a new plaything for Violet and Peony; and that they themselves had been created, as the snowbirds were, to take delight only in the tempest, and in the white mantle which is spread over the earth.

At last, when they had frosted one another all over with handfuls of snow, Violet, after laughing heartily at little Peony's figure, was struck with a new idea.

"You look exactly like a snow-image, Peony," said she, "if your cheeks were not so red. And that puts me in mind! Let us make an image out of snow,—an image of a little girl,—and it shall be our sister, and shall run about and play with us all winter long. Won't it be nice?"

"O, yes!" cried Peony, as plainly as he could speak, for he was but a little boy. "That will be nice! And mamma shall see it!"

"Yes," answered Violet; "mamma shall see the new little girl. But she must not make her come into the warm parlor; for, you know, our little snow-sister will not love the warmth."

And forthwith the children began this great business of making a snow-image that should run about; while their mother, who was sitting at the window and overheard some of their talk, could not help smiling at the gravity with which they set about it. They really seemed to imagine that there would be no difficulty whatever in creating a live little girl out of the snow. And, to say the truth, if miracles are ever to be wrought, it will be by putting our hands to the work in precisely such a simple and undoubting frame of mind as that in which Violet and Peony now undertook to perform one, without so much as knowing that it was a miracle. So thought the mother; and thought, likewise, that the new snow, just fallen from heaven, would be excellent material to make new beings of, if it were not so very cold. She gazed at the children a moment longer, delighting to watch their little figures,—the girl, tall for her age, graceful and agile, and so delicately colored that she looked like a cheerful thought more than a physical reality; while Peony expanded in breadth rather than height, and rolled along on his short and sturdy legs as substantial as an elephant, though not quite so big. Then the mother resumed her work. What it was I forget; but she was either trimming a silken bonnet for Violet, or darning a pair of stockings for little Peony's short legs. Again, however, and again, and yet other agains, she could not help turning her head to the window to see how the children got on with their snow-image.

Indeed, it was an exceedingly pleasant sight, those bright little souls at their task! Moreover, it was really wonderful to observe how knowingly and skilfully they managed the matter. Violet assumed the chief direction, and told Peony what to do, while, with her own delicate fingers, she shaped out all the nicer parts of the snow-figure. It seemed, in fact, not so much to be made by the children, as to grow up under their hands, while they were playing and prattling about it. Their mother was quite surprised at this; and the longer she looked, the more and more surprised she grew.

"What remarkable children mine are!" thought she, smiling with a mother's pride; and, smiling at herself, too, for being so proud of them. "What other children could have made anything so like a little girl's figure out of snow at the first trial? Well; but now I must finish Peony's new frock, for his grandfather is coming to-morrow, and I want the little fellow to look handsome."

So she took up the frock, and was soon as busily at work again with her needle as the two children with their snow-image. But still, as the needle travelled hither and thither through the seams of the dress, the mother made her toil light and happy by listening to the airy voices of Violet and Peony. They kept talking to one another all the time, their tongues being quite as active as their feet and hands. Except at intervals, she could not distinctly hear what was said, but had merely a sweet impression that they were in a most loving mood, and were enjoying themselves highly, and that the business of making the snow-image went prosperously on. Now and then, however, when Violet and Peony happened to raise their voices, the words were as audible as if they had been spoken in the very parlor where the mother sat. O, how delightfully those words echoed in her heart, even though they meant nothing so very wise or wonderful, after all!

But you must know a mother listens with her heart much more than with her ears; and thus she is often delighted with the trills of celestial music, when other people can hear nothing of the kind.

"Peony, Peony!" cried Violet to her brother, who had gone to another part of the garden, "bring me some of that fresh snow, Peony, from the very farthest corner, where we have not been trampling. I want it to shape our little snow-sister's bosom with. You know that part must be quite pure, just as it came out of the sky!"

"Here it is, Violet!" answered Peony, in his bluff tone,—but a very sweet tone, too,—as he came floundering through the half-trodden drifts. "Here is the snow for her little bosom. O Violet, how beau-ti-ful she begins to look!"

"Yes," said Violet thoughtfully and quietly; our snow-sister does look very lovely. I did not quite know, Peony, that we could make such a sweet little girl as this."

The mother, as she listened, thought how fit and delightful an incident it would be, if fairies, or still better, if angel-children were to come from paradise, and play invisibly with her own darlings, and help them to make their snow-image, giving it the features of celestial babyhood! Violet and Peony would not be aware of their immortal playmates,— only they would see that the image grew very beautiful while they worked at it, and would think that they themselves had done it all.

"My little girl and boy deserve such playmates, if mortal children ever did!" said the mother to herself; and then she smiled again at her own motherly pride.

Nevertheless, the idea seized upon her imagination; and, ever and anon, she took a glimpse out of the window, half dreaming that she might see the golden-haired children of paradise sporting with her own golden-haired Violet and bright-cheeked Peony.

Now, for a few moments, there was a busy and earnest but indistinct hum of the two children's voices, as Violet and Peony wrought together with one happy consent. Violet still seemed to be the guiding spirit, while Peony acted rather as a laborer, and brought her the snow from far and near. And yet the little urchin evidently had a proper understanding of the matter, too!

"Peony, Peony!" cried Violet; for her brother was again at the other side of the garden. "Bring me those light wreaths of snow that have rested on the lower branches of the pear-tree. You can clamber on the snowdrift, Peony, and reach them easily. I must have them to make some ringlets for our snow-sister's head!"

"Here they are, Violet!" answered the little boy. "Take care you do not break them. Well done! Well done! How pretty!"

"Does she not look sweetly?" said Violet, with a very satisfied tone; "and now we must have some little shining bits of ice, to make the brightness of her eyes. She is not finished yet. Mamma will see how very beautiful she is; but papa will say, 'Tush! nonsense!—come in out of the cold!'"

"Let us call mamma to look out," said Peony; and then he shouted lustily, "Mamma! mamma!! mamma!!! Look out, and see what a nice 'ittle girl we are making!"

The mother put down her work for an instant, and looked out of the window. But it so happened that the sun—for this was one of the shortest days of the whole year—had sunken so nearly to the edge of the world that his setting shine came obliquely into the lady's eyes. So she was dazzled, you must understand, and could not very distinctly observe what was in the garden. Still, however, through all that bright, blinding dazzle of the sun and the new snow, she beheld a small white figure in the garden, that seemed to have a wonderful deal of human likeness about it. And she saw Violet and Peony,—indeed, she looked more at them than at the image,—she saw the two children still at work; Peony bringing fresh snow, and Violet applying it to the figure as scientifically as a sculptor adds clay to his model. Indistinctly as she discerned the snow-child, the mother thought to herself that never before was there a snow-figure so cunningly made, nor ever such a dear little girl and boy to make it.

"They do everything better than other children," said she very complacently. "No wonder they make better snow-images!"

She sat down again to her work, and made as much haste with it as possible; because twilight would soon come, and Peony's frock was not yet finished, and grandfather was expected, by railroad, pretty early in the morning. Faster and faster, therefore, went her flying fingers. The children, likewise, kept busily at work in the garden, and still the mother listened, whenever she could catch a word. She was amused to observe how their little imaginations had got mixed up with what they were doing, and carried away by it. They seemed positively to think that the snow-child would run about and play with them.

"What a nice playmate she will be for us, all winter long!" said Violet. "I hope papa will not be afraid of her giving us a cold! Sha'n't you love her dearly, Peony?"

"O, yes!" cried Peony. "And I will hug her, and she shall sit down close by me, and drink some of my warm milk!"

"O, no, Peony!" answered Violet, with grave wisdom. "That will not do at all. Warm milk will not be wholesome for our little snow-sister. Little snow-people, like her, eat nothing but icicles. No, no, Peony we must not give her anything warm to drink!"

There was a minute or two of silence; for Peony, whose short legs were never weary, had gone on a pilgrimage again to the other side of the garden. All of a sudden, Violet cried out, loudly and joyfully,—

"Look here, Peony! Come quickly! A light has been shining on her cheek out of that rose-colored cloud! And the color does not go away! Is not that beautiful!"

"Yes; it is beau-ti-ful," answered Peony, pronouncing the three syllables with deliberate accuracy. "O Violet, only look at her hair! It is all like gold!

"O, certainly," said Violet with tranquillity, as if it were very much a matter of course. "That color, you know, comes from the golden clouds that we see up there in the sky. She is almost finished now. But her lips must be made very red,—redder than her cheeks. Perhaps, Peony, it will make them red if we both kiss them!"

Accordingly, the mother heard two smart little smacks, as if both her children were kissing the snow-image on its frozen mouth. But, as this did not seem to make the lips quite red enough, Violet next proposed that the snow-child should be invited to kiss Peony's scarlet cheek.

"Come, 'ittle snow-sister, kiss me!" cried Peony.

"There! she has kissed you," added Violet, and now her lips are very red. And she blushed a little, too!"

"O, what a cold kiss!" cried Peony.

Just then, there came a breeze of the pure west wind, sweeping through the garden and rattling the parlor windows. It sounded so wintry cold, that the mother was about to tap on the window-pane with her thimbled finger, to summon the two children in, when they both cried out to her with one voice. The tone was not a tone of surprise, although they were evidently a good deal excited; it appeared rather as if they were very much rejoiced at some event that had now happened, but which they had been looking for, and had reckoned upon all along.

"Mamma! mamma! We have finished our little snow-sister, and she is running about the garden with us!"

"What imaginative little beings my children are!" thought the mother, putting the last few stitches into Peony's frock. "And it is strange, too, that they make me almost as much a child as they themselves are! I can hardly help believing, now, that the snow-image has really come to life!"

"Dear mamma!" cried Violet, "pray look out and see what a sweet playmate we have!"

The mother, being thus entreated, could no longer delay to look forth from the window. The sun was now gone out of the sky, leaving, however, a rich inheritance of his brightness among those purple and golden clouds which make the sunsets of winter so magnificent. But there was not the slightest gleam or dazzle, either on the window or on the snow; so that the good lady could look all over the garden, and see everything and everybody in it. And what do you think she saw there? Violet and Peony, of course, her own two darling children. Ah, but whom or what did she see besides? Why, if you will believe me, there was a small figure of a girl, dressed all in white, with rose-tinged cheeks and ringlets of golden hue, playing about the garden with the two children! A stranger though she was, the child seemed to be on as familiar terms with Violet and Peony, and they with her, as if all the three had been playmates during the whole of their little lives. The mother thought to herself that it must certainly be the daughter of one of the neighbors, and that, seeing Violet and Peony in the garden, the child had run across the street to play with them. So this kind lady went to the door, intending to invite the little runaway into her comfortable parlor; for, now that the sunshine was withdrawn, the atmosphere, out of doors, was already growing very cold.

But, after opening the house door, she stood an instant on the threshold, hesitating whether she ought to ask the child to come in, or whether she should even speak to her. Indeed, she almost doubted whether it were a real child after all, or only a light wreath of the new-fallen snow, blown hither and thither about the garden by the intensely cold west wind. There was certainly something very singular in the aspect of the little stranger. Among all the children of the neighborhood, the lady could remember no such face, with its pure white, and delicate rose color, and the golden ringlets tossing about the forehead and cheeks. And as for her dress, which was entirely of white, and fluttering in the breeze, it was such as no reasonable woman would put upon a little girl, when sending her out to play, in the depth of winter. It made this kind and careful mother shiver only to look at those small feet, with nothing in the world on them, except a very thin pair of white slippers. Nevertheless, airily as she was clad, the child seemed to feel not the slightest inconvenience from the cold, but danced so lightly over the snow that the tips of her toes left hardly a print in its surface; while Violet could but just keep pace with her, and Peony's short legs compelled him to lag behind.

Once, in the course of their play, the strange child placed herself between Violet and Peony, and, taking a hand of each, skipped merrily forward and they along with her. Almost immediately, however, Peony pulled away his little fist, and began to rub it as if the fingers were tingling with cold; while Violet also released herself, though with less abruptness, gravely remarking that it was better not to take hold of hands. The white-robed damsel said not a word, but danced about, just as merrily as before. If Violet and Peony did not choose to play with her, she could make just as good a playmate of the brisk and cold west wind, which kept blowing her all about the garden, and took such liberties with her, that they seemed to have been friends for a long time. All this while, the mother stood on the threshold, wondering how a little girl could look so much like a flying snowdrift, or how a snowdrift could look so very like a little girl. She called Violet, and whispered to her.

"Violet, my darling, what is this child's name?" asked she. "Does she live near us?"

"Why, dearest mamma," answered Violet, laughing to think that her mother did not comprehend so very plain an affair, "this is our little snow-sister whom we have just been making!"

"Yes, dear mamma," cried Peony, running to his mother, and looking up simply into her face. "This is our snow-image! Is it not a nice 'ittle child?"

At this instant a flock of snowbirds came flitting through the air. As was very natural, they avoided Violet and Peony. But—and this looked strange—they flew at once to the white-robed child, fluttered eagerly about her head, alighted on her shoulders, and seemed to claim her as an old acquaintance. She, on her part, was evidently as glad to see these little birds, old Winter's grandchildren, as they were to see her, and welcomed them by holding out both her hands. Hereupon, they each and all tried to alight on her two palms and ten small fingers and thumbs, crowding one another off, with an immense fluttering of their tiny wings. One dear little bird nestled tenderly in her bosom; another put its bill to her lips. They were as joyous, all the while, and seemed as much in their element, as you may have seen them when sporting with a snowstorm.

Violet and Peony stood laughing at this pretty sight; for they enjoyed the merry time which their new playmate was having with these small-winged visitants, almost as much as if they themselves took part in it.

"Violet," said her mother, greatly perplexed, "tell me the truth, without any jest. Who is this little girl?"

"My darling mamma," answered Violet, looking seriously into her mother's face, and apparently surprised that she should need any further explanation, "I have told you truly who she is. It is our little snow-image, which Peony and I have been making. Peony will tell you so, as well as I."

"Yes, mamma," asseverated Peony, with much gravity in his crimson little phiz; "this is 'ittle snow-child. Is not she a nice one? But, mamma, her hand is, O, so very cold!"

While mamma still hesitated what to think and what to do, the street gate was thrown open, and the father of Violet and Peony appeared, wrapped in a pilot-cloth sack, with a fur cap drawn down over his ears, and the thickest of gloves upon his hands. Mr. Lindsey was a middle-aged man, with a weary and yet a happy look in his wind-flushed and frost-pinched face, as if he had been busy all the day long, and was glad to get back to his quiet home. His eyes brightened at the sight of his wife and children, although he could not help uttering a word or two of surprise, at finding the whole family in the open air, on so bleak a day, and after sunset too. He soon perceived the little white stranger sporting to and fro in the garden, like a dancing snow-wreath, and the flock of snowbirds fluttering about her head.

"Pray, what little girl may that be?" inquired this very sensible man. "Surely her mother must be crazy to let her go out in such bitter weather as it has been to-day, with only that flimsy white gown and those thin slippers!"

"My dear husband," said his wife, "I know no more about the little thing than you do. Some neighbor's child, I suppose. Our Violet and Peony," she added, laughing at herself for repeating so absurd a story, "insist that she is nothing but a snow-image, which they have been busy about in the garden almost all the afternoon."

As she said this, the mother glanced her eyes toward the spot where the children's snow-image had been made. What was her surprise, on perceiving that there was not the slightest trace of so much labor!—no image at all!—no piled-up heap of snow!—nothing whatever, save the prints of little footsteps around a vacant space! "This is very strange!" said she.

"What is strange, dear mother?" asked Violet. "Dear father, do not you see how it is? This is our snow-image, which Peony and I have made, because we wanted another playmate. Did not we, Peony?"

"Yes, papa," said crimson Peony. "This be our 'ittle snow-sister. Is she not beautiful? But she gave me such a cold kiss!"

"Poh, nonsense, children!" cried their good, honest father, who, as we have already intimated had an exceedingly common-sensible way of looking at matters. "Do not tell me of making live figures out of snow. Come, wife; this little stranger must not stay out in the bleak air a moment longer. We will bring her into the parlor; and you shall give her a supper of warm bread and milk, and make her as comfortable as you can. Meanwhile, I will inquire among the neighbors; or, if necessary, send the city-crier about the streets, to give notice of a lost child."

So saying, this honest and very kind-hearted man was going toward the little white damsel, with the best intentions in the world. But Violet and Peony, each seizing their father by the hand, earnestly besought him not to make her come in.

"Dear father," cried Violet, putting herself before him, "it is true what I have been telling you! This is our little snow-girl, and she cannot live any longer than while she breathes the cold west wind. Do not make her come into the hot room!"

"Yes, father," shouted Peony, stamping his little foot, so mightily was he in earnest, "this be nothing but our 'ittle snow-child! She will not love the hot fire!"

"Nonsense, children, nonsense, nonsense!" cried the father, half vexed, half laughing at what he considered their foolish obstinacy. "Run into the house this moment! It is too late to play any longer now. I must take care of this little girl immediately, or she will catch her death-a-cold!"

"Husband! dear husband!" said his wife, in a low voice,—for she had been looking narrowly at the snow-child, and was more perplexed than ever,—"there is something very singular in all this. You will think me foolish,—but—but—may it not be that some invisible angel has been attracted by the simplicity and good faith with which our children set about their undertaking? May he not have spent an hour of his immortality in playing with those dear little souls? and so the result is what we call a miracle. No, no! Do not laugh at me; I see what a foolish thought it is!"

"My dear wife," replied the husband, laughing heartily, "you are as much a child as Violet and Peony."

And in one sense so she was, for all through life she had kept her heart full of childlike simplicity and faith, which was as pure and clear as crystal; and, looking at all matters through this transparent medium, she sometimes saw truths so profound that other people laughed at them as nonsense and absurdity.

But now kind Mr. Lindsey had entered the garden, breaking away from his two children, who still sent their shrill voices after him, beseeching him to let the snow-child stay and enjoy herself in the cold west wind. As he approached, the snowbirds took to flight. The little white damsel, also, fled backward, shaking her head, as if to say, "Pray, do not touch me!" and roguishly, as it appeared, leading him through the deepest of the snow. Once, the good man stumbled, and floundered down upon his face, so that, gathering himself up again, with the snow sticking to his rough pilot-cloth sack, he looked as white and wintry as a snow-image of the largest size. Some of the neighbors, meanwhile, seeing him from their windows, wondered what could possess poor Mr. Lindsey to be running about his garden in pursuit of a snowdrift, which the west wind was driving hither and thither! At length, after a vast deal of trouble, he chased the little stranger into a corner, where she could not possibly escape him. His wife had been looking on, and, it being nearly twilight, was wonderstruck to observe how the snow-child gleamed and sparkled, and how she seemed to shed a glow all round about her; and when driven into the corner, she positively glistened like a star! It was a frosty kind of brightness, too, like that of an icicle in the moonlight. The wife thought it strange that good Mr. Lindsey should see nothing remarkable in the snow-child's appearance.

"Come, you odd little thing!" cried the honest man, seizing her by the hand, "I have caught you at last, and will make you comfortable in spite of yourself. We will put a nice warm pair of worsted stockings on your frozen little feet, and you shall have a good thick shawl to wrap yourself in. Your poor white nose, I am afraid, is actually frost-bitten. But we will make it all right. Come along in."

And so, with a most benevolent smile on his sagacious visage, all purple as it was with the cold, this very well-meaning gentleman took the snow-child by the hand and led her toward the house. She followed him, droopingly and reluctant; for all the glow and sparkle was gone out of her figure; and whereas just before she had resembled a bright, frosty, star-gemmed evening, with a crimson gleam on the cold horizon, she now looked as dull and languid as a thaw. As kind Mr. Lindsey led her up the steps of the door, Violet and Peony looked into his face,—their eyes full of tears, which froze before they could run down their cheeks,—and again entreated him not to bring their snow-image into the house.

"Not bring her in!" exclaimed the kindhearted man. "Why, you are crazy, my little Violet!—quite crazy, my small Peony! She is so cold, already, that her hand has almost frozen mine, in spite of my thick gloves. Would you have her freeze to death?"

His wife, as he came up the steps, had been taking another long, earnest, almost awe-stricken gaze at the little white stranger. She hardly knew whether it was a dream or no; but she could not help fancying that she saw the delicate print of Violet's fingers on the child's neck. It looked just as if, while Violet was shaping out the image, she had given it a gentle pat with her hand, and had neglected to smooth the impression quite away.

"After all, husband," said the mother, recurring to her idea that the angels would be as much delighted to play with Violet and Peony as she herself was,—"after all, she does look strangely like a snow-image! I do believe she is made of snow!"

A puff of the west wind blew against the snow-child, and again she sparkled like a star.

"Snow!" repeated good Mr. Lindsey, drawing the reluctant guest over his hospitable threshold. "No wonder she looks like snow. She is half frozen, poor little thing! But a good fire will put everything to rights!"

Without further talk, and always with the same best intentions, this highly benevolent and common-sensible individual led the little white damsel—drooping, drooping, drooping, more and more—out of the frosty air, and into his comfortable parlor. A Heidenberg stove, filled to the brim with intensely burning anthracite, was sending a bright gleam through the isinglass of its iron door, and causing the vase of water on its top to fume and bubble with excitement. A warm, sultry smell was diffused throughout the room. A thermometer on the wall farthest from the stove stood at eighty degrees. The parlor was hung with red curtains, and covered with a red carpet, and looked just as warm as it felt. The difference betwixt the atmosphere here and the cold, wintry twilight out of doors, was like stepping at once from Nova Zembla to the hottest part of India, or from the North Pole into an oven. O, this was a fine place for the little white stranger!

The common-sensible man placed the snow-child on the hearth-rug, right in front of the hissing and fuming stove.

"Now she will be comfortable!" cried Mr. Lindsey, rubbing his hands and looking about him, with the pleasantest smile you ever saw. Make yourself at home, my child."

Sad, sad and drooping, looked the little white maiden, as she stood on the hearth-rug, with the hot blast of the stove striking through her like a pestilence. Once, she threw a glance wistfully toward the windows, and caught a glimpse, through its red curtains, of the snow covered roofs, and the stars glimmering frostily, and all the delicious intensity of the cold night. The bleak wind rattled the window-panes, as if it were summoning her to come forth. But there stood the snow-child, drooping, before the hot stove!

But the common-sensible man saw nothing amiss.

"Come, wife," said he, "let her have a pair of thick stockings and a woollen shawl or blanket directly; and tell Dora to give her some warm supper as soon as the milk boils. You, Violet and Peony, amuse your little friend. She is out of spirits, you see, at finding herself in a strange place. For my part, I will go around among the neighbors, and find out where she belongs."

The mother, meanwhile, had gone in search of the shawl and stockings; for her own view of the matter, however subtle and delicate, had given way, as it always did, to the stubborn materialism of her husband. Without heeding the remonstrances of his two children, who still kept murmuring that their little snow-sister did not love the warmth, good Mr. Lindsey took his departure, shutting the parlor door carefully behind him. Turning up the collar of his sack over his ears, he emerged from the house, and had barely reached the street gate, when he was recalled by the screams of Violet and Peony, and the rapping of a thimbled finger against the parlor window.

"Husband! husband!" cried his wife, showing her horror-stricken face through the window-panes. "There is no need of going for the child's parents!"

"We told you so, father!" screamed Violet and Peony, as he reentered the parlor. "You would bring her in; and now our poor—dear beautiful little snow-sister is thawed!"

And their own sweet little faces were already dissolved in tears; so that their father, seeing what strange things occasionally happen in this every-day world, felt not a little anxious lest his children might be going to thaw too! In the utmost perplexity, he demanded an explanation of his wife. She could only reply, that, being summoned to the parlor by the cries of Violet and Peony, she found no trace of the little white maiden, unless it were the remains of a heap of snow, which, while she was gazing at it, melted quite away upon the hearth-rug.

"And there you see all that is left of it!" added she, pointing to a pool of water in front of the stove.

"Yes, father," said Violet, looking reproachfully at him through her tears, "there is all that is left of our dear little snow-sister!"

"Naughty father!" cried Peony, stamping his foot, and—I shudder to say—shaking his little fist at the common-sensible man. "We told you how it would be! What for did you bring her in?"

And the Heidenberg stove, through the isinglass of its door, seemed to glare at good Mr. Lindsey, like a red-eyed demon, triumphing in the mischief which it had done!

This, you will observe, was one of those rare cases, which yet will occasionally happen, where common-sense finds itself at fault. The remarkable story of the snow-image, though to that sagacious class of people to whom good Mr. Lindsey belongs it may seem but a childish affair is, nevertheless, capable of being moralized in various methods, greatly for their edification. One of its lessons, for instance, might be, that it behooves men, and especially men of benevolence, to consider well what they are about, and, before acting on their philanthropic purposes, to be quite sure that they comprehend the nature and all the relations of the business in hand. What has been established as an element of good to one being may prove absolute mischief to another; even as the warmth of the parlor was proper enough for children of flesh and blood, like Violet and Peony,—though by no means very wholesome, even for them, but involved nothing short of annihilation to the unfortunate snow-image.

But, after all, there is no teaching anything to wise men of good Mr. Lindsey's stamp. They know everything,—O, to be sure!— everything that has been, and everything that is, and everything that, by any future possibility, can be. And, should some phenomenon of nature or Providence transcend their system, they will not recognize it, even if it come to pass under their very noses.

"Wife," said Mr. Lindsey, after a fit of silence, "see what a quantity of snow the children have brought in on their feet! It has made quite a puddle here before the stove. Pray tell Dora to bring some towels and sop it up!"

5

A GHOST OF
THE SIERRAS

BY BRET HARTE

Born in Albany, New York, to parents who did not support his aspirations as a writer, Bret Harte (1836–1902) moved to California at age seventeen, hoping to strike it rich in the gold fields. He later worked as a schoolmaster and journalist. His most famous stories, including "The Outcasts of Poker Flat" and "The Luck of Roaring Camp," are set in frontier California. Later he served as a U.S. consul in Germany and Scotland. "A Ghost of the Sierras" first appeared in 1876.

It was a vast silence of pines, redolent with balsamic breath, and muffled with the dry dust of dead bark and matted mosses. Lying on our backs, we looked upward through a hundred feet of clear, unbroken interval to the first lateral branches that formed the flat canopy above us. Here and there the fierce sun, from whose active persecution we had just escaped, searched for us through the woods, but its keen blade was dulled and turned aside by intercostal boughs, and its brightness dissipated in nebulous mists throughout the roofing of the dim, brown aisles around us. We were in another atmosphere, under another sky; indeed, in another world than the dazzling one we had just quitted. The grave silence seemed so much a part of the grateful coolness, that we hesitated to speak, and for some moments lay quietly outstretched on the pine tassels where we had first thrown ourselves. Finally, a voice broke the silence:—

"Ask the old Major; he knows all about it!"

The person here alluded to under that military title was myself. I hardly need explain to any Californian that it by no means followed that I was a "Major," or that I was "old," or that I knew anything about "it," or indeed what "it" referred to. The whole remark was merely one of the usual conventional feelers to conversation,—a kind of social preamble, quite common to our slangy camp intercourse. Nevertheless, as I was always known as the Major, perhaps for no better reason than that the speaker, an old journalist, was always called Doctor, I recognized the fact so far as to kick aside an intervening saddle, so that I could see the speaker's face on a level with my own, and said nothing.

"About ghosts!" said the Doctor, after a pause, which nobody broke or was expected to break. "Ghosts, sir! That's what we want to know. What are we doing here in this blanked old mausoleum of Calaveras County, if it isn't to find out something about 'em, eh?"

Nobody replied.

"Thar's that haunted house at Cave City. Can't be more than a mile or two away, anyhow. Used to be just off the trail."

A dead silence.

The Doctor (addressing space generally), "Yes, sir; it *was* a mighty queer story."

Still the same reposeful indifference. We all knew the Doctor's skill as a *raconteur*; we all knew that a story was coming, and we all knew that any interruption would be fatal. Time and time again, in our prospecting experience, had a word of polite encouragement, a rash expression of interest, even a too eager attitude of silent expectancy, brought the Doctor to a sudden change of subject. Time and time again have we seen the unwary stranger stand amazed and bewildered between our own indifference and the sudden termination of a promising anecdote, through his own unlucky interference. So we said nothing. "The Judge"—another instance of arbitrary nomenclature—pretended to sleep. Jack began to twist a *cigarrito*. Thornton bit off the ends of pine needles reflectively.

"Yes, sir," continued the Doctor, coolly resting the back of his head on the palms of his hands, "it *was* rather curious. All except the murder. *That's* what gets me, for the murder had no new points, no fancy touches, no sentiment, no mystery. Was just one of the old style, 'sub-head' paragraphs. Old-fashioned miner scrubs along on hardtack and beans, and saves up a little money to go home and see relations. Old-fashioned assassin sharpens up knife, old style; loads old flint-lock, brass-mounted pistol; walks in on old-fashioned miner one dark night, sends him home to his relations away back to several generations, and walks off with the swag. No mystery *there*; nothing to clear up; subsequent revelations only impertinence. Nothing for any ghost to do—who meant business. More than that, over forty murders, same old kind, committed every year in Calaveras, and no spiritual post obits coming due every anniversary; no assessments made on the peace and quiet of the surviving community. I tell you what, boys, I've always been inclined to throw off on the Cave City ghost for that alone. It's a bad precedent, sir. If that kind o' thing is going to obtain in the foot-hills, we'll have the trails full of chaps formerly knocked over by Mexicans and road agents; every little camp and grocery will have stock enough on hand to go into business, and where's there any security for surviving life and property, eh? What's your opinion, Judge, as a fair-minded legislator?"

Of course there was no response. Yet it was part of the Doctor's system of aggravation to become discursive at these moments, in the hope of interruption, and he continued for some moments to dwell on the terrible possibility of a state of affairs in which a gentleman could no longer settle a dispute with an enemy without being subjected to succeeding spiritual embarrassment. But all this digression fell upon apparently inattentive ears.

"Well, sir, after the murder, the cabin stood for a long time deserted and tenantless. Popular opinion was against it. One day a ragged prospector, savage with hard labor and harder luck, came to the camp, looking for a place to live and a chance to prospect. After the boys had taken his measure, they concluded that he'd already tackled so much in the way of difficulties that a ghost more or less wouldn't be of much account. So they sent him to the haunted cabin. He had a big yellow dog with him, about as ugly and as savage as himself; and the boys sort o' congratulated themselves, from a practical view-point, that while they were giving the old ruffian a shelter, they were helping in the cause of Christianity against ghosts and goblins. They had little faith in the old man, but went their whole pile on that dog. That's where they were mistaken.

"The house stood almost three hundred feet from the nearest cave, and on dark nights, being in a hollow, was as lonely as if it had been on the top of Shasta. If you ever saw the spot when there was just moon enough to bring out the little surrounding clumps of chaparral until they looked like crouching figures, and make the bits of broken quartz glisten like skulls, you'd begin to understand how big a contract that man and that yellow dog undertook.

"They went into possession that afternoon, and old Hard Times set out to cook his supper. When it was over he sat down by the embers and lit his pipe, the yellow dog lying at his feet. Suddenly 'Rap! rap!' comes from the door. 'Come in,' says the man, gruffly. 'Rap!' again. 'Come in and be d—d to you,' says the man, who has no idea of getting up to open the door. But no one responded, and the next moment smash goes the only sound pane in the only window. Seeing this, old Hard Times gets up, with the devil in his eye, and a revolver in his hand, followed by the yellow dog, with every tooth showing, and swings open the door. No one there! But as the man opened the door, that yellow dog, that had been so chipper before, suddenly begins to crouch and step backward, step by step, trembling and shivering, and at last crouches down in the chimney, without even so much as looking at his master. The man slams the door shut again, but there comes another smash.

"This time it seems to come from inside the cabin, and it isn't until the man looks around and sees everything quiet that he gets up, without speaking, and makes a dash for the door, and tears round outside the cabin like mad, but finds nothing but silence and darkness. Then he comes back swearing and calls the dog. But that great yellow dog that the boys would have staked all their money on is crouching under the bunk, and has to be dragged out like a coon from a hollow tree, and lies there, his eyes starting from their sockets; every limb and muscle quivering with fear, and his very hair drawn up in bristling ridges. The man calls him to the door. He drags himself a few steps, stops, sniffs, and refuses to go further. The man calls him again, with an oath and a threat. Then, what does that yellow dog do? He crawls edgewise towards the door, crouching himself against the bunk till he's flatter than a knife blade; then, half way, he stops. Then that d—d yellow dog begins to walk gingerly—lifting each foot up in the air, one after the other, still trembling in every limb. Then he stops again. Then he crouches. Then he gives one little shuddering leap—not straight forward, but up—clearing the floor about six inches, as if—"

"Over something," interrupted the Judge, hastily, lifting himself on his elbow.

The Doctor stopped instantly. "Juan," he said coolly, to one of the Mexican packers, "quit foolin' with that *riata*. You'll have that stake out and that mule loose in another minute. Come over this way!"

The Mexican turned a scared, white face to the Doctor, muttering something, and let go the deer-skin hide. We all up-raised our voices with one accord, the Judge most penitently and apologetically, and implored the Doctor to go on. "I'll shoot the first man who interrupts you again," added Thornton, persuasively.

But the Doctor, with his hands languidly under his head, had lost his interest. "Well, the dog ran off to the hills, and neither the threats nor cajoleries of his master could ever make him enter the cabin again. The next day the man left the camp. What time is it? Getting on to sundown, ain't it? Keep off my leg, will you, you d—d Greaser, and stop stumbling round there! Lie down."

But we knew that the Doctor had not completely finished his story, and we waited patiently for the conclusion. Meanwhile the old, gray silence of the woods again asserted itself, but shadows were now beginning to gather in the heavy beams of the roof above, and the dim aisles seemed to be narrowing and closing in around us. Presently the Doctor recommenced lazily, as if no interruption had occurred.

"As I said before, I never put much faith in that story, and shouldn't have told it, but for a rather curious experience of my own. It was in the spring of '62, and I was one of a party of four, coming up from O'neill's, when we had been snowed up. It was awful weather; the snow had changed to sleet and rain after we crossed the divide, and the water was out everywhere; every ditch was a creek, every creek a river. We had lost two horses on the North Fork, we were dead beat, off the trail, and sloshing round, with night coming on, and the level hail like shot in our faces. Things were looking bleak and scary when, riding a little ahead of the party, I saw a light twinkling in a hollow beyond. My horse was still fresh, and calling out to the boys to follow me and bear for the light, I struck out for it. In another moment I was before a little cabin that half burrowed in the black chaparral; I dismounted and rapped at the door. There was no response. I then tried to force the door, but it was fastened securely from within. I was all the more surprised when one of the boys, who had overtaken me, told me that he had just seen through a window a man reading by the fire. Indignant at this inhospitality, we both made a resolute onset against the door, at the same time raising our angry voices to a yell. Suddenly there was a quick response, the hurried withdrawing of a bolt, and the door opened.

"The occupant was a short, thick-set man, with a pale, careworn face, whose prevailing expression was one of gentle good humor and patient suffering. When we entered, he asked us hastily why we had not 'sung out' before.

"'But we *knocked!*' I said, impatiently, 'and almost drove your door in.'

"'That's nothing,' he said, patiently. 'I'm used to *that.*'

"I looked again at the man's patient, fateful face, and then around the cabin. In an instant the whole situation flashed before me. 'Are we not near Cave City?' I asked.

"'Yes,' he replied, 'it's just below. You must have passed it in the storm.'

"'I see.' I again looked around the cabin. 'Isn't this what they call the haunted house?'

"He looked at me curiously. 'It is,' he said, simply.

"You can imagine my delight! Here was an opportunity to test the whole story, to work down to the bed rock, and see how it would pan out! We were too many and too well armed to fear tricks or dangers from outsiders. If—as one theory had been held—the disturbance was kept up by a band of concealed marauders or road agents, whose purpose was to preserve their haunts from intrusion, we were quite able to pay them back in kind for any assault. I need not say that the boys were delighted with this prospect when the fact was revealed to them. The only one doubtful or apathetic spirit there was our host, who quietly resumed his seat and his book, with his old expression of patient martyrdom. It would have been easy for me to have drawn him out, but I felt that I did not want to corroborate anybody else's experience; only to record my own. And I thought it better to keep the boys from any predisposing terrors.

"We ate our supper, and then sat, patiently and expectant, around the fire. An hour slipped away, but no disturbance; another hour passed as monotonously. Our host read his book; only the dash of hail against the roof broke the silence. But—"

The Doctor stopped. Since the last interruption, I noticed he had changed the easy slangy style of his story to a more perfect, artistic, and even studied manner. He dropped now suddenly into his old colloquial speech, and quietly said: "If you don't quit stumbling over those *riatas*, Juan, I'll hobble *you*. Come here, there; lie down, will you?"

We all turned fiercely on the cause of this second dangerous interruption, but a sight of the poor fellow's pale and frightened face withheld our vindictive tongues. And the Doctor, happily, of his own accord, went on:—

"But I had forgotten that it was no easy matter to keep these high-spirited boys, bent on a row, in decent subjection; and after the third hour passed without a supernatural exhibition, I observed, from certain winks and whispers, that they were determined to get up indications of their own. In a few moments violent rappings were heard from all parts of the cabin; large stones (adroitly thrown up the chimney) fell with a heavy thud on the roof. Strange groans and ominous yells seemed to come from the outside (where the interstices between the logs were wide enough). Yet, through all this uproar, our host sat still and patient, with no sign of indignation or reproach upon his good-humored but haggard features. Before long it became evident that this exhibition was exclusively for *his* benefit. Under the thin disguise of asking him to assist them in discovering the disturbers *outside* the cabin, those inside took advantage of his absence to turn the cabin topsy-turvy.

"'You see what the spirits have done, old man,' said the arch leader of this mischief. 'They've upset that there flour barrel while we wasn't looking, and then kicked over the water jug and spilled all the water!'

"The patient man lifted his head and looked at the flour-strewn walls. Then he glanced down at the floor, but drew back with a slight tremor.

"'It ain't water!' he said, quietly.

"'What is it, then?'

"'It's BLOOD! Look!'"

The nearest man gave a sudden start and sank back white as a sheet.

"For there, gentlemen, on the floor, just before the door, where the old man had seen the dog hesitate and lift his feet, there! there!—gentlemen—upon my honor, slowly widened and broadened a dark red pool of human blood! Stop him! Quick! Stop him, I say!"

There was a blinding flash that lit up the dark woods, and a sharp report! When we reached the Doctor's side he was holding the smoking pistol, just discharged, in one hand, while with the other he was pointing to the rapidly disappearing figure of Juan, our Mexican *vaquero*!

"Missed him! by G-d!" said the Doctor. "But did you hear him? Did you see his livid face as he rose up at the name of blood? Did you see his guilty conscience in his face. Eh? Why don't you speak? What are you staring at?"

"Was it the murdered man's ghost, Doctor?" we all panted in one quick breath.

"Ghost be d—d! No! But in that Mexican *vaquero*—that cursed Juan Ramirez!—I saw and shot at his murderer!"

6

THE LADY'S MAID'S BELL

BY EDITH WHARTON

Edith Wharton (1862–1937) was the first woman to win the Pulitzer Prize for Literature (in 1921, for her novel The Age of Innocence*). Born into a wealthy and prominent New York City family, as a child Wharton traveled in Europe with her parents, becoming fluent in French, German, and Italian. She began writing stories and poems by age eleven, though her mother discouraged this, wanting her to marry well, as befitted a young woman of her social standing. Wharton was friends with many of the elite people of her day, including Henry James, George Washington Vanderbilt II, and Theodore Roosevelt. In addition to fiction, she wrote books about travel and interior and garden design. After 1911, she lived the rest of her life in France, where she was awarded the Légion d'Honneur for her charitable work and support of the French war effort in World War I. "The Lady's Maid's Bell" was first published in 1902.*

I

It was the autumn after I had the typhoid. I'd been three months in hospital, and when I came out I looked so weak and tottery that the two or three ladies I applied to were afraid to engage me. Most of my money was gone, and after I'd boarded for two months, hanging about the employment agencies, and answering any advertisement that looked any way respectable, I pretty nearly lost heart, for fretting hadn't made me fatter, and I didn't see why my luck should ever turn. It did though—or I thought so at the time. A Mrs. Railton, a friend of the lady that first brought me out to the States, met me one day and stopped to speak to me: she was one that had always a friendly way with her. She asked me what ailed me to look so white, and when I told her, "Why, Hartley," says she, "I believe I've got the very place for you. Come in to-morrow and we'll talk about it."

The next day, when I called, she told me the lady she'd in mind was a niece of hers, a Mrs. Brympton, a youngish lady, but something of an invalid, who lived all the year round at her country-place on the Hudson, owing to not being able to stand the fatigue of town life.

"Now, Hartley," Mrs. Railton said, in that cheery way that always made me feel things must be going to take a turn for the better—"now understand me; it's not a cheerful place I'm sending you to. The house is big and gloomy; my niece is nervous, vaporish; her husband—well, he's generally away; and the two children are dead. A year ago I would as soon have thought of shutting a rosy active girl like you into a vault; but you're not particularly brisk yourself just now, are you? and a quiet place, with country air and wholesome food and early hours, ought to be the very thing for you. Don't mistake me," she added, for I suppose I looked a trifle downcast; "you may find it dull but you won't be unhappy. My niece is an angel. Her former maid, who died last spring, had been with her twenty years and worshiped the ground she walked on. She's a kind mistress to all, and where the mistress is kind, as you know, the servants are generally good-humored, so you'll probably get on well enough with the rest of the household. And you're the very woman I want for my niece: quiet, well-mannered, and educated above your station. You read aloud well, I think? That's a good thing; my niece likes to be read to. She wants a maid that can be something of a companion: her last was, and I can't say how she misses her. It's a lonely life . . .well, have you decided?"

"Why, ma'am," I said, "I'm not afraid of solitude."

"Well, then, go; my niece will take you on my recommendation. I'll telegraph her at once and you can take the afternoon train. She has no one to wait on her at present, and I don't want you to lose any time."

I was ready enough to start, yet something in me hung back; and to gain time I asked, "And the gentleman, ma'am?"

"The gentleman's almost always away, I tell you," said Mrs. Railton, quick-like—"and when he's there," says she suddenly, "you've only to keep out of his way."

I took the afternoon train and got out at D—— station at about four o'clock. A groom in a dog-cart was waiting, and we drove off at a smart pace. It was a dull October day, with rain hanging close overhead, and by the time we turned into Brympton Place woods the daylight was almost gone. The drive wound through the woods for a mile or two, and came out on a gravel court shut in with thickets of tall black-looking shrubs. There were no lights in the windows, and the house *did* look a bit gloomy.

I had asked no questions of the groom, for I never was one to get my notion of new masters from their other servants: I prefer to wait and see for myself. But I could tell by the look of everything that I had got into the right kind of house, and that things were done handsomely. A pleasant-faced cook met me at the back door and called the house-maid to show me up to my room. "You'll see madam later," she said. "Mrs. Brympton has a visitor."

I hadn't fancied Mrs. Brympton was a lady to have many visitors, and somehow the words cheered me. I followed the house-maid upstairs, and saw, through a door on the upper landing, that the main part of the house seemed well-furnished, with dark paneling and a number of old portraits. Another flight of stairs led us up to the servants' wing. It was almost dark now, and the house-maid excused herself for not having brought a light. "But there's matches in your room," she said, "and if you go careful you'll be all right. Mind the step at the end of the passage. Your room is just beyond."

I looked ahead as she spoke, and half-way down the passage I saw a woman standing. She drew back into a doorway as we passed and the house-maid didn't appear to notice her. She was a thin woman with a white face, and a darkish stuff gown and apron. I took her for the housekeeper and thought it odd that she didn't speak, but just gave me a long look as she went by. My room opened into a square hall at the end of the passage. Facing my door was another which stood open: the house-maid exclaimed when she saw it:

"There—Mrs. Blinder's left that door open again!" said she, closing it.

"Is Mrs. Blinder the housekeeper?"

"There's no housekeeper: Mrs. Blinder's the cook."

"And is that her room?"

"Laws, no," said the house-maid, cross-like. "That's nobody's room. It's empty, I mean, and the door hadn't ought to be open. Mrs. Brympton wants it kept locked."

She opened my door and led me into a neat room, nicely furnished, with a picture or two on the walls; and having lit a candle she took leave, telling me that the servants'-hall tea was at six, and that Mrs. Brympton would see me afterward.

I found them a pleasant-spoken set in the servants' hall, and by what they let fall I gathered that, as Mrs. Railton had said, Mrs. Brympton was the kindest of ladies; but I didn't take much notice of their talk, for I was watching to see the pale woman in the dark gown come in. She didn't show herself, however, and I wondered if she ate apart; but if she wasn't the housekeeper, why should she? Suddenly it struck me that she might be a trained nurse, and in that case her meals would of course be served in her room. If Mrs. Brympton was an invalid it was likely enough she had a nurse. The idea annoyed me, I own, for they're not always the easiest to get on with, and if I'd known I shouldn't have taken the place. But there I was and there was no use pulling a long face over it; and not being one to ask questions I waited to see what would turn up.

When tea was over the house-maid said to the footman: "Has Mr. Ranford gone?" and when he said yes, she told me to come up with her to Mrs. Brympton.

Mrs. Brympton was lying down in her bedroom. Her lounge stood near the fire and beside it was a shaded lamp. She was a delicate-looking lady, but when she smiled I felt there was nothing I wouldn't do for her. She spoke very pleasantly, in a low voice, asking me my name and age and so on, and if I had everything I wanted, and if I wasn't afraid of feeling lonely in the country.

"Not with you I wouldn't be, madam," I said, and the words surprised me when I'd spoken them, for I'm not an impulsive person; but it was just as if I'd thought aloud.

She seemed pleased at that, and said she hoped I'd continue in the same mind; then she gave me a few directions about her toilet, and said Agnes the house-maid would show me next morning where things were kept.

"I am tired to-night, and shall dine upstairs," she said. "Agnes will bring me my tray, that you may have time to unpack and settle yourself; and later you may come and undress me."

"Very well, ma'am," I said. "You'll ring, I suppose?"

I thought she looked odd.

"No—Agnes will fetch you," says she quickly, and took up her book again.

Well—that was certainly strange: a lady's maid having to be fetched by the house-maid whenever her lady wanted her! I wondered if there were no bells in the house; but the next day I satisfied myself that there was one in every room, and a special one ringing from my mistress's room to mine; and after that it did strike me as queer that, whenever Mrs. Brympton wanted anything, she rang for Agnes, who had to walk the whole length of the servants' wing to call me.

But that wasn't the only queer thing in the house. The very next day I found out that Mrs. Brympton had no nurse; and then I asked Agnes about the woman I had seen in the passage the afternoon before. Agnes said she had seen no one, and I saw that she thought I was dreaming. To be sure, it was dusk when we went down the passage, and she had excused herself for not bringing a light; but I had seen the woman plain enough to know her again if we should meet. I decided that she must have been a friend of the cook's, or of one of the other women servants: perhaps she had come down from town for a night's visit, and the servants wanted it kept secret. Some ladies are very stiff about having their servants' friends in the house overnight. At any rate, I made up my mind to ask no more questions.

In a day or two another odd thing happened. I was chatting one afternoon with Mrs. Blinder, who was a friendly disposed woman, and had been longer in the house than the other servants, and she asked me if I was quite comfortable and had everything I needed. I said I had no fault to find with my place or with my mistress, but I thought it odd that in so large a house there was no sewing-room for the lady's maid.

"Why," says she, "there *is* one: the room you're in is the old sewing-room."

"Oh," said I; "and where did the other lady's maid sleep?"

At that she grew confused, and said hurriedly that the servants' rooms had all been changed about last year, and she didn't rightly remember.

That struck me as peculiar, but I went on as if I hadn't noticed: "Well, there's a vacant room opposite mine, and I mean to ask Mrs. Brympton if I mayn't use that as a sewing-room."

To my astonishment, Mrs. Blinder went white, and gave my hand a kind of squeeze. "Don't do that, my dear," said she, trembling-like. "To tell you the truth, that was Emma Saxon's room, and my mistress has kept it closed ever since her death."

"And who was Emma Saxon?"

"Mrs. Brympton's former maid."

"The one that was with her so many years?" said I, remembering what Mrs. Railton had told me.

Mrs. Blinder nodded.

"What sort of woman was she?"

"No better walked the earth," said Mrs. Blinder. "My mistress loved her like a sister."

"But I mean—what did she look like?"

Mrs. Blinder got up and gave me a kind of angry stare. "I'm no great hand at describing," she said; "and I believe my pastry's rising." And she walked off into the kitchen and shut the door after her.

II

I had been near a week at Brympton before I saw my master. Word came that he was arriving one afternoon, and a change passed over the whole household. It was plain that nobody loved him below stairs. Mrs. Blinder took uncommon care with the dinner that night, but she snapped at the kitchen-maid in a way quite unusual with her; and Mr. Wace, the butler, a serious, slow-spoken man, went about his duties as if he'd been getting ready for a funeral. He was a great Bible-reader, Mr. Wace was, and had a beautiful assortment of texts at his command; but that day he used such dreadful language, that I was about to leave the table, when he assured me it was all out of Isaiah; and I noticed that whenever the master came Mr. Wace took to the prophets.

About seven, Agnes called me to my mistress's room; and there I found Mr. Brympton. He was standing on the hearth; a big fair bull-necked man, with a red face and little bad-tempered blue eyes: the kind of man a young simpleton might have thought handsome, and would have been like to pay dear for thinking it.

He swung about when I came in, and looked me over in a trice. I knew what the look meant, from having experienced it once or twice in my former places. Then he turned his back on me, and went on talking to his wife; and I knew what *that* meant, too. I was not the kind of morsel he was after. The typhoid had served me well enough in one way: it kept that kind of gentleman at arm's length.

"This is my new maid, Hartley," says Mrs. Brympton in her kind voice; and he nodded and went on with what he was saying.

In a minute or two he went off, and left my mistress to dress for dinner, and I noticed as I waited on her that she was white, and chill to the touch.

Mr. Brympton took himself off the next morning, and the whole house drew a long breath when he drove away. As for my mistress, she put on her hat and furs (for it was a fine winter morning) and went out for a walk in the gardens, coming back quite fresh and rosy, so that for a minute, before her color faded, I could guess what a pretty young lady she must have been, and not so long ago, either.

She had met Mr. Ranford in the grounds, and the two came back together, I remember, smiling and talking as they walked along the terrace under my window. That was the first time I saw Mr. Ranford, though I had often heard his name mentioned in the hall. He was a neighbor, it appeared, living a mile or two beyond Brympton, at the end of the village; and as he was in the habit of spending his winters in the country he was almost the only company my mistress had at that season. He was a slight tall gentleman of about thirty, and I thought him rather melancholy-looking till I saw his smile, which had a kind of surprise in it, like the first warm day in spring. He was a great reader, I heard, like my mistress, and the two were forever borrowing books of one another, and sometimes (Mr. Wace told me) he would read aloud to Mrs. Brympton by the hour, in the big dark library where she sat in the winter afternoons. The servants all liked him, and perhaps that's more of a compliment than the masters suspect. He had a friendly word for every one of us, and we were all glad to think that Mrs. Brympton had a pleasant companionable gentleman like that to keep her company when the master was away. Mr. Ranford seemed on excellent terms with Mr. Brympton too; though I couldn't but wonder that two gentlemen so unlike each other should be so friendly. But then I knew how the real quality can keep their feelings to themselves.

As for Mr. Brympton, he came and went, never staying more than a day or two, cursing the dullness and the solitude, grumbling at everything, and (as I soon found out) drinking a deal more than was good for him. After Mrs. Brympton left the table he would sit half the night over the old Brympton port and madeira, and once, as I was leaving my mistress's room rather later than usual, I met him coming up the stairs in such a state that I turned sick to think of what some ladies have to endure and hold their tongues about.

The servants said very little about their master; but from what they let drop I could see it had been an unhappy match from the beginning. Mr. Brympton was coarse, loud, and pleasure-loving; my mistress quiet, retiring, and perhaps a trifle cold. Not that she was not always pleasant-spoken to him: I thought her wonderfully forbearing; but to a gentleman as free as Mr. Brympton I dare say she seemed a little offish.

Well, things went on quietly for several weeks. My mistress was kind, my duties were light, and I got on well with the other servants. In short, I had nothing to complain of; yet there was always a weight on me. I can't say why it was so, but I know it was not the loneliness that I felt. I soon got used to that; and being still languid from the fever, I was thankful for the quiet and the good country air. Nevertheless, I was never quite easy in my mind. My mistress, knowing I had been ill, insisted that I should take my walk regularly, and often invented errands for me:—a yard of ribbon to be fetched from the village, a letter posted, or a book returned to Mr. Ranford. As soon as I was out of doors my spirits rose, and I looked forward to my walks through the bare moist-smelling woods; but the moment I caught sight of the house again my heart dropped down like a stone in a well. It was not a gloomy house exactly, yet I never entered it but a feeling of gloom came over me.

Mrs. Brympton seldom went out in winter; only on the finest days did she walk an hour at noon on the south terrace. Excepting Mr. Ranford, we had no visitors but the doctor, who, drove over from D—— about once a week. He sent for me once or twice to give me some trifling direction about my mistress, and though he never told me what her illness was, I thought, from a waxy look she had now and then of a morning, that it might be the heart that ailed her. The season was soft and unwholesome, and in January we had a long spell of rain. That was a sore trial to me, I own, for I couldn't go out, and sitting over my sewing all day, listening to the drip, drip of the eaves, I grew so nervous that the least sound made me jump. Somehow, the thought of that locked room across the passage began to weigh on me. Once or twice, in the long rainy nights, I fancied I heard noises there; but that was nonsense, of course, and the daylight drove such notions out of my head. Well, one morning Mrs. Brympton gave me quite a start of pleasure by telling me she wished me to go to town for some shopping. I hadn't known till then how low my spirits had fallen. I set off in high glee, and my first sight of the crowded streets and the cheerful-looking shops quite took me out of myself. Toward afternoon, however, the noise and confusion began to tire me, and I was actually looking forward to the quiet of Brympton, and thinking how I should enjoy the drive home through the dark woods, when I ran across an old acquaintance, a maid I had once been in service with. We had lost sight of each other for a number of years, and I had to stop and tell her what had happened to me in the interval. When I mentioned where I was living she rolled up her eyes and pulled a long face.

"What! The Mrs. Brympton that lives all the year at her place on the Hudson? My dear, you won't stay there three months."

"Oh, but I don't mind the country," says I, offended somehow at her tone. "Since the fever I'm glad to be quiet."

She shook her head. "It's not the country I'm thinking of. All I know is she's had four maids in the last six months, and the last one, who was friend of mine, told me nobody could stay in the house."

"Did she say why?" I asked.

"No—she wouldn't give me her reason. But she says to me, *Mrs. Ansey*, she says, *if ever a young woman as you know of thinks of going there, you tell her it's not worth while to unpack her boxes.*"

"Is she young and handsome?" said I, thinking of Mr. Brympton.

"Not her! She's the kind that mothers engage when they've gay young gentlemen at college."

Well, though I knew the woman was an idle gossip, the words stuck in my head, and my heart sank lower than ever as I drove up to Brympton in the dusk. There *was* something about the house—I was sure of it now . . .

When I went in to tea I heard that Mr. Brympton had arrived, and I saw at a glance that there had been a disturbance of some kind. Mrs. Blinder's hand shook so that she could hardly pour the tea, and Mr. Wace quoted the most dreadful texts full of brimstone. Nobody said a word to me then, but when I went up to my room Mrs. Blinder followed me.

"Oh, my dear," says she, taking my hand, "I'm so glad and thankful you've come back to us!"

That struck me, as you may imagine. "Why," said I, "did you think I was leaving for good?"

"No, no, to be sure," said she, a little confused, "but I can't a-bear to have madam left alone for a day even." She pressed my hand hard, and, "Oh, Miss Hartley," says she, "be good to your mistress, as you're a Christian woman." And with that she hurried away, and left me staring.

A moment later Agnes called me to Mrs. Brympton. Hearing Mr. Brympton's voice in her room, I went round by the dressing-room, thinking I would lay out her dinner-gown before going in. The dressing-room is a large room with a window over the portico that looks toward the gardens. Mr. Brympton's apartments are beyond. When I went in, the door into the bedroom was ajar, and I heard Mr. Brympton saying angrily:—"One would suppose he was the only person fit for you to talk to."

"I don't have many visitors in winter," Mrs. Brympton answered quietly.

"You have *me!*" he flung at her, sneeringly.

"You are here so seldom," said she.

"Well—whose fault is that? You make the place about as lively as the family vault—"

With that I rattled the toilet things, to give my mistress warning, and she rose and called me in.

The two dined alone, as usual, and I knew by Mr. Wace's manner at supper that things must be going badly. He quoted the prophets something terrible, and worked on the kitchen-maid so that she declared she wouldn't go down alone to put the cold meat in the icebox. I felt nervous myself, and after I had put my mistress to bed I was half tempted to go down again and persuade Mrs. Blinder to sit up awhile over a game of cards. But I heard her door closing for the night and so I went on to my own room. The rain had begun again, and the drip, drip, drip seemed to be dropping into my brain. I lay awake listening to it, and turning over what my friend in town had said. What puzzled me was that it was always the maids who left . . .

After a while I slept; but suddenly a loud noise wakened me. My bell had rung. I sat up, terrified by the unusual sound, which seemed to go on jangling through the darkness. My hands shook so that I couldn't find the matches. At length I struck a light and jumped out of bed. I began to think I must have been dreaming; but I looked at the bell against the wall, and there was the little hammer still quivering.

I was just beginning to huddle on my clothes when I heard another sound. This time it was the door of the locked room opposite mine softly opening and closing. I heard the sound distinctly, and it frightened me so that I stood stock still. Then I heard a footstep hurrying down the passage toward the main house. The floor being carpeted, the sound was very faint, but I was quite sure it was a woman's step. I turned cold with the thought of it, and for a minute or two I dursn't breathe or move. Then I came to my senses.

"Alice Hartley," says I to myself, "someone left that room just now and ran down the passage ahead of you. The idea isn't pleasant, but you may as well face it. Your mistress has rung for you, and to answer her bell you've got to go the way that other woman has gone."

Well—I did it. I never walked faster in my life, yet I thought I should never get to the end of the passage or reach Mrs. Brympton's room. On the way I heard nothing and saw nothing: all was dark and quiet as the grave. When I reached my mistress's door the silence was so deep that I began to think I must be dreaming, and was half minded to turn back. Then a panic seized me, and I knocked.

There was no answer, and I knocked again, loudly. To my astonishment the door was opened by Mr. Brympton. He started back when he saw me, and in the light of my candle his face looked red and savage.

"You?" he said, in a queer voice. "How many of you are there, in God's name?"

At that I felt the ground give under me; but I said to myself that he had been drinking, and answered as steadily as I could: "May I go in, sir? Mrs. Brympton has rung for me."

"You may all go in, for what I care," says he, and, pushing by me, walked down the hall to his own bedroom. I looked after him as he went, and to my surprise I saw that he walked as straight as a sober man.

I found my mistress lying very weak and still, but she forced a smile when she saw me, and signed to me to pour out some drops for her.

After that she lay without speaking, her breath coming quick, and her eyes closed. Suddenly she groped out with her hand, and *"Emma,"* says she, faintly.

"It's Hartley, madam," I said. "Do you want anything?"

She opened her eyes wide and gave me a startled look.

"I was dreaming," she said. "You may go, now, Hartley, and thank you kindly. I'm quite well again, you see." And she turned her face away from me.

III

There was no more sleep for me that night, and I was thankful when daylight came.

Soon afterward, Agnes called me to Mrs. Brympton. I was afraid she was ill again, for she seldom sent for me before nine, but I found her sitting up in bed, pale and drawn-looking, but quite herself.

"Hartley," says she quickly, "will you put on your things at once and go down to the village for me? I want this prescription made up—" here she hesitated a minute and blushed—"and I should like you to be back again before Mr. Brympton is up."

"Certainly, madam," I said.

"And—stay a moment—" she called me back as if an idea had just struck her—"while you're waiting for the mixture, you'll have time to go on to Mr. Ranford's with this note."

It was a two-mile walk to the village, and on my way I had time to turn things over in my mind. It struck me as peculiar that my mistress should wish the prescription made up without Mr. Brympton's knowledge; and, putting this together with the scene of the night before, and with much else that I had noticed and suspected, I began to wonder if the poor lady was weary of her life, and had come to the mad resolve of ending it. The idea took such hold on me that I reached the village on a run, and dropped breathless into a chair before the chemist's counter. The good man, who was just taking down his shutters, stared at me so hard that it brought me to myself.

"Mr. Limmel," I says, trying to speak indifferently, "will you run your eye over this, and tell me if it's quite right?"

He put on his spectacles and studied the prescription.

"Why, it's one of Dr. Walton's," says he. "What should be wrong with it?"

"Well—is it dangerous to take?"

"Dangerous—how do you mean?"

I could have shaken the man for his stupidity.

"I mean—if a person was to take too much of it—by mistake of course—" says I, my heart in my throat.

"Lord bless you, no. It's only lime-water. You might feed it to a baby by the bottleful."

I gave a great sigh of relief and hurried on to Mr. Ranford's. But on the way another thought struck me. If there was nothing to conceal about my visit to the chemist's, was it my other errand that Mrs. Brympton wished me to keep private? Somehow, that thought frightened me worse than the other. Yet the two gentlemen seemed fast friends, and I would have staked my head on my mistress's goodness. I felt ashamed of my suspicions, and concluded that I was still disturbed by the strange events of the night. I left the note at Mr. Ranford's, and hurrying back to Brympton, slipped in by a side door without being seen, as I thought.

An hour later, however, as I was carrying in my mistress's breakfast, I was stopped in the hall by Mr. Brympton.

"What were you doing out so early?" he says, looking hard at me.

"Early—me, sir?" I said, in a tremble.

"Come, come," he says, an angry red spot coming out on his forehead, "didn't I see you scuttling home through the shrubbery an hour or more ago?"

I'm a truthful woman by nature, but at that a lie popped out ready-made. "No, sir, you didn't," said I and looked straight back at him.

He shrugged his shoulders and gave a sullen laugh. "I suppose you think I was drunk last night?" he asked suddenly.

"No, sir, I don't," I answered, this time truthfully enough.

He turned away with another shrug. "A pretty notion my servants have of me!" I heard him mutter as he walked off.

Not till I had settled down to my afternoon's sewing did I realize how the events of the night had shaken me. I couldn't pass that locked door without a shiver. I knew I had heard someone come out of it, and walk down the passage ahead of me. I thought of speaking to Mrs. Blinder or to Mr. Wace, the only two in the house who appeared to have an inkling of what was going on, but I had a feeling that if I questioned them they would deny everything, and that I might learn more by holding my tongue and keeping my eyes open. The idea of spending another night opposite the locked room sickened me, and once I was seized with the notion of packing my trunk and taking the first train to town; but it wasn't in me to throw over a kind mistress in that manner, and I tried to go on with my sewing as if nothing had happened.

I hadn't worked ten minutes before the sewing machine broke down. It was one I had found in the house, a good machine but a trifle out of order: Mrs. Blinder said it had never been used since Emma Saxon's death. I stopped to see what was wrong, and as I was working at the machine a drawer which I had never been able to open slid forward and a photograph fell out. I picked it up and sat looking at it in a maze. It was a woman's likeness, and I knew I had seen the face somewhere—the eyes had an asking look that I had felt on me before. And suddenly I remembered the pale woman in the passage.

I stood up, cold all over, and ran out of the room. My heart seemed to be thumping in the top of my head, and I felt as if I should never get away from the look in those eyes. I went straight to Mrs. Blinder. She was taking her afternoon nap, and sat up with a jump when I came in.

"Mrs. Blinder," said I, "who is that?" And I held out the photograph. She rubbed her eyes and stared.

"Why, Emma Saxon," says she. "Where did you find it?"

I looked hard at her for a minute. "Mrs. Blinder," I said, "I've seen that face before."

Mrs. Blinder got up and walked over to the looking-glass. "Dear me! I must have been asleep," she says. "My front is all over one ear. And now do run along, Miss Hartley, dear, for I hear the clock striking four, and I must go down this very minute and put on the Virginia ham for Mr. Brympton's dinner."

IV

To all appearances, things went on as usual for a week or two. The only difference was that Mr. Brympton stayed on, instead of going off as he usually did, and that Mr. Ranford never showed himself. I heard Mr. Brympton remark on this one afternoon when he was sitting in my mistress's room before dinner:

"Where's Ranford?" says he. "He hasn't been near the house for a week. Does he keep away because I'm here?"

Mrs. Brympton spoke so low that I couldn't catch her answer.

"Well," he went on, "two's company and three's trumpery; I'm sorry to be in Ranford's way, and I suppose I shall have to take myself off again in a day or two and give him a show." And he laughed at his own joke.

The very next day, as it happened, Mr. Ranford called. The footman said the three were very merry over their tea in the library, and Mr. Brympton strolled down to the gate with Mr. Ranford when he left.

I have said that things went on as usual; and so they did with the rest of the household; but as for myself, I had never been the same since the night my bell had rung. Night after night I used to lie awake, listening for it to ring again, and for the door of the locked room to open stealthily. But the bell never rang, and I heard no sound across the passage. At last the silence began to be more dreadful to me than the most mysterious sounds. I felt that *someone* was cowering there, behind the locked door, watching and listening as I watched and listened, and I could almost have cried out, "Whoever you are, come out and let me see you face to face, but don't lurk there and spy on me in the darkness!"

Feeling as I did, you may wonder I didn't give warning. Once I very nearly did so; but at the last moment something held me back. Whether it was compassion for my mistress, who had grown more and more dependent on me, or unwillingness to try a new place, or some other feeling that I couldn't put a name to, I lingered on as if spell-bound, though every night was dreadful to me, and the days but little better.

For one thing, I didn't like Mrs. Brympton's looks. She had never been the same since that night, no more than I had. I thought she would brighten up after Mr. Brympton left, but though she seemed easier in her mind, her spirits didn't revive, nor her strength either. She had grown attached to me, and seemed to like to have me about; and Agnes told me one day that, since Emma Saxon's death, I was the only maid her mistress had taken to. This gave me a warm feeling for the poor lady, though after all there was little I could do to help her.

After Mr. Brympton's departure, Mr. Ranford took to coming again, though less often than formerly. I met him once or twice in the grounds, or in the village, and I couldn't but think there was a change in him too; but I set it down to my disordered fancy.

The weeks passed, and Mr. Brympton had now been a month absent. We heard he was cruising with a friend in the West Indies, and Mr. Wace said that was a long way off, but though you had the wings of a dove and went to the uttermost parts of the earth, you couldn't get away from the Almighty. Agnes said that as long as he stayed away from Brympton the Almighty might have him and welcome; and this raised a laugh, though Mrs. Blinder tried to look shocked, and Mr. Wace said the bears would eat us.

We were all glad to hear that the West Indies were a long way off, and I remember that, in spite of Mr. Wace's solemn looks, we had a very merry dinner that day in the hall. I don't know if it was because of my being in better spirits, but I fancied Mrs. Brympton looked better too, and seemed more cheerful in her manner. She had been for a walk in the morning, and after luncheon she lay down in her room, and I read aloud to her. When she dismissed me I went to my own room feeling quite bright and happy, and for the first time in weeks walked past the locked door without thinking of it. As I sat down to my work I looked out and saw a few snow-flakes falling. The sight was pleasanter than the eternal rain, and I pictured to myself how pretty the bare gardens would look in their white mantle. It seemed to me as if the snow would cover up all the dreariness, indoors as well as out.

The fancy had hardly crossed my mind when I heard a step at my side. I looked up, thinking it was Agnes.

"Well, Agnes—," said I, and the words froze on my tongue; for there, in the door, stood Emma Saxon.

I don't know how long she stood there. I only know I couldn't stir or take my eyes from her. Afterward I was terribly frightened, but at the time it wasn't fear I felt, but something deeper and quieter. She looked at me long and hard, and her face was just one dumb prayer to me—but how in the world was I to help her? Suddenly she turned, and I heard her walk down the passage. This time I wasn't afraid to follow—I felt that I must know what she wanted. I sprang up and ran out. She was at the other end of the passage, and I expected her to take the turn toward my mistress's room; but instead of that she pushed open the door that led to the backstairs. I followed her down the stairs, and across the passageway to the back door. The kitchen and hall were empty at that hour, the servants being off duty, except for the footman, who was in the pantry. At the door she stood still a moment, with another look at me; then she turned the handle, and stepped out. For a minute I hesitated. Where was she leading me to? The door had closed softly after her, and I opened it and looked out, half-expecting to find that she had disappeared. But I saw her a few yards off hurrying across the courtyard to the path through the woods. Her figure looked black and lonely in the snow, and for a second my heart failed me and I thought of turning back. But all the while she was drawing me after her; and catching up an old shawl of Mrs. Blinder's I ran out into the open.

Emma Saxon was in the wood path now. She walked on steadily, and I followed at the same pace, till we passed out of the gates and reached the high-road. Then she struck across the open fields to the village. By this time the ground was white, and as she climbed the slope of a bare hill ahead of me I noticed that she left no footprints behind her. At sight of that my heart shriveled up within me, and my knees were water. Somehow, it was worse here than indoors. She made the whole countryside seem lonely as the grave, with none but us two in it, and no help in the wide world.

Once I tried to go back; but she turned and looked at me, and it was as if she had dragged me with ropes. After that I followed her like a dog. We came to the village and she led me through it, past the church and the blacksmith's shop, and down the lane to Mr. Ranford's. Mr. Ranford's house stands close to the road: a plain old-fashioned building, with a flagged path leading to the door between box-borders. The lane was deserted, and as I turned into it I saw Emma Saxon pause under the old elm by the gate. And now another fear came over me. I saw that we had reached the end of our journey, and that it was my turn to act. All the way from Brympton I had been asking myself what she wanted of me, but I had followed in a trance, as it were, and not till I saw her stop at Mr. Ranford's gate did my brain begin to clear itself. I stood a little way off in the snow, my heart beating fit to strangle me, and my feet frozen to the ground; and she stood under the elm and watched me.

I knew well enough that she hadn't led me there for nothing. I felt there was something I ought to say or do—but how was I to guess what it was? I had never thought harm of my mistress and Mr. Ranford, but I was sure now that, from one cause or another, some dreadful thing hung over them. *She* knew what it was; she would tell me if she could; perhaps she would answer if I questioned her.

It turned me faint to think of speaking to her; but I plucked up heart and dragged myself across the few yards between us. As I did so, I heard the house door open and saw Mr. Ranford approaching. He looked handsome and cheerful, as my mistress had looked that morning, and at sight of him the blood began to flow again in my veins.

"Why, Hartley," said he, "what's the matter? I saw you coming down the lane just now, and came out to see if you had taken root in the snow." He stopped and stared at me. "What are you looking at?" he says.

I turned toward the elm as he spoke, and his eyes followed me; but there was no one there. The lane was empty as far as the eye could reach.

A sense of helplessness came over me. She was gone, and I had not been able to guess what she wanted. Her last look had pierced me to the marrow; and yet it had not told me! All at once, I felt more desolate than when she had stood there watching me. It seemed as if she had left me all alone to carry the weight of the secret I couldn't guess. The snow went round me in great circles, and the ground fell away from me . . .

A drop of brandy and the warmth of Mr. Ranford's fire soon brought me to, and I insisted on being driven back at once to Brympton. It was nearly dark, and I was afraid my mistress might be wanting me. I explained to Mr. Ranford that I had been out for a walk and had been taken with a fit of giddiness as I passed his gate. This was true enough; yet I never felt more like a liar than when I said it.

When I dressed Mrs. Brympton for dinner she remarked on my pale looks and asked what ailed me. I told her I had a headache, and she said she would not require me again that evening, and advised me to go to bed.

It was a fact that I could scarcely keep on my feet; yet I had no fancy to spend a solitary evening in my room. I sat downstairs in the hall as long as I could hold my head up; but by nine I crept upstairs, too weary to care what happened if I could but get my head on a pillow. The rest of the household went to bed soon afterward; they kept early hours when the master was away, and before ten I heard Mrs. Blinder's door close, and Mr. Wace's soon after.

It was a very still night, earth and air all muffled in snow. Once in bed I felt easier, and lay quiet, listening to the strange noises that come out in a house after dark. Once I thought I heard a door open and close again below: it might have been the glass door that led to the gardens. I got up and peered out of the window; but it was in the dark of the moon, and nothing visible outside but the streaking of snow against the panes.

I went back to bed and must have dozed, for I jumped awake to the furious ringing of my bell. Before my head was clear I had sprung out of bed, and was dragging on my clothes. *It is going to happen now*, I heard myself saying; but what I meant I had no notion. My hands seemed to be covered with glue—I thought I should never get into my clothes. At last I opened my door and peered down the passage. As far as my candle flame carried, I could see nothing unusual ahead of me. I hurried on, breathless; but as I pushed open the baize door leading to the main hall my heart stood still, for there at the head of the stairs was Emma Saxon, peering dreadfully down into the darkness.

For a second I couldn't stir; but my hand slipped from the door, and as it swung shut the figure vanished. At the same instant there came another sound from below stairs—a stealthy mysterious sound, as of a latchkey turning in the house door. I ran to Mrs. Brympton's room and knocked.

There was no answer, and I knocked again. This time I heard someone moving in the room; the bolt slipped back and my mistress stood before me. To my surprise I saw that she had not undressed for the night. She gave me a startled look.

"What is this, Hartley?" she says in a whisper. "Are you ill? What are you doing here at this hour?"

"I am not ill, madam; but my bell rang."

At that she turned pale, and seemed about to fall.

"You are mistaken," she said harshly; "I didn't ring. You must have been dreaming." I had never heard her speak in such a tone. "Go back to bed," she said, closing the door on me.

But as she spoke I heard sounds again in the hall below: a man's step this time; and the truth leaped out on me.

"Madam," I said, pushing past her, "there is someone in the house—"

"Someone—?"

"Mr. Brympton, I think—I hear his step below—"

A dreadful look came over her, and without a word, she dropped flat at my feet. I fell on my knees and tried to lift her: by the way she breathed I saw it was no common faint. But as I raised her head there came quick steps on the stairs and across the hall: the door was flung open, and there stood Mr. Brympton, in his traveling clothes, the snow dripping from him. He drew back with a start as he saw me kneeling by my mistress.

"What the devil is this?" he shouted. He was less high-colored than usual, and the red spot came out on his forehead.

"Mrs. Brympton has fainted, sir," said I.

He laughed unsteadily and pushed by me. "It's a pity she didn't choose a more convenient moment. I'm sorry to disturb her, but—"

I raised myself up aghast at the man's action.

"Sir," said I, "are you mad? What are you doing?"

"Going to meet a friend," said he, and seemed to make for the dressing-room.

At that my heart turned over. I don't know what I thought or feared; but I sprang up and caught him by the sleeve.

"Sir, sir," said I, "for pity's sake look at your wife!"

He shook me off furiously.

"It seems that's done for me," says he, and caught hold of the dressing-room door.

At that moment I heard a slight noise inside. Slight as it was, he heard it too, and tore the door open; but as he did so he dropped back.

On the threshold stood Emma Saxon. All was dark behind her, but I saw her plainly, and so did he. He threw up his hands as if to hide his face from her; and when I looked again she was gone.

He stood motionless, as if the strength had run out of him; and in the stillness my mistress suddenly raised herself, and opening her eyes fixed a look on him. Then she fell back, and I saw the death-flutter pass over her . . .

We buried her on the third day, in a driving snow-storm. There were few people in the church, for it was bad weather to come from town, and I've a notion my mistress was one that hadn't many near friends. Mr. Ranford was among the last to come, just before they carried her up the aisle. He was in black, of course, being such a friend of the family, and I never saw a gentleman so pale. As he passed me, I noticed that he leaned a trifle on a stick he carried; and I fancy Mr. Brympton noticed it too, for the red spot came out sharp on his forehead, and all through the service he kept staring across the church at Mr. Ranford, instead of following the prayers as a mourner should.

When it was over and we went out to the graveyard, Mr. Ranford had disappeared, and as soon as my poor mistress's body was underground, Mr. Brympton jumped into the carriage nearest the gate and drove off without a word to any of us. I heard him call out, "To the station," and we servants went back alone to the house.

7

A GHOST STORY

BY MARK TWAIN

*One of America's most celebrated authors and humorists, Mark Twain
(1835–1910) was born Samuel Langhorne Clemens, in Missouri. He
adopted the pen name Mark Twain from his days as a Mississippi
riverboat pilot. Boat hands would shout "Mark twain!" upon measuring a safe depth of two fathoms. Widely acclaimed for his many
books, especially* The Adventures of Tom Sawyer *and its sequel,*
The Adventures of Huckleberry Finn, *Twain became a friend of
wealthy industrialists, U.S. presidents, and European royalty. Twain
was also popular for his lectures, which nowadays might be called
stand-up comedy. "A Ghost Story" appeared in 1875.*

I took a large room, far up Broadway, in a huge old building whose
upper stories had been wholly unoccupied for years until I came. The
place had long been given up to dust and cobwebs, to solitude and
silence. I seemed groping among the tombs and invading the privacy

of the dead, that first night I climbed up to my quarters. For the first time in my life a superstitious dread came over me; and as I turned a dark angle of the stairway and an invisible cobweb swung its hazy woof in my face and clung there, I shuddered as one who had encountered a phantom.

I was glad enough when I reached my room and locked out the mold and the darkness. A cheery fire was burning in the grate, and I sat down before it with a comforting sense of relief. For two hours I sat there, thinking of bygone times; recalling old scenes, and summoning half-forgotten faces out of the mists of the past; listening, in fancy, to voices that long ago grew silent for all time, and to once familiar songs that nobody sings now. And as my reverie softened down to a sadder and sadder pathos, the shrieking of the winds outside softened to a wail, the angry beating of the rain against the panes diminished to a tranquil patter, and one by one the noises in the street subsided, until the hurrying footsteps of the last belated straggler died away in the distance and left no sound behind.

The fire had burned low. A sense of loneliness crept over me. I arose and undressed, moving on tiptoe about the room, doing stealthily what I had to do, as if I were environed by sleeping enemies whose slumbers it would be fatal to break. I covered up in bed, and lay listening to the rain and wind and the faint creaking of distant shutters, till they lulled me to sleep.

I slept profoundly, but how long I do not know. All at once I found myself awake, and filled with a shuddering expectancy. All was still. All but my own heart—I could hear it beat. Presently the bedclothes began to slip away slowly toward the foot of the bed, as if some one were pulling them! I could not stir; I could not speak. Still the blankets slipped deliberately away, till my breast was uncovered. Then with a great effort I seized them and drew them over my head. I waited, listened, waited. Once more that steady pull began, and once more I lay torpid a century of dragging seconds till my breast was naked again. At last I roused my energies and snatched the covers back to their place and held them with a strong grip. I waited. By and by I felt a faint tug, and took a fresh grip. The tug strengthened to a steady strain—it grew stronger and stronger. My hold parted, and for the third time the blankets slid away. I groaned. An answering groan came from the foot of the bed! Beaded drops of sweat stood upon my forehead. I was more dead than alive. Presently I heard a heavy footstep in my room—the step of an elephant, it seemed to me—it was not like anything human. But it was moving from me—there was relief in that. I heard it approach the door—pass out without moving bolt or lock—and wander away among the dismal corridors, straining the floors and joists till they creaked again as it passed—and then silence reigned once more.

When my excitement had calmed, I said to myself, "This is a dream—simply a hideous dream." And so I lay thinking it over until I convinced myself that it was a dream, and then a comforting laugh relaxed my lips and I was happy again. I got up and struck a light; and when I found that the locks and bolts were just as I had left them, another soothing laugh welled in my heart and rippled from my lips. I took my pipe and lit it, and was just sitting down before the fire, when—down went the pipe out of my nerveless fingers, the blood forsook my cheeks, and my placid breathing was cut short with a gasp! In the ashes on the hearth, side by side with my own bare footprint, was another, so vast that in comparison mine was but an infant's! Then I had had a visitor, and the elephant tread was explained.

I put out the light and returned to bed, palsied with fear. I lay a long time, peering into the darkness, and listening.—Then I heard a grating noise overhead, like the dragging of a heavy body across the floor; then the throwing down of the body, and the shaking of my windows in response to the concussion. In distant parts of the building I heard the muffled slamming of doors. I heard, at intervals, stealthy footsteps creeping in and out among the corridors, and up and down the stairs. Sometimes these noises approached my door, hesitated, and went away again. I heard the clanking of chains faintly, in remote passages, and listened while the clanking grew nearer— while it wearily climbed the stairways, marking each move by the loose surplus of chain that fell with an accented rattle upon each succeeding step as the goblin that bore it advanced. I heard muttered sentences; half uttered screams that seemed smothered violently; and the swish of invisible garments, the rush of invisible wings. Then I became conscious that my chamber was invaded—that I was not alone. I heard sighs and breathings about my bed, and mysterious whisperings. Three little spheres of soft phosphorescent light appeared on the ceiling directly over my head, clung and glowed there a moment, and then dropped—two of them upon my face and one upon the pillow. They spattered, liquidly, and felt warm. Intuition told me they had turned to gouts of blood as they fell—I needed no light to satisfy myself of that. Then I saw pallid faces, dimly luminous, and white uplifted hands, floating bodiless in the air—floating a moment and then disappearing. The whispering ceased, and the voices and the sounds, and a solemn stillness followed. I waited and listened. I felt that I must have light or die. I was weak with fear. I slowly raised myself toward a sitting posture, and my face came in contact with a clammy hand! All strength went from me apparently, and I fell back like a stricken invalid. Then I heard the rustle of a garment—it seemed to pass to the door and go out.

When everything was still once more, I crept out of bed, sick and feeble, and lit the gas with a hand that trembled as if it were aged with a hundred years. The light brought some little cheer to my spirits.

I sat down and fell into a dreamy contemplation of that great footprint in the ashes. By and by its outlines began to waver and grow dim. I glanced up and the broad gas flame was slowly wilting away. In the same moment I heard that elephantine tread again. I noted its approach, nearer and nearer, along the musty halls, and dimmer and dimmer the light waned. The tread reached my very door and paused—the light had dwindled to a sickly blue, and all things about me lay in a spectral twilight. The door did not open, and yet I felt a faint gust of air fan my cheek, and presently was conscious of a huge, cloudy presence before me. I watched it with fascinated eyes. A pale glow stole over the Thing; gradually its cloudy folds took shape—an arm appeared, then legs, then a body, and last a great sad face looked out of the vapor. Stripped of its filmy housings, naked, muscular and comely, the majestic Cardiff Giant loomed above me!

All my misery vanished—for a child might know that no harm could come with that benignant countenance. My cheerful spirits returned at once, and in sympathy with them the gas flamed up brightly again. Never a lonely outcast was so glad to welcome company as I was to greet the friendly giant. I said:

"Why, is it nobody but you? Do you know, I have been scared to death for the last two or three hours? I am most honestly glad to see you. I wish I had a chair—Here, here, don't try to sit down in that thing—"

But it was too late. He was in it before I could stop him and down he went—I never saw a chair shivered so in my life.

"Stop, stop, you'll ruin ev—"

Too late again. There was another crash, and another chair was resolved into its original elements.

"Confound it, haven't you got any judgment at all? Do you want to ruin all the furniture in the place? Here, here, you petrified fool—"

But it was no use. Before I could arrest him he had sat down on the bed, and it was a melancholy ruin.

"Now what sort of a way is that to do? First you come lumbering about the place bringing a legion of vagabond goblins along with you to worry me to death, and then when I overlook an indelicacy of costume which would not be tolerated anywhere by cultivated people except in a respectable theater, and not even there if the nudity were of your sex, you repay me by wrecking all the furniture you can find to sit down on. And why will you? You damage yourself as much as you do me. You have broken off the end of your spinal column, and littered up the floor with chips of your hams till the place looks like a marble yard. You ought to be ashamed of yourself—you are big enough to know better."

"Well, I will not break any more furniture. But what am I to do? I have not had a chance to sit down for a century." And the tears came into his eyes.

"Poor devil," I said, "I should not have been so harsh with you. And you are an orphan, too, no doubt. But sit down on the floor here— nothing else can stand your weight—and besides, we cannot be sociable with you away up there above me; I want you down where I can perch on this high countinghouse stool and gossip with you face to face." So he sat down on the floor, and lit a pipe which I gave him, threw one of my red blankets over his shoulders, inverted my sitz-bath on his head, helmet fashion, and made himself picturesque and comfortable. Then he crossed his ankles, while I renewed the fire, and exposed the flat, honeycombed bottoms of his prodigious feet to the grateful warmth.

"What is the matter with the bottom of your feet and the back of your legs, that they are gouged up so?"

"Infernal chilblains—I caught them clear up to the back of my head, roosting out there under Newell's farm. But I love the place;

I love it as one loves his old home. There is no peace for me like the peace I feel when I am there."

We talked along for half an hour, and then I noticed that he looked tired, and spoke of it.

"Tired?" he said. "Well, I should think so. And now I will tell you all about it, since you have treated me so well. I am the spirit of the Petrified Man that lies across the street there in the museum. I am the ghost of the Cardiff Giant. I can have no rest, no peace, till they have given that poor body burial again. Now what was the most natural thing for me to do, to make men satisfy this wish? Terrify them into it! haunt the place where the body lay! So I haunted the museum night after night. I even got other spirits to help me. But it did no good, for nobody ever came to the museum at midnight. Then it occurred to me to come over the way and haunt this place a little. I felt that if I ever got a hearing I must succeed, for I had the most efficient company that perdition could furnish. Night after night we have shivered around through these mildewed halls, dragging chains, groaning, whispering, tramping up and down stairs, till, to tell you the truth, I am almost worn out. But when I saw a light in your room tonight I roused my energies again and went at it with a deal of the old freshness. But I am tired out—entirely fagged out. Give me, I beseech you, give me some hope!"

I lit off my perch in a burst of excitement, and exclaimed:

"This transcends everything! Everything that ever did occur! Why you poor blundering old fossil, you have had all your trouble for nothing—you have been haunting a plaster cast of yourself—the real Cardiff Giant is in Albany!

"Confound it, don't you know your own remains?"

I never saw such an eloquent look of shame, of pitiable humiliation, overspread a countenance before.

The Petrified Man rose slowly to his feet, and said:

"Honestly, is that true?"

"As true as I am sitting here."

He took the pipe from his mouth and laid it on the mantel, then stood irresolute a moment (unconsciously, from old habit, thrusting his hands where his pantaloons pockets should have been, and meditatively dropping his chin on his breast); and finally said:

"Well—I never felt so absurd before. The Petrified Man has sold everybody else, and now the mean fraud has ended by selling its own ghost! My son, if there is any charity left in your heart for a poor friendless phantom like me, don't let this get out. Think how you would feel if you had made such an ass of yourself."

I heard his stately tramp die away, step by step down the stairs and out into the deserted street, and felt sorry that he was gone, poor fellow—and sorrier still that he had carried off my red blanket and my bathtub.

8

THE NIGHT CALL

BY HENRY VAN DYKE

Born in Pennsylvania, prolific author, poet, and clergyman Henry van Dyke (1852–1933) graduated from Princeton University and Princeton Theological Seminary. Van Dyke's former Princeton classmate President Woodrow Wilson appointed him ambassador to the Netherlands and Luxembourg on the eve of World War I. Van Dyke related his experiences in Europe in his book Pro Patria. *For many years he was a professor of English literature at Princeton, and wrote many books, poems, and stories. "The Night Call" was first published in 1913.*

I

The first caprice of November snow had sketched the world in white for an hour in the morning. After mid-day, the sun came out, the wind turned warm, and the whiteness vanished from the landscape.

By evening, the low ridges and the long plain of New Jersey were rich and sad again, in russet and dull crimson and old gold; for the foliage still clung to the oaks and elms and birches, and the dying monarchy of autumn retreated slowly before winter's cold republic.

In the old town of Calvinton, stretched along the highroad, the lamps were lit early as the saffron sunset faded into humid night. A mist rose from the long, wet street and the sodden lawns, muffling the houses and the trees and the college towers with a double veil, under which a pallid aureole encircled every light, while the moon above, languid and tearful, waded slowly through the mounting fog. It was a night of delay and expectation, a night of remembrance and mystery, lonely and dim and full of strange, dull sounds.

In one of the smaller houses on the main street the light in the window burned late. Leroy Carmichael was alone in his office reading Balzac's story of "The Country Doctor." He was not a gloomy or despondent person, but the spirit of the night had entered into him. He had yielded himself, as young men of ardent temperament often do, to the subduing magic of the fall. In his mind, as in the air, there was a soft, clinging mist, and blurred lights of thought, and a still foreboding of change. A sense of the vast tranquil movement of Nature, of her sympathy and of her indifference, sank deeply into his heart. For a time he realised that all things, and he, too, some day, must grow old; and he felt the universal pathos of it more sensitively, perhaps, than he would ever feel it again.

If you had told Carmichael that this was what he was thinking about as he sat in his bachelor quarters on that November night, he would have stared at you and then laughed.

"Nonsense," he would have answered, cheerfully. "I'm no sentimentalist: only a bit tired by a hard afternoon's work and a rough ride home. Then, Balzac always depresses me a little. The next time I'll take some quinine and Dumas: he is a tonic."

But, in fact, no one came in to interrupt his musings and rouse him to that air of cheerfulness with which he always faced the world, and to which, indeed (though he did not know it), he owed some measure of his delay in winning the confidence of Calvinton.

He had come there some five years ago with a particularly good outfit to practice medicine in that quaint and alluring old burgh, full of antique hand-made furniture and traditions. He had not only been well trained for his profession in the best medical school and hospital of New York, but he was also a graduate of Calvinton College (in which his father had been a professor for a time), and his granduncle was a Grubb, a name high in the Golden Book of Calvintonian aristocracy and inscribed upon tombstones in every village within a radius of fifteen miles. Consequently the young doctor arrived well accredited, and was received in his first year with many tokens of hospitality in the shape of tea-parties and suppers.

But the final and esoteric approval of Calvinton was a thing apart from these mere fashionable courtesies and worldly amenities—a thing not to be bestowed without due consideration and satisfactory reasons. Leroy Carmichael failed, somehow or other, to come up to the requirements for a leading physician in such a conservative community. In the judgment of Calvinton he was a clever young man; but he lacked poise and gravity. He walked too lightly along the streets, swinging his stick, and greeting his acquaintances blithely, as if he were rather glad to be alive. Now this is a sentiment, if you analyse it, near akin to vanity, and, therefore, to be discountenanced in your neighbour and concealed in yourself. How can a man be glad that he is alive, and frankly show it, without a touch of conceit and a reprehensible forgetfulness of the presence of original sin even in the best families? The manners of a professional man, above all, should at once express and impose humility.

Young Dr. Carmichael, Calvinton said, had been spoiled by his life in New York. It had made him too gay, light-hearted, almost frivolous. It was possible that he might know a good deal about medicine, though doubtless that had been exaggerated; but it was certain that his temperament needed chastening before he could win the kind of confidence that Calvinton had given to the venerable Dr. Coffin, whose face was like a monument, and whose practice rested upon the two pillars of podophyllin and predestination.

So Carmichael still felt, after his five years' work, that he was an outsider; felt it rather more indeed than when he had first come. He had enough practice to keep him in good health and spirits. But his patients were along the side streets and in the smaller houses and out in the country. He was not called, except in a chance emergency, to the big houses with the white pillars. The inner circle had not yet taken him in.

He wondered how long he would have to work and wait for that. He knew that things in Calvinton moved slowly; but he knew also that its silent and subconscious judgments sometimes crystallised with incredible rapidity and hardness. Was it possible that he was already classified in the group that came near but did not enter, an inhabitant but not a real burgher, a half-way citizen and a lifelong new-comer? That would be rough; he would not like growing old in that way.

But perhaps there was no such invisible barrier hemming in his path. Perhaps it was only the naturally slow movement of things that hindered him. Some day the gate would open. He would be called in behind those white pillars into the world of which his father had often told him stories and traditions. There he would prove his skill and his worth. He would make himself useful and trusted by his work. Then he could marry the girl he loved, and win a firm place and a real home in the old town whose strange charm held him so strongly even in the vague sadness of this autumnal night.

He turned again from these musings to his Balzac, and read the wonderful pages in which Benassis tells the story of his consecration to his profession and Captain Genestas confides the little Adrien to his care, and then the beautiful letter in which the boy describes the country doctor's death and burial. The simple pathos of it went home to Carmichael's heart.

"It is a fine life, after all," said he to himself, as he shut the book at midnight and laid down his pipe. "No man has a better chance than a doctor to come close to the real thing. Human nature is his patient, and each case is a symptom. It's worth while to work for the sake of getting nearer to the reality and doing some definite good by the way. I'm glad that this isn't one of those mystical towns where Christian Science and Buddhism and all sorts of vagaries flourish. Calvinton may be difficult, but it's not obscure. And some day I'll feel its pulse and get at the heart of it."

The silence of the little office was snapped by the nervous clamour of the electric bell, shrilling with a night call.

II

Dr. Carmichael turned on the light in the hall, and opened the front door. A tall, dark man of military aspect loomed out of the mist, and, behind him, at the curbstone, the outline of a big motorcar was dimly visible. He held out a visiting-card inscribed "Baron de Mortemer," and spoke slowly and courteously, but with a strong nasal accent and a tone of insistent domination.

"You are the Dr. Carmichael, yes? You speak French—no? It is a pity. There is need of you at once—a patient—it is very pressing. You will come with me, yes?"

"But I do not know you, sir," said the doctor; "you are—"

"The Baron de Mortemer," broke in the stranger, pointing to the card as if it answered all questions. "It is the Baroness who is very suffering—I pray you to come without delay."

"But what is it?" asked the doctor. "What shall I bring with me? My instrument-case?"

The Baron smiled with his lips and frowned with his eyes. "Not at all," he said, "Madame expects not an arrival—it is not so bad as that—but she has had a sudden access of anguish—she has demanded you. I pray you to come at the instant. Bring what pleases you, what you think best, but come!"

The man's manner was not agitated, but it was strangely urgent, overpowering, constraining; his voice was like a pushing hand. Carmichael threw on his coat and hat, hastily picked up his medicine-satchel and a portable electric battery, and followed the Baron to the motor.

The great car started easily and rolled softly purring down the deserted street. The houses were all asleep, and the college buildings dark as empty fortresses. The moon-threaded mist clung closely to the town like a shroud of gauze, not concealing the form beneath, but making its immobility more mysterious. The trees drooped and dripped with moisture, and the leaves seemed ready, almost longing, to fall at a touch. It was one of those nights when the solid things of the world, the houses and the hills and the woods and the very earth itself, grow unreal to the point of vanishing; while the impalpable things, the presences of life and death which travel on the unseen air, the influences of the far-off starry lights, the silent messages and presentiments of darkness, the ebb and flow of vast currents of secret existence all around us, seem so close and vivid that they absorb and overwhelm us with their intense reality.

Through this realm of indistinguishable verity and illusion, strangely imposed upon the familiar, homely street of Calvinton, the machine ran smoothly, faintly humming, as the Frenchman drove it with master-skill—itself a dream of embodied power and speed. Gliding by the last cottages of Town's End where the street became the highroad, the car ran swiftly through the open country for a mile until it came to a broad entrance. The gate was broken from the leaning posts and thrown to one side. Here the machine turned in and laboured up a rough, grass-grown carriage-drive.

Carmichael knew that they were at Castle Gordon, one of the "old places" of Calvinton, which he often passed on his country drives. The house stood well back from the road, on a slight elevation, looking down over the oval field that was once a lawn, and the scattered elms and pines and Norway firs that did their best to preserve the memory of a noble plantation. The building was colonial; heavy stone walls covered with yellow stucco; tall white wooden pillars ranged along a narrow portico; a style which seemed to assert that a Greek temple was good enough for the residence of an American gentleman. But the clean buff and white of the house had long since faded. The stucco had cracked, and, here and there, had fallen from the stones. The paint on the pillars was dingy, peeling in round blisters and narrow strips from the grey wood underneath. The trees were ragged and untended, the grass uncut, the driveway overgrown with weeds and gullied by rains— the whole place looked forsaken. Carmichael had always supposed that it was vacant. But he had not passed that way for nearly a month, and, meantime, it might have been reopened and tenanted.

The Baron drove the car around to the back of the house and stopped there.

"Pardon," said he, "that I bring you not to the door of entrance; but this is the more convenient."

He knocked hurriedly and spoke a few words in French. The key grated in the lock and the door creaked open. A withered, wiry little man, dressed in dark grey, stood holding a lighted candle, which flickered in the draught. His head was nearly bald; his sallow, hairless face might have been of any age from twenty to a hundred years; his eyes between their narrow red lids were glittering and inscrutable as those of a snake. As he bowed and grinned, showing his yellow, broken teeth, Carmichael thought that he had never seen a more evil face or one more clearly marked with the sign of the drug-fiend.

"My chauffeur, Gaspard," said the Baron, "also my valet, my cook, my chambermaid, my man to do all, what you call factotum, is it not? But he speaks not English, so pardon me once more."

He spoke a few words to the man, who shrugged his shoulders and smiled with the same deferential grimace while his unchanging eyes gleamed through their slits. Carmichael caught only the word "Madame" while he was slipping off his overcoat, and understood that they were talking of his patient.

"Come," said the Baron, "he says that it goes better, at least not worse—that is always something. Let us mount at the instant."

The hall was bare, except for a table on which a kitchen lamp was burning, and two chairs with heavy automobile coats and rugs and veils thrown upon them. The stairway was uncarpeted, and the dust lay thick under the banisters. At the door of the back room on the second floor the Baron paused and knocked softly. A low voice answered, and he went in, beckoning the doctor to follow.

III

If Carmichael lived to be a hundred he could never forget that first impression. The room was but partly furnished, yet it gave at once the idea that it was inhabited; it was even, in some strange way, rich and splendid. Candles on the mantelpiece and a silver travelling-lamp on the dressing-table threw a soft light on little articles of luxury, and photographs in jewelled frames, and a couple of well-bound books, and a gilt clock marking the half-hour after midnight. A wood fire burned in the wide chimney-place, and before it a rug was spread. At one side there was a huge mahogany four-post bedstead, and there, propped up by the pillows, lay the noblest-looking woman that Carmichael had ever seen.

She was dressed in some clinging stuff of soft black, with a diamond at her breast, and a deep-red cloak thrown over her feet. She must have been past middle age, for her thick, brown hair was already touched with silver, and one lock of snow-white lay above her forehead. But her face was one of those which time enriches; fearless and tender and high-spirited, a speaking face in which the dark-lashed grey eyes were like words of wonder and the sensitive mouth like a clear song. She looked at the young doctor and held out her hand to him.

"I am glad to see you," she said, in her low, pure voice, "very glad! You are Roger Carmichael's son. Oh, I am glad to see you indeed."

"You are very kind," he answered, "and I am glad also to be of any service to you, though I do not yet know who you are."

The Baron was bending over the fire rearranging the logs on the andirons. He looked up sharply and spoke in his strong nasal tone.

"*Pardon! Madame la Baronne de Mortemer, j'ai l'honneur de vous presenter Monsieur le Docteur Carmichael.*"

The accent on the "doctor" was marked. A slight shadow came upon the lady's face. She answered, quietly:

"Yes, I know. The doctor has come to see me because I was ill. We will talk of that in a moment. But first I want to tell him who I am— and by another name. Dr. Carmichael, did your father ever speak to you of Jean Gordon?"

"Why, yes," he said, after an instant of thought, "it comes back to me now quite clearly. She was the young girl to whom he taught Latin when he first came here as a college instructor. He was very fond of her. There was one of her books in his library—I have it now—a little volume of Horace, with a few translations in verse written on the fly-leaves, and her name on the title-page—Jean Gordon. My father wrote under that, 'My best pupil, who left her lessons unfinished.' He was very fond of the book, and so I kept it when he died."

The lady's eyes grew moist, but the tears did not fall. They trembled in her voice.

"I was that Jean Gordon—a girl of fifteen—your father was the best man I ever knew. You look like him, but he was handsomer than you. Ah, no, I was not his best pupil, but his most wilful and ungrateful one. Did he never tell you of my running away—of the unjust suspicions that fell on him—of his voyage to Europe?"

"Never," answered Carmichael. "He only spoke, as I remember, of your beauty and your brightness, and of the good times that you all had when this old house was in its prime."

"Yes, yes," she said, quickly and with strong feeling, "they were good times, and he was a man of honour. He never took an unfair advantage, never boasted of a woman's favour, never tried to spare himself. He was an American man. I hope you are like him."

The Baron, who had been leaning on the mantel, crossed the room impatiently and stood beside the bed. He spoke in French again, dragging the words in his insistent, masterful voice, as if they were something heavy which he laid upon his wife.

Her grey eyes grew darker, almost black, with enlarging pupils. She raised herself on the pillows as if about to get up. Then she sank back again and said, with an evident effort:

"Rene, I must beg you not to speak in French again. The doctor does not understand it. We must be more courteous. And now I will tell him about my sudden illness to-night. It was the first time—like a flash of lightning—an ice-cold hand of pain—"

Even as she spoke a swift and dreadful change passed over her face. Her colour vanished in a morbid pallor; a cold sweat lay like death-dew on her forehead; her eyes were fixed on some impending horror; her lips, blue and rigid, were strained with an unspeakable, intolerable anguish. Her left arm stiffened as if it were gripped in a vise of pain. Her right hand fluttered over her heart, plucking at an unseen weight. It seemed as if an invisible, silent death-wind were quenching the flame of her life. It flickered in an agony of strangulation.

"Be quick," cried the doctor; "lay her head lower on the pillows, loosen her dress, warm her hands."

He had caught up his satchel, and was looking for a little vial. He found it almost empty. But there were four or five drops of the yellowish, oily liquid. He poured them on his handkerchief and held it close to the lady's mouth. She was still breathing regularly though slowly, and as she inhaled the pungent, fruity smell, like the odour of a jargonelle pear, a look of relief flowed over her face, her breathing deepened, her arm and her lips relaxed, the terror faded from her eyes.

He went to his satchel again and took out a bottle of white tablets marked "Nitroglycerin." He gave her one of them, and when he saw her look of peace grow steadier, after a minute, he prepared the electric battery. Softly he passed the sponges charged with their mysterious current over her temples and her neck and down her slender arms and blue-veined wrists, holding them for a while in the palms of her hands, which grew rosy.

In all this the Baron had helped as he could, and watched closely, but without a word. He was certainly not indifferent; neither was he distressed; the expression of his black eyes and heavy, passionless face was that of presence of mind, self-control covering an intense curiosity. Carmichael conceived a vague sentiment of dislike for the man.

When the patient rested easily they stepped outside the room together for a moment.

"It is the *angina*, I suppose," droned the Baron, "*hein*? That is of great inconvenience. But I think it is the false one, that is much less grave—not truly dangerous, *hein*?"

"My dear sir," answered Carmichael, "who can tell the difference between a false and a true *angina pectoris*, except by a post-mortem? The symptoms are much alike, the result is sometimes identical, if the paroxysm is severe enough. But in this case I hope that you may be right. Your wife's illness is severe, dangerous, but not necessarily fatal. This attack has passed and may not recur for months or even years."

The lip-smile came back under the Baron's sullen eyes.

"Those are the good news, my dear doctor," said he, slowly. "Then we shall be able to travel soon, perhaps to-morrow or the next day. It is of an extreme importance. This place is insufferable to me. We have engagements in Washington—a gay season."

Carmichael looked at him steadily and spoke with deliberation.

"Baron, you must understand me clearly. This is a serious case. If I had not come in time your wife might be dead now. She cannot possibly be moved for a week, perhaps it may take a month fully to restore her strength. After that she must have a winter of absolute quiet and repose."

The Frenchman's face hardened; his brows drew together in a black line, and he lifted his hand quickly with a gesture of irritation. Then he bowed.

"As you will, doctor! And for the present moment, what is it that I may have the honour to do for your patient?"

"Just now," said the doctor, "she needs a stimulant—a glass of sherry or of brandy, if you have it—and a hot-water bag—you have none? Well, then, a couple of bottles filled with hot water and wrapped in a cloth to put at her feet. Can you get them?"

The Baron bowed again, and went down the stairs. As Carmichael returned to the bedroom he heard the droning, insistent voice below calling "Gaspard, Gaspard!"

The great grey eyes were open as he entered the room, and there was a sense of release from pain and fear in them that was like the deepest kind of pleasure.

"Yes, I am much better," said she; "the attack has passed. Will it come again? No? Not soon, you mean. Well, that is good. You need not tell me what it is—time enough for that to-morrow. But come and sit by me. I want to talk to you. Your first name is—"

"Leroy," he answered. "But you are weak; you must not talk much."

"Only a little," she replied, smiling; "it does me good. Leroy was your mother's name—yes? It is not a Calvinton name. I wonder where your father met her. Perhaps in France when he came to look for me. But he did not find me—no, indeed—I was well hidden then—but he found your mother. You are young enough to be my son. Will you be a friend to me for your father's sake?"

She spoke gently, in a tone of infinite kindness and tender grace, with pauses in which a hundred unspoken recollections and appeals were suggested. The young man was deeply moved. He took her hand in his firm clasp.

"Gladly," he said, "and for your sake too. But now I want you to rest."

"Oh," she answered, "I am resting now. But let me talk a little more. It will not harm me. I have been through so much! Twice married—a great fortune to spend—all that the big world can give. But now I am very tired of the whirl. There is only one thing I want—to stay here in Calvinton. I rebelled against it once; but it draws me back. There is a strange magic in the place. Haven't you felt it? How do you explain it?"

"Yes," he said, "I have felt it surely, but I can't explain it, unless it is a kind of ancient peace that makes you wish to be at home here even while you rebel."

She nodded her head and smiled softly.

"That is it," she said, hesitating for a moment. "But my husband—you see he is a very strong man, and he loves the world, the whirling life—he took a dislike to this place at once. No wonder, with the house in such a state! But I have plenty of money—it will be easy to restore the house. Only, sometimes I think he cares more for the money than—but no matter what I think. He wishes to go on at once—to-morrow, if we can. I hate the thought of it. Is it possible for me to stay? Can you help me?"

"Dear lady," he answered, lifting her hand to his lips, "set your mind at rest. I have already told him that it is impossible for you to go for many days. You can arrange to move to the inn to-morrow, and stay there while you direct the putting of your house in order."

A sound in the hallway announced the return of the Baron and Gaspard with the hot-water bottles and the cognac. The doctor made his patient as comfortable as possible for the night, prepared a sleeping-draught, and gave directions for the use of the tablets in an emergency.

"Good night," he said, bending over her. "I will see you in the morning. You may count upon me."

"I do," she said, with her eyes resting on his; "thank you for all. I shall expect you—*au revoir*."

As they went down the stairs he said to the Baron, "Remember, absolute repose is necessary. With that you are safe enough for to-night. But you may possibly need more of the nitrite of amyl. My vial is empty. I will write the prescription, if you will allow me."

"In the dining-room," said the Baron, taking up the lamp and throwing open the door of the back room on the right. The floor had been hastily swept and the rubbish shoved into the fireplace. The heavy chairs stood along the wall. But two of them were drawn up at the head of the long mahogany table, and dishes and table utensils from a travelling-basket were lying there, as if a late supper had been served.

"You see," said the Baron, drawling, "our banquet-hall! Madame and I have dined in this splendour to-night. Is it possible that you write here?"

His secret irritation, his insolence, his contempt spoke clearly enough in his tone. The remark was almost like an intentional insult. For a second Carmichael hesitated. "No," he thought, "why should I quarrel with him? He is only sullen. He can do no harm."

He pulled a chair to the foot of the table, took out his tablet and his fountain-pen, and wrote the prescription. Tearing off the leaf, he folded it crosswise and left it on the table.

In the hall, as he put on his coat he remembered the paper.

"My prescription," he said, "I must take it to the druggist to-night."

"Permit me," said the Baron, "the room is dark. I will take the paper, and procure the drug as I return from escorting the doctor to his residence."

He went into the dark room, groped about for a moment, and returned, closing the door behind him.

"Come, Monsieur," he said, "your work at the Chateau Gordon is finished for this night. I shall leave you with yourself—at home, as you say—in a few moments. Gaspard—Gaspard, *fermez la porte a clé!*"

The strong nasal voice echoed through the house, and the servant ran lightly down the stairs. His master muttered a few sentences to him, holding up his right hand as he did so, with the five fingers extended, as if to impress something on the man's mind.

"*Pardon,*" he said, turning to Carmichael, "that I speak always French, after the rebuke. But this time it is of necessity. I repeat the instruction for the *pilules*. One at each hour until eight o'clock—five, not more—it is correct? Come, then, our equipage is always harnessed, always ready, how convenient!"

The two men did not speak as the car rolled through the brumous night. A rising wind was sifting the fog. The moon had set. The loosened leaves came whirling, fluttering, sinking through the darkness like a flight of huge dying moths. Now and then they brushed the faces of the travellers with limp, moist wings.

The red night-lamp in the drug-store was still burning. Carmichael called the other's attention to it.

"You have the prescription?"

"Without doubt!" he answered. "After I have escorted you, I shall procure the drug."

The doctor's front door was lit up as he had left it. The light streamed out rather brightly and illumined the Baron's sullen black eyes and smiling lips as he leaned from the car, lifting his cap.

"A thousand thanks, my dear doctor, you have been excessively kind; yes, truly of an excessive goodness for us. It is a great pleasure—how do you tell it in English?—it is a great pleasure to have met you. *Adieu.*"

"Till to-morrow morning!" said Carmichael, cheerfully, waving his hand.

The Baron stared at him curiously, and lifted his cap again.

"*Adieu!*" droned the insistent voice, and the great car slid into the dark.

IV

The next morning was of crystal. It was after nine when Carmichael drove his electric-phaeton down the leaf-littered street, where the country wagons and the decrepit hacks were already meandering placidly, and out along the highroad, between the still green fields. It seemed to him as if the experience of the past night were "such stuff as dreams are made of." Yet the impression of what he had seen and heard in that firelit chamber—of the eyes, the voice, the hand of that strangely lovely lady—of her vision of sudden death, her essentially lonely struggle with it, her touching words to him when she came back to life—all this was so vivid and unforgettable that he drove straight to Castle Gordon.

The great house was shut up like a tomb: every door and window was closed, except where half of one of the shutters had broken loose and hung by a single hinge. He drove around to the back. It was the same there. A cobweb was spun across the lower corner of the door and tiny drops of moisture jewelled it. Perhaps it had been made in the early morning. If so, no one had come out of the door since night.

Carmichael knocked, and knocked again. No answer. He called. No reply. Then he drove around to the portico with the tall white pillars and tried the front door. It was locked. He peered through the half-open window into the drawing-room. The glass was crusted with dirt and the room was dark. He was trying to make out the outlines of the huddled furniture when he heard a step behind him. It was the old farmer from the nearest cottage on the road.

"Mornin', doctor! I seen ye comin' in, and tho't ye might want to see the house."

"Good morning, Scudder! I do, if you'll let me in. But first tell me about these automobile tracks in the drive."

The old man gazed at him with a kind of dull surprise as if the question were foolish.

"Why, ye made 'em yerself, comin' up, didn't ye?"

"I mean those larger tracks—they were made by a much heavier car than mine."

"Oh," said the old man, nodding, "them was made by a big machine that come in here las' week. You see this house's bin shet up 'bout ten years, ever sence ol' Jedge Gordon died. B'longs to Miss Jean—her that run off with the Eye-talyin. She kinder wants to sell it, and kinder not—ye see—"

"Yes," interrupted Carmichael, "but about that big machine—when did you say it was here?"

"P'raps four or five days ago; I think it was a We'nsday. Two fellers from Philadelfy—said they wanted to look at the house, tho't of buyin' it. So I bro't 'em in, but when they seen the outside of it they said they didn't want to look at it no more—too big and too crumbly!"

"And since then no one has been here?"

"Not a soul—leastways nobody that I seen. I don't s'pose you think o' buyin' the house, doc'! It's too lonely for an office, ain't it?"

"You're right, Scudder, much too lonely. But I'd like to look through the old place, if you will take me in."

The hall, with the two chairs and the table, on which a kitchen lamp with a half-inch of oil in it was standing, gave no sign of recent habitation. Carmichael glanced around him and hurried up the stairway to the bedroom. A tall four-poster stood in one corner, with a coverlet apparently hiding a mattress and some pillows. A dressing-table stood against the wall, and in the middle of the floor there were a few chairs. A half-open closet door showed a pile of yellow linen. The daylight sifted dimly into the room through the cracks of the shutters.

"Scudder," said Carmichael, "I want you to look around carefully and tell me whether you see any signs of any one having been here lately."

The old man stared, and turned his eyes slowly about the room. Then he shook his head.

"Can't say as I do. Looks pretty much as it did when me and my wife breshed it up in October. Ye see it's kinder clean fer an old house—not much dust from the road here. That linen and that bed's bin here sence I c'n remember. Them burnt logs mus' be left over from old Jedge Gordon's time. He died in here. But what's the matter, doc'? Ye think tramps or burglers—"

"No," said Carmichael, "but what would you say if I told you that I was called here last night to see a patient, and that the patient was the Miss Jean Gordon of whom you have just told me?"

"What d'ye mean?" said the old man, gaping. Then he gazed at the doctor pityingly, and shook his head. "I know ye ain't a drinkin' man, doc', so I wouldn't say nothin'. But I guess ye bin dreamin'. Why, las' time Miss Jean writ to me—her name's Mortimer now, and her husband's a kinder Barrin or some sorter furrin noble,—she was in Paris, not mor'n two weeks ago! Said she was dyin' to come back to the ol' place agin, but she wa'n't none too well, and didn't guess she c'd manage it. Ef ye said ye seen her here las' night—why—well, I'd jest think ye'd bin dreamin'. P'raps ye're a little under the weather—bin workin' too hard?"

"I never was better, Scudder, but sometimes curious notions come to me. I wanted to see how you would take this one. Now we'll go downstairs again."

The old man laughed, but doubtfully, as if he was still puzzled by the talk, and they descended the creaking, dusty stairs. Carmichael turned at once into the dining-room.

The rubbish was still in the fireplace, the chairs ranged along the wall. There were no dishes on the long table; but at the head of it two chairs; and at the foot, one; and in front of that, lying on the table, a folded bit of paper. Carmichael picked it up and opened it.

It was his prescription for the nitrite of amyl.

He hesitated a moment; then refolded the paper and put it in his vest-pocket.

Seated in his car, with his hand on the lever, he turned to Scudder, who was watching him with curious eyes.

"I'm very much obliged to you, Scudder, for taking me through the house. And I'll be more obliged to you if you'll just keep it to yourself—what I said to you about last night."

"Sure," said the old man, nodding gravely. "I like ye, doc', and that kinder talk might do ye harm here in Calvinton. We don't hold much to dreams and visions down this way. But, say, 'twas a mighty interestin' dream, wa'n't it? I guess Miss Jean hones for them white pillars, many a day—they sorter stand for old times. They draw ye, don't they?"

"Yes, my friend," said Carmichael as he moved the lever, "they speak of the past. There is a magic in those white pillars. They draw you."

9

TOM TOOTHACRE'S GHOST STORY

BY HARRIET BEECHER STOWE

Known in her day as a devoted abolitionist and women's rights activist as well as an author, Harriet Beecher Stowe (1811–1896) was born in Litchfield, Connecticut, the daughter of a famous Calvinist preacher. She and her husband, Calvin Stowe, participated in the Underground Railroad, helping fugitive slaves escape the U.S. to Canada. She is most famous today as the author of the novel (later also a play) Uncle Tom's Cabin, *which detailed and condemned the mistreatment of black slaves. But she also wrote many other novels and stories. "Tom Toothacre's Ghost Story" appeared in 1871.*

"What is it about that old house in Sherbourne?" said Aunt Nabby to Sam Lawson, as he sat drooping over the coals of a great fire one October evening.

Aunt Lois was gone to Boston on a visit; and, the smart spice of her scepticism being absent, we felt the more freedom to start our story-teller on one of his legends.

Aunt Nabby sat trotting her knitting-needles on a blue-mixed yarn stocking. Grandmamma was knitting in unison at the other side of the fire. Grandfather sat studying "The Boston Courier." The wind outside was sighing in fitful wails, creaking the pantry-doors, occasionally puffing in a vicious gust down the broad throat of the chimney. It was a drizzly, sleety evening; and the wet lilac bushes now and then rattled and splashed against the window as the wind moaned and whispered through them.

We boys had made preparation for a comfortable evening. We had enticed Sam to the chimney corner, and drawn him a mug of cider. We had set down a row of apples to roast on the hearth, which even now were giving faint sighs and sputters as their plump sides burst in the genial heat. The big oak back-log simmered and bubbled, and distilled large drops down amid the ashes; and the great hickory fore-stick had just burned out into solid bright coals, faintly skimmed over with white ashes. The whole area of the big chimney was full of a sleepy warmth and brightness just calculated to call forth fancies and visions. It only wanted somebody now to set Sam off; and Aunt Nabby broached the ever-interesting subject of haunted houses.

"Wal, now, Miss Badger," said Sam, "I ben over there, and walked round that are house consid'able; and I talked with Granny Hokum and Aunt Polly, and they've putty much come to the conclusion that they'll hev to move out on't. Ye see these 'ere noises, they keep 'em awake nights; and Aunt Polly, she gets 'stericky; and Hannah Jane, she says, ef they stay in the house, *she* can't live with 'em no longer. And what can them lone women do without Hannah Jane? Why, Hannah Jane, she says these two months past she's seen a woman, regular, walking up and down the front hall between twelve and one o'clock at night; and it's jist the image and body of old Ma'am Tillotson, Parson Hokum's mother, that everybody know'd was a thunderin' kind o' woman, that kep' every thing in a muss while she was alive. What the old crittur's up to now there ain't no knowin'. Some folks seems to think it's a sign Granny Hokum's time's comin'. But Lordy massy I says she to me, says she, 'Why, Sam, I don't know nothin' what I've done, that Ma'am Tillotson should be set loose on me.' Anyway they've all got so narvy, that Jed Hokum has ben up from Needham, and is goin' to cart 'em all over to live with him. Jed, he's for hushin' on't up, 'cause he says it brings a bad name on the property. Wal, I talked with Jed about it; and says I to Jed, says I, 'now, ef you'll take my advice, jist you give that are old house a regular overhaulin, and paint it over with tew coats o' paint, and that are'll clear 'em out, if any thing will. Ghosts is like bedbugs,—they can't stan fresh paint,' says I. 'They allers clear out. I've seen it tried on a ship that got haunted.'"

"Why, Sam, do ships get haunted?"

"To be sure they do!—haunted the wust kind. Why, I could tell ye a story'd make your har rise on e'end, only I'm 'fraid of frightening boys when they're jist going to bed."

"Oh! you can't frighten Horace," said my grandmother. "He will go and sit out there in the graveyard till nine o'clock nights, spite of all I tell him."

"Do tell, Sam!" we urged. "What was it about the ship?" Sam lifted his mug of cider, deliberately turned it round and round in his hands, eyed it affectionately, took a long drink, and set it down in front of him on the hearth, and began:—

"Ye 'member I told you how I went to sea down East, when I was a boy, 'long with Tom Toothacre. Wal, Tom, he reeled off a yarn one night that was 'bout the toughest I ever hed the pullin' on. And it come all straight, too, from Tom. 'Twa'n't none o' yer hearsay: 'twas what he seen with his own eyes. Now, there wa'n't no nonsense 'bout Tom, not a bit on't ; and he wa'n't afeard o' the divil himself; and he ginally saw through things about as straight as things could be seen through. This 'ere happened when Tom was mate o' 'The Albatross,' and they was a-runnin' up to the Banks for a fare o' fish. 'The Albatross' was as handsome a craft as ever ye see; and Cap'n Sim Witherspoon, he was skipper—a rail nice likely man he was. I heard Tom tell this 'ere one night to the boys on 'The Brilliant,' when they was all a-settin' round the stove in the cabin one foggy night that we was to anchor in French-man's Bay, and all kind o' layin' off loose.

"Tom, he said they was having a famous run up to the Banks. There was a spankin' southerly, that blew 'em along like all natur'; and they was hevin' the best kind of a time, when this 'ere southerly brought a pesky fog down on 'em, and it grew thicker than hasty-puddin'. Ye see, that are's the pester o' these 'ere southerlies: they's the biggest fog-breeders there is goin'. And so, putty soon, you couldn't see half ship's length afore you.

"Wal, they all was down to supper, except Dan Sawyer at the wheel, when there come sich a crash as if heaven and earth was a-splittin', and then a scrapin' and thump bumpin' under the ship, and gin 'em sich a h'ist that the pot o' beans went rollin', and brought up jam ag'in the bulk-head; and the fellers was keeled over,—men and pork and beans kinder permiscus.

"'The divil!' says Tom Toothacre, 'we've run down somebody. Look out, up there !'

"Dan, he shoved the helm hard down, and put her up to the wind, and sung out, 'Lordy massy! we've struck her right amidships!'

"'Struck what?' they all yelled, and tumbled up on deck.

"'Why, a little schooner,' says Dan. 'Didn't see her till we was right on her. She's gone down tack and sheet. Look! there's part o' the wreck a-floating off: don't ye see?'

"Wal, they didn't see, 'cause it was so thick you couldn't hardly see your hand afore your face. But they put about, and sent out a boat, and kind o' sarched round; but, Lordy massy ye might as well looked for a drop of water in the Atlantic Ocean. Whoever they was, it was all done gone and over with 'em for this life, poor critturs!

"Tom says they felt confoundedly about it; but what could they do? Lordy massy! what can any on us do? There's places where folks jest lets go 'cause they hes to. Things ain't as they want 'em, and they can't alter 'em. Sailors ain't so rough as they look: they'z feelin' critturs, come to put things right to 'em. And there wasn't one on 'em who wouldn't 'a' worked all night for a chance o' saving some o' them poor fellows. But there 'twas, and 'twa'n't no use trying.

"Wal, so they sailed on; and by 'm by the wind kind o' chopped round no'theast, and then come round east, and sot in for one of them regular east blows and drizzles that takes the starch out o' fellers more'n a regular storm. So they concluded they might as well put into a little bay there, and come to anchor.

"So they sot an anchor-watch, and all turned in.

"Wal, now comes the particular curus part o' Tom's story; and it was more curus 'cause Tom was one that wouldn't 'a' believed no other man that had told it. Tom was one o' your sort of philosophers. He was fer lookin' into things, and wa'n't in no hurry 'bout believin'; so that this 'un was more 'markable on account of it's bein' Tom that seen it than ef it had ben others.

"Tom says that night he hed a pesky toothache that sort o' kep' grumblin' and jumpin' so he couldn't go to sleep; and he lay in his bunk, a-turnin' this way and that, till long past twelve o'clock.

"Tom had a 'thwart-ship bunk where he could see into every bunk on board, except Bob Coffin's; and Bob was on the anchor-watch. Wal, he lay there, tryin' to go to sleep, hearin' the men snorin' like bull-frogs in a swamp, and watchin' the lantern a-swingin' back and forward; and the sou'westers and pea-jackets were kinder throwin' their long shadders up and down as the vessel sort o' rolled and pitched,—for there was a heavy swell on,—and then he'd hear Bob Coffin tramp, tramp, trampin' overhead,—for Bob had a pretty heavy foot of his own,—and all sort o' mixed up together with Tom's tooth-ache, so he couldn't get to sleep. Finally, Tom, he bit off a great chaw o' 'baccy, and got it well sot in his cheek, and kind o' turned over to lie on't, and ease the pain. Wal, he says he laid a spell, and dropped off in a sort o' doze, when he woke in sich a chill his teeth chattered, and the pain come on like a knife, and he bounced over, thinking the fire had gone out in the stove.

"Wal, sure enough, he see a man a-crouchin' over the stove, with his back to him, a-stretchin' out his hands to warm 'em. He had on a sou'wester and a pea-jacket, with a red tippet round his neck; and his clothes was drippin' as if he'd just come in from a rain.

"'What the divil!' says Tom. And he riz right up, and rubbed his eyes. 'Bill Bridges,' says he, 'what shine be you up to now?' For Bill was a master oneasy crittur, and allers a-gettin' up and walkin' nights; and Tom, he thought it was Bill. But in a minute he looked over, and there, sure enough, was Bill, fast asleep in his bunk, mouth wide open, snoring like a Jericho ram's-horn. Tom looked round, and counted every man in his bunk, and then says he, 'Who the devil is this? for there's Bob Coffin on deck, and the rest is all here.'

"Wal, Tom wa'n't a man to be put under too easy. He hed his thoughts about him allers; and the fust he thought in every pinch was what to do. So he sot considerin' a minute, sort o' winkin' his eyes to be sure he saw straight, when, sure enough, there come another man backin' down the companion-way.

"'Wal, there's Bob Coffin, anyhow,' says Tom to himself. But no, the other man, he turned: Tom see his face; and, sure as you live, it was the face of a dead corpse. Its eyes was sot, and it jest came as still across the cabin, and sot down by the stove, and kind o' shivered, and put out its hands as if it was gettin' warm.

"Tom said that there was a cold air round in the cabin, as if an iceberg was comin' near, and he felt cold chills running down his back; but he jumped out of his bunk, and took a step forward. 'Speak!' says he. 'Who be you? and what do you want?'

"They never spoke, nor looked up, but kept kind o' shivering and crouching over the stove.

"'Wal,' says Tom, 'I'll see who you be, anyhow.' And he walked right up to the last man that come in, and reached out to catch hold of his coat-collar; but his hand jest went through him like moonshine, and in a minute he all faded away; and when he turned round the other one was gone too. Tom stood there, looking this way and that; but there warn't nothing but the old stove, and the lantern swingin', and the men all snorin' round in their bunks. Tom, he sung out to Bob Coffin. 'Hullo, up there!' says he. But Bob never answered, and Tom, he went up, and found Bob down on his knees, his teeth a-chatterin' like a bag o' nails, trying to say his prayers; and all he could think of was, 'Now I lay me,' and he kep going that over and over. Ye see, boys, Bob was a dreful wicked, swearin' crittur, and hadn't said no prayers since he was tew years old, and it didn't come natural to him. Tom give a grip on his collar, and shook him. 'Hold yer yawp,' said he. 'What you howlin' about? What's up?'

"'Oh, Lordy massy!' says Bob, 'we're sent for,—all on us,—there's been two on 'em: both on 'em went right by me!'

"Wal, Tom, he hed his own thoughts; but he was bound to get to the bottom of things, anyway. Ef 'twas the devil, well and good—he wanted to know it. Tom jest wanted to hev the matter settled one way or t'other: so he got Bob sort o' stroked down, and made him tell what he saw.

"Bob, he stood to it that he was a-standin' right for'ard, a-leanin' on the windlass, and kind o' hummin' a tune, when he looked down, and see a sort o' queer light in the fog; and he went and took a look over the bows, when up came a man's head in a sort of sou'wester, and then a pair of hands, and catched at the bob-stay; and then the hull figger of a man riz right out o' the water, and clim up on the martingale till he could reach the jib-stay with his hands, and then he swung himself right up onto the bowsprit, and stepped aboard, and went past Bob, right aft, and down into the cabin. And he hadn't more'n got down, afore he turned round, and there was another comin' in over the bowsprit, and he went by him, and down below: so there was two on 'em, jest as Tom had seen in the cabin.

"Tom he studied on it a spell, and finally says he, 'Bob, let you and me keep this 'ere to ourselves, and see ef it'll come again. Ef it don't, well and good: ef it does—why, we'll see about it.'

"But Tom he told Cap'n Witherspoon, and the Cap'n he agreed to keep an eye out the next night. But there warn't nothing said to the rest o' the men.

"Wal, the next night they put Bill Bridges on the watch. The fog had lifted, and they had a fair wind, and was going on steady. The men all turned in, and went fast asleep, except Cap'n Witherspoon, Tom and Bob Coffin. Wal, sure enough, 'twixt twelve and one o'clock, the same thing came over, only there war four men 'stead o' two. They come in jes' so over the bowsprit, and they looked neither to right nor left, but clim down stairs, and sot down, and crouched and shivered over the stove jist like the others. Wal, Bill Bridges, he came tearin' down like a wild-cat, frightened half out o' his wits, screechin', 'Lord, have mercy! we're all goin' to the devil!' And then they all vanished.

"'Now, Cap'n, what's to be done?' says Tom. 'Ef these 'ere fellows is to take passage, we can't do nothin' with the boys: that's clear.'

"Wal, so it turned out; for, come next night, there was six on 'em come in, and the story got round, and the boys was all on eend. There wa'n't no doin' nothin' with 'em. Ye see, it's allers jest so. Not but what dead folks is jest as 'spectable as they was afore they's dead. These might 'a' been as good fellers as any aboard; but it's human natur'. The minute a feller's dead, why, you sort o' don't know 'bout him; and it's kind o' skeery hevin' on him round; and so 'twan't no wonder the boys didn't feel as if they could go on with the vy'ge, ef these 'ere fellers was all to take passage. Come to look, too, there war consid'able of a leak stove in the vessel; and the boys, they all stood to it, ef they went farther, that they'd all go to the bottom. For, ye see, once the story got a-goin', every one on 'em saw a new thing every night. One on 'em saw the baitmill a-grindin', without no hands to grind it; and another saw fellers up aloft, workin' in the sails. Wal, the fact war, they jest had to put about,—run back to Castine.

"Wal, the owners, they hushed up things the best they could; and they put the vessel on the stocks, and worked her over, and put a new coat o' paint on her, and called her 'The Betsey Ann'; and she went a good vy'ge to the Banks, and brought home the biggest fare o' fish that had been for a long time; and she's made good vy'ges ever since; and that jest proves what I've been a-saying,—that there's nothin' to drive out ghosts like fresh paint.'"

10

A STRANGE STORY
FROM THE COAST

BY REBECCA HARDING DAVIS

Born in Pennsylvania, Rebecca Harding Davis (1831–1910) was a pro-
lific writer, best known for her novel Life in the Iron Mills, *a realistic*
depiction of the difficulties of life among working-class people. She
was also one of the first American female authors to explore the moral
independence of women in a patriarchal society. She was the mother
of the internationally famous war correspondent Richard Harding
Davis. Though her work was largely forgotten at the time of her death,
it was rediscovered in the 1970s. "A Strange Story from the Coast" first
appeared in 1879.

The incident of which you have asked me to give you an account
occurred six years ago, but the details are still fresh in my memory.
The matter impressed me at the time with peculiar force. I am quite

sure that I cannot convey any of this impression to you. I can only give you the facts, and very probably your shrewd common sense will readily find a rational explanation of them. I confess honestly, however, that I have never been able to account for them to myself on any ordinary basis of reasoning.

In February of 1873 her physician ordered C—— to the seashore. Our medical men were then just beginning to find out that the tonic of a bath of salt air for lungs and body, even in winter, was a surer restorer of exhausted vitality than the usual prescriptions of interminable quinine and beef-tea.

We went down together to an old farmhouse on the New Jersey coast in which we had spent a summer years before. The farmer, who was also, according to a common custom there, captain of a coast-schooner, was trading in the South that winter, and had taken his wife with him. We rented the house, opened it, built up fires and began housekeeping in a couple of hours. The older part of the house, built long before the Revolution, consisted of log huts joined one to another, through whose vacant rooms and fireless chimneys the wind from the sea whistled drearily, but the living-room and chamber which we occupied, with their double doors, red rag-carpets and hearths heaped with blazing logs from the wrecks which strewed the beach, were snug and comfortable enough. Outside, the solitude and silence, even at noonday, were so profound that it was incredible to us that we were but a day's journey from New York. This was surely some forgotten outskirt of the world which we had first discovered. The windows on one side of the living-room opened on the vast sweep of water, swelling and sinking that day gray and sullen under the low wintry sky; and on the other upon a plane of sand as interminable, broken at intervals by swamps overgrown with black bare laurel-bushes, by pine woods and by a few lonely fishermen's houses, the surf-boats set up on end against them, rows of crab-cars and seine-reels fronting the leafless orchards.

When C—— and I had visited this coast before it had borrowed a certain gayety and lightness from the summer. The marshes were rich in color; artists were camping under their yellow umbrellas here and there, catching brilliant effects of sky or water; sportsmen from New York in irreproachable shooting-rig were popping at the snipe among the reeds; the sea and bay were full of white scudding sails. But in winter it lapsed back to its primitive condition: the land seemed to answer the sea out of depths of immeasurable age and silence. The only sign of life was the trail of smoke upward to the clouds from some distant cabin, or a ghostly sail flitting along the far horizon. The sand heaped itself day by day in fantastic unbroken ridges along the beach. The very fences and houses had grown hoary with lichen and gray moss that shivered unwholesomely in the wind. Some of these old log houses had been built two centuries ago by Quaker refugees from England under the Proprietary Barclay. They built the houses and settled down in them, so far barred out of the world on this lonely coast that they did not know when their old persecutor Charles was dead. We were almost persuaded that they had forgotten to die themselves when we saw the old graycoated, slow-moving folk going in and out of these houses, with the same names as those of the men who built them, the same features and inexorable habits of hard work and prosy gossip, the same formal tricks of speech and strange superstitions. Indeed, these people usually live to an old age so extreme that it seems as if Death himself forgot this out-of-the-way corner of the world on his rounds. In many of the houses there had been but two generations since the days of the Stuarts, son and father living far beyond the ninetieth year.

A wiry, withered youth of seventy-six, Captain Jeremiah Holdcomb (who is still living, by the way), whom we met one day on the beach, constituted himself our guide and protector: he took us from farm-house to farmhouse by day to make friends with the "old people," always coming in at night to tell us the histories of them and of their houses, and to chuckle boyishly over the "onaccountable notions of them as was gettin' on in years," and to sip a glass of toddy, unctuously smacking his withered lips and wagging his white poll.

One day, as a storm was rising, C—— and I led the old man across the garden at an earlier hour than usual to set him safely on his way homeward. A raw nor'easter blew heavily off sea that evening; the sun had not been seen for two days; the fog was banked up to landward in solid wet masses; the landscape was walled in by it until nothing was left in view but our house and the rotted leaves of the garden-beds, half buried now in drifted sand.

"You have never told us the history of this house, captain?" said C——, looking back at the dilapidated log building behind us.

Holdcomb, as I thought, evaded the question at first. The house, he said when C—— urged it, had been built by a family named Whynne, and still belonged to them, the young man from whom we rented it being himself only a tenant. The Whynnes were of the oldest Quaker stock; the men had always followed the water; they "took to brandy," Holdcomb said, "as a lamb to its dam's milk. Men and women was oneasy, wanderin' folk." But they all came home to this house at the last, which was the reason, he supposed, they were so longlived. He referred here to a belief which we had found current among these people, that a man's hold upon life was stronger in the house in which he was born than in any other.

"Because thar," explained the captain, "is where the yerth first got a grip on him, and thar's the last place it'll be loosened. Now, the Whynnes all lived in this house to an oncommon old age. Thar was a kind of backbone of obstinacy in them all. I reckon Death himself had to have a tough fight with them before he got them under. Old Abner Whynne lived to be a hunderd and four. He died—let me see—he died just sixty year ago, come January. Priscilla was his youngest da'ater. She's livin' yet: she's got no notion of dyin'. She's the only Whynne, though, that is livin'."

On further inquiry it appeared that this said Priscilla had married a Perot, and, being now a childless widow, occupied the Perot house, another decayed old habitation on the other side of the marshes, to the north.

"She was ninety-two last June," said Holdcomb. "It's thirty years since she has been able to hear thunder. But she keeps a-watchin' and a-watchin' out of them black eyes of hern. God knows what fur. But whenever I see her I says to myself, 'It'll come to you some day, Priscilla,' says I, whatever it be. She's got an awful holt on livin', that ther woman. All the Whynnes had, as I told you. She's a mere shackle of bones, and as deaf as that dead sherk yander, but she's got a kind of life in her yet, sech as these pink-an'-white mishy young gells never knowed. I'll take you to see her to-morrow. If she gets a sight of anybody that's come from out of the towns and the crowd, it kind of gives her a fresh start. Yes, we'll go and see her to-morrow," climbing over the bars. "Well, I'll be goin' now. That's all ther is to tell about this house."

"No, no," said C——. "One moment, captain. Those queer squares of brick at the end of the garden, what are they?"

The old man shuffled uneasily: "I don't see no brick. I don't know nothin about 'em."

"Surely, you can see them—close to the house, almost covered with the sand. They look like the entrance to a vault—or they might be graves."

By this time Holdcomb had succeeded in ridding his startled face of every glimmer of meaning, "Oh, them?" staring at them with unconcern. "They were ther long before I was born. I wouldn't worry myself about them if I was you. They've somethin' to do, 's likely, with them old Whynnes that's dead an' gone. I'd let 'em rest. Never dig deep into a rotten ma'ash, 's we say hereabouts."

With that old Jeremiah hobbled quickly away, and C—— and I returned to the house, pausing to look curiously at the sunken squares of brick over which the sand had drifted deep. I remember that C—— remarked irritably that it was evident that the old man knew for what purpose they had been built there, and chose to conceal it from us.

"There is something evil about them," she added, declaring that whenever she passed them she was conscious of some sudden unpleasant physical influence, as though she had breathed miasma. Her illness had made her peculiarly susceptible to outside influences, real or imaginary. I thought nothing more at the time, therefore, of her assertion, though later circumstances reminded me of it.

The next day we crossed the marshes under Jeremiah's guidance, and found Priscilla in the old Perot house. This woman differed from any other human being I had ever seen in some indescribable way. The peculiar effect of it upon me returns whenever I remember her: I would rather see a ghost than think of that nightmare of a woman.

Age had ravaged and gnawed her away mercilessly: nothing was left of her in the world but a little quick-moving shadow. The delicate features, the restless, birdlike hands, the shrunken outline of shape, made but a silhouette of the actual woman that she once had been. The brown flannel gown and crossed white handkerchief which she wore after the Quaker fashion seemed to me like a load hung upon a ghost. For the rest, she was vivacious, keen, hard; she talked incessantly in a shrill, vehement pipe; our answers necessarily were written or by signs. She welcomed us with a kind of fierce eagerness, examined the cut and material of our clothes, and questioned us about the city and the news of the day with the delight of a prisoner to whose dungeon had come a glimmer of light from the world outside. She chattered in return the gossip of the neighborhood—gossip which from her lips obscurely hinted at malignant and foul meanings—occasionally rebuffing old Holdcomb with savage contempt.

"But she's not such a bad un," he said, turning deprecatingly to us. "Naterally, she's a kind, decent soul, Priscilla is. But, you see, it's excitement to her to talk that way: all them Whynnes must have excitement of one sort or another. The men took to liquor, and the women— Now, Priscilla—" suddenly checking himself: "it's like bein' shut up in jail, what with livin' here alone and that dreadful deafness."

The old creature had gone, moving with a quick, nervous step, to a corner cupboard, from which she brought out a plate of seed-cakes. She stood holding them out to me, poising herself on tiptoe, her dark luminous eyes fixed on me from underneath the shaggy white brows.

"No, C——," I said, "this is not a bad woman: she is not immodest nor malignant." Yet I drew back from her. Now I was conscious wherein she differed from other aged people. It was a young woman who looked out of those strange eyes at me. Old Priscilla Perot, in the isolation of her thirty years of deafness, had grown vulgar and bitter in her speech, but back of that was another creature, who was not vulgar, who never spoke. I fancied that it looked out with all the unsatisfied passion and longing of youth through these eyes before me. They seemed perpetually challenging the world to give back something that was lost with a silent, sad entreaty strangely at variance with the shrill, mean talk that came from the woman's lips. I wondered idly when this creature in her had ever lived, and what had killed it, and whether it would ever, in all the ages to come, waken and live again. How many possible human beings, after all, die in each of us and are forgotten before the body gives up too and has to be hidden out of sight!

Old Priscilla went out into the kitchen and bustled aimlessly about. Our coming had made her restless; she laughed without cause; frequent nervous shudders passed over her lean body.

"It's always the way when any one from the city comes near her," said Jeremiah. "She was main fond of the crowd and of town."

"So I should have guessed," said C——. "Do you notice the dainty dress and the high shoes and jaunty bit of ribbon in her cap? Yet she impresses me strangely, as though she might have had once a much finer, more delicate, nature than she shows to us.—She has not always lived here? What is her history?" turning to Holdcomb.

The old fellow gave a scared look at the wan little figure skipping in and out of the dark kitchen: "Lord! how should I know? She belongs to them as was dead and gone before my time." To stop short all further inquiry he began talking to her by signs. She perched herself upon the high wooden chair at one side of the fireplace, looking at C——, her head a little on one side.

"She wants to know what changes I remember in this place?" for so Holdcomb had interpreted C——'s question. "Not many—not many: my time has been so short. Now, my father could remember when a good part of Ocean and Monmouth counties was under the sea. But *he* lived to a good age. Under this house where you are there's been dug up sherks' teeth and the backbones of whales. My grandfather, 's likely, could remember when they swam over this field," pursing up her thin lips thoughtfully. "Thee wasn't here in the war of 1812?" turning sharply on C——.

"No."

"I was here: I had come home for the first time from New York then. I watched the English vessels come up the inlet: it was a gusty afternoon like this. They had come up to plunder the farms. The men that weren't Friends took their guns and went down to fire on them from the shore."

"And those that were Friends?" asked C——.

"Took their guns and went along," with a shrill laugh and nod. "Oh, the young people in the house were terribly frightened. It was all I could do to keep their courage up, silly children."

"Were you not afraid?"

"No. I wasn't young, and I had nothing to lose." She had turned her head, with her back to us, and was talking into the darkness. She hurled out the last words with a kind of defiance. "I had nothing to lose."

"True enough!" said Jeremiah, with many wags of the head and senile blinks of sympathy; but, catching our inquiring looks, he recovered himself with a sudden deprecatory cough and leaned his chin on his cane, silent and attentive.

"I set the children to barring up the windows," continued Priscilla after a moment's pause, "and then I took a ladder and climbed on to the roof. I put my back against the chimney and my feet on the top rung, and there I saw the fight. Our men hid among the salt grass of the ma'ash and picked 'em off one by one. They was main good shots. I saw Ben Stover aim at a man up on the foremast, and then there was a whiff of smoke and down he went in a lump into the water. They said his dyin' yell was terrible to hear," she added with a chuckle.

"What became of Stover after that?" asked Jeremiah.

"He died when he was a young man—only sixty or thereabout. He used to go up and down the beach lookin' for Kidd's treasure, muttering to himself. They said he went mad because there was blood on his hands, him bein' a Quaker. But I knew different from that: it was the money drove him mad—Kidd's money—he was so sure of finding it."

She fell back in her chair, breathless with her vehemence. But in a few minutes she sat upright again and thrust her bloodless, peaked face into mine. "Where did thee say thee came from?"

"New York, mother," signed Jeremiah.

"New York—a-ah!" drawing in her breath. "I lived nigh New York— in a country-place three mile from town, but now they tell me it's in the heart of the city, built over with huckster-shops. Does thee know it?"

I shook my head.

"No, nobody would remember it." she said gently. "I would know it: nothing they could build on it would hide it from me." Her eyes deepened in their sad quiet, the shrill tones softened. For the moment it was the voice of a young woman that we heard.

C—— was about to question her, but Jeremiah interposed: "Take care! Don't ask her what she means. Never before sin' I've known her has she spoken of the time she was in New York. God knows what's drove them words out of her now!"

To change the current of her thoughts he leaned forward and told her by signs the story of our coming to the Whynne house. I was quite willing that she should be turned from any dangerous subjects: I had the uncomfortable feeling when with her that we were dealing with Death himself, or with some forgotten part of a past age more alien and incomprehensible than Death.

"Thee is living in my house?" turning sharply on us. "Yes, it's mine: it will never belong to any but a Whynne. I know every board in it."

Her head dropped on her breast and her eyes were fixed on vacancy. After waiting a few moments, finding that she had apparently forgotten us, we rose to leave her. As C—— came up to bid her good-bye she said, "You will come to your house while we are there?"

"I ?" She started up, standing erect without her staff: her voice was feebler than a whisper, her hands were clasped over her head. But it was the voice and gesture of a young, passionate woman. "Into that house? I'll never cross the threshold while I'm living. It's just a step across the ma'ash, thee knows," appealing to Jeremiah, "but it's nigh sixty year since I put my foot in it. I've never forgot that I was Josiah Perot's wife. There's them waitin' for me there as Josiah never could abide. But when I'm dead—" She threw out her arms with a sudden indescribable gesture of freedom. "I'll have done with Josiah Perot when I'm dead."

C—— drew me away, and we hurried homeward. Glancing back, we could see the woman standing in the doorway: her back was turned toward us, looking out to Sea.

It was a gusty, chilly afternoon. Spectral whitish drifts of fog were blown inland across the marshes. The sun went down in an angry yellow glare which foreboded ill; and then the night fell suddenly, unusually dark, full of shrill whispers of the wind through the swamps and the threatening roar of the sea.

We had, however, I remember, a comfortable hot supper soon ready, and we closed the curtains and heaped up the fire in the living-room to shut out the darkness and strange noises without.

When supper was over and Captain Holdcomb was seated with his pipe in the chimney-corner, we urged him to tell us the history of Priscilla without reserve.

"There's not much to tell," he said. "She was born in this house, and she married Josiah Perot well on in life; and if Josiah was a bit stupid he was a steady, God-fearin' fellow; and that's more than could be said of any Whynne that ever lived."

"But before she married Perot?"

"Well, nothin' happened remarkable—onless," he added reluctantly, "that curious occurrence at Abner Whynne's death. I kin tell you about that," dropping into the singsong of an oft-told tale. "Abner

Whynne was this woman's father. He lived to be a hunderd and four. He lived with his wife down to Sherk River, for the old people had give up this house to their da'ater Peggy, who married Sam Volk."

"Where was Priscilla?"

"Well, I might as well tell the whole on't. It was like this. She wa'n't like the rest on 'em. She wa'n't ez handsome as Peggy, but she was of a different sort, I've heard say—finer an' harder to please. She went up to New York, and ther she fell in with a Captain John Salterre, commanding a brig that run to the Mediterranean. He war a handsome fellow, 'cordin' to accounts, and of a high family—very different from the Whynnes. Word came back that she war married to him, and next (that al'ays was the queer part of it to me) that he had sent her to school. Oh, I've heard my father say when she came back in 1812 she could speak one of them foreign tongues quite fluent. Her father al'ays set great store by Priscilla, though she never come anigh him. Peggy grew to be a humble, hard-workin' woman in middle age, and war a faithful da'ater. But, Lord! he cared not a copper cent for her. It was all 'My da'ater Priscilla,' because she had made the grand marriage in New York. When her mother died down to Sherk River, Peggy war ther. She said, 'now, daddy, thee must come along home to me.'—'I will not, Margaret, he says.—'But thee must,' says she: 'thee cannot live here alone.' For he was then ninety-eight.—'I hev my lines to watch,' says he. For he was a fisherman, thee knows. 'Very well, daddy,' says Peggy, 'thee can set thee lines in the inlet jest as well as Sherk River.' Then she ups and packs his clock and his wooden chair (it's this one I'm sittin' on, only it had a sheep-skin cover on then) and his tea-kettle and his fire-dogs, so's he might feel at home, and she fixed them all up in this hyar room back of me." Jeremiah, with his staff, pushed open the door into the half-ruined chamber behind him. The log walls had fallen to decay half a century ago, but there was the fireplace with rusted irons on the hearth—the very fire-dogs he had mentioned, perhaps.

"That was his room, and he could do as he pleased in it. He used to set by the door yander, his old deaf yaller dog Turk lyin' atween his knees, both on 'em a-lookin' out at the sea hour in an' hour out. He lived on here with Peggy for six year. In that time no word came from Priscilla. He used to talk about her and her grandeur to the men a-fishin', but we all knowed it was jest his notions, for she never sent him a letter or made a sign. I was a peart young lad then, rising sixteen. It's jest sixty year ago, last October, when one mornin' Peggy went in to get the old man's coffee for him. She al'ays made his bite of break-fast ready afore anything else. 'I'll have no coffee, Peggy,' says he.—'Is thee sick, daddy?' says she. For it was the first time he had ever refused his breakfast. As for sickness, he had never been sick an hour since any living man could remember, though as to his boyhood nobody was left on this yerth that remembered that. So Peggy was sort of stunned. 'Is thee sick?' says she.—'No: I never was better, he says; but I'll eat naught, I tell thee.' So he fell asleep, and Peggy went out. But she could not 'tend to her work, she was that dazed. She told me she was mendin' Sam's nets that mornin' (Sam was her husband), and presently out comes daddy dressed and leanin' on his staff as usual. He sat down in this chair by the fire yander, and she brought him his breakfast, and he ate it. About an hour after Joshua Van Dorn came in, and he and Peggy talked of the blue mackerel, for there was a school of them in, and Sam hed made a good haul that mornin'. Joshua was but a boy about twenty, but a strong, rugged fellow. Abner said nothin' to him until he was on his feet to go: then he says, 'Joshua, Sam'll be out eel-fishin' to-night, and I want thee to come an' watch with me. I'll die to-night when the tide goes out.' Joshua thought it was jest his notions. 'All right, daddy' says he, winkin' at Peggy. 'I'll come and watch with thee, and eat breakfast with thee too in the mornin'. Who'll I bring with me? Jeremiah Holdcomb?'—'Jeremiah'll do as well as another: it's the same to me. It'll not take a strong man to streak me,' says the old man; and he laughed, looking down at himself. For he was lean like Priscilla. The Whynnes wear away with age. Peggy said he sot 'most all day by the door yander, lookin' out to sea. Ther's some think that old sea-farin' men hes a warnin' from the water when their time's come. I dunno how that may be. But old Abner he sot lookin' out all day. When Sam come in he talked about the blue-mackerel haul. Sam watched him keerful, but he couldn't see as there was aught the matter with him."

"Was no clergyman sent for ?" demanded C——. "Did nobody remind him of the God that he was going to meet?"

Jeremiah looked up startled, chuckled and grew suddenly grave: "Nobody'd go to a Whynne with that sort of talk. I doubt ef old Abner in all his hunderd year had ever thought of a God, any more than his dog Turk hed. Him and Priscilla war jest alike. They belonged to this yerth. But as to their turnin' up agen in any other—I dunno: I reckon they won't," shaking his head decisively.

"Go on with the story," said C——.

"Well, come evenin', Sam started out eel-fishin'. Daddy nodded to him. 'Good-bye, Sam Volk, says he: 'I'll be gone afore thee gets back. Sam humored him. 'Good-bye, daddy,' he says. 'Is there aught I ken do for thee afore I go?'—'No,' he says, 'no.' But he took Sam's hand and kept looking up at him. 'Onless,' he says, 'thee could fetch Priscilla hyar. I'd like to hev seen the girl afore I go. I hev it on my mind ther's somethin' she wants to say to me.'—I can't do that, thee knows, daddy,' says Sam. For we all thought she was in foreign parts. But she'd been livin' in New York for four year, and that very night, as it turned out, she was on her way home in John Van Dorn's schooner.

"Well, Joshua and I come in to watch. We sent Peggy to bed at the usual time, eight o'clock, for neither she nor we thought aught ra'aly ailed the old man. He took no notice of her when she went, nor of the children: he never could abide children. 'I'll make you some toddy, boys, to keep you awake,' he says; and we war willin'. Ther was not a man on the Jarsey coast could brew toddy like old Abner. It was prime toddy, that's a fact. He drank a bit, and then he went to bed (he wouldn't hev any help in ondressin'), and when he was stretched out he whistled for old Turk, and the brute lay down across his feet. 'Good fellow! good fellow!' he says, and he put his hand on the dog's head and straightened himself, and so went to sleep. About ten o'clock Joshua called to me: he was standin' by the bed. 'Jerry,' says he, 'ther's a queer settlin' in the old man's face, and his pulse is mighty low. Shouldn't wonder ef he'd been in the right of it about himself, after all.'—'Shell I call Peggy?' I says— 'no,' says he: 'wait a bit.' But in a hour he says, 'Jerry, go and call Peggy.' So I called her. But what could we do? He was goin' out with the tide. He didn't move or speak, and his eyes were shet: he didn't hear Peggy or the children when they was cryin' about him. His breath got slowly thinner and thinner, and his flesh colder. When Peggy called to him he took no notice, but the dog raised himself after a while on his fore legs and looked in his face and gave a howl. I declar' it skeert me, it was so like a human bein'. The old man stirred at that, and sort of smiled, and his lips moved as if to say 'Good fellow!' But he was too far gone to speak. Then it was all quiet. I opened the window yander" (pointing to the square opening in the ruined wall of the room outside), "and I stood by it watchin' the tide go down, jest as you might be doin' now. And he lay on the bed hyar jest by the door. It was a clear night, and I could see the line of white surf sinkin' lower and lower. I knowed by Peggy's face, leanin' over him, that he was goin' with it fast. At last the sea fell out of sight into the darkness. Then I shut the window: I knowed it was all over. When I come up to the bed he was dead: Joshua was closin' his eyes. We folded his hands and straightened him. It seemed to me but a few minutes till he was stark and stiff and dreadful cold. I remember Joshua said it was onusual, and was because there was so little blood in his body, but how that might be I dunno. We sot with him till mornin'. Now, here's the cur'ous part of the story. You'll likely not believe it, but I'll tell you word for word, jest as it happened. An hour after Abner Whynne died his da'ater Priscilla come to the house. She had landed at the inlet, where the men war a-fishin', and Sam brought her over. She war not a very young woman, but she was like a lady—very fine appearing. She was greatly excited when she found her father dead, though she skercely spoke a word. 'You come too late,' says Peggy. 'You might have given him a deal of comfort. But you're too late.' I didn't know before that Peggy war so bitter agen her.—'I must speak to him,' she said; and she tore off the sheet and put her hand to his heart. I could see her start when she felt the cold. 'Daddy!' she cried, 'daddy!'—'Let the dead rest, Priscilla,' says Peggy.—'Go out, all of you,' she says, motionin' to the door. 'Let me have him to myself.'

"I went out, an' took Peggy. Priscilla kept a-cryin' in a low voice, 'Daddy! daddy!' I went outside—I was that cur'ous—and looked in the window. Fur God! I tell you the truth. The dead man opened his eyes and sat up. 'Why did you bring me back?' he said. 'Why did you not let me alone, Priscilla? I was at rest.' She leaned over him, sobbin'. Presently he says, 'Is your husband here?' Then she whispered something. God knows what. But I reckon the whole truth was wrenched out of her. You can't lie to the dead. He sat up in the bed, and I saw him point with one hand to the door. 'Begone!' says he: 'you are no da'ater of mine.' She stood a minute, and then came out, and ran a-past me, cryin', into the dark."

"Of course you only fancied that you saw the man alive through the window?" said C——.

"I dunno," said Holdcomb doggedly. "I do know as she has never crossed the doorway from that night, and that's sixty year gone. And," lowering his voice, "when we come back into the room the old man was dead and stark as we had left him. *But he was sitting bolt upright in the bed.*"

"What do you suppose she had told him?"

"Oh, that soon come out. She never had been John Salterre's wife. A sort of shame had seized her at last, and she had left him and come home. She's lived hyar ever since. Four year later she married Josiah Perot, who was a heap better husband than she deserved. She married him for a home: she never could abide to work. But nobody ever thought she cared aught for him. The Whynnes never forget, and I believe she thinks of John Salterre at this minute, and keers for him jest the same as she did when she war a young girl."

"What became of him? Did he ever find her?" I asked.

Jeremiah hesitated: "I didn't mean to tell thee that. A year after her father died Salterre found out whar she was, and put off straight from New York on a schooner for this inlet. The schooner—the Petrel it was—struck the bar out yander, and the crew was lost, Salterre and all. They war buried in the sand on the beach, jest where they come ashore, 's the custom was."

The old man rose and began to put on his coat. We were not sorry to have him go. His ghastly story made us quite willing to close the door on the dilapidated apartment outside and to turn our thoughts to cheerfuller matters.

For a week afterward the threatened nor'-east storm kept us in-doors. The captain did not come to pay his daily visit, and we heard from a neighbor that he "was attendin' on Priscilla Perot, who was waitin' her call."

"Jerry's a main good doctor," she added. "But I doubt he'll not keep old Priscilla. She's bein' took off afore her time: the Whynnes live to a great old age. But they say she's been restlesslike ever since she talked to thee about her young days in this house."

The storm continued to rage so heavily that it shut us in to an absolute solitude. Even the hardiest fishermen did not venture out upon the beach. On the second night it abated. C—— and I were sitting by the fire reading between ten and eleven o'clock, when, finding that the beating of the rain upon the roof had ceased, I opened the door into the ruined room of which Holdcomb had told the story, and looked out. The wind had changed: the storm-clouds were driving to the east, and were banked on that horizon in a solid rampart; the moon shone out whitely on the surging sea and on the drenched marshes webbed with the swollen black lines of the creeks. The tide-water had risen to an unprecedented height, and was within three feet of our door.

I called C—— to look. "If the storm had lasted a few hours longer," I said, "the Whynne house would have gone at last."

We both stood in the doorway between the living-room, in which we had been sitting, and Abner Whynne's old chamber. The latter was clearly lighted by the moon and by the fire and lamplight in the room behind us. As I looked down through the broken wall to the marsh, C—— touched my arm, whispering, "Who is this?"

I turned. A small dark figure was crossing the beach, coming up toward the house. It came with such rapidity that before I had time to speak it stood in the outer doorway, and was in the room beside us.

"Priscilla!" cried C——.

The woman had reached the spot where, as Jeremiah told us, her father had died. She halted there a moment. I saw her face as distinctly as that of C——, being about the same distance from both. It was Priscilla, and yet not Priscilla. The weight of age had dropped away.

This was the creature which I had fancied still lived in the woman, young, passionate, it might be wicked, but in no sense Perot's vulgar, malignant widow.

She hesitated but a moment, and then passed through the back door into the garden, where the sand lay heaped by the storm in deep wet drifts. C—— and I hurried after her, each with the same thought, that the dying woman had become deranged and had escaped from her attendants with the wild fancy of reaching her old home. She suddenly flung out her arms with a vehement gesture of triumph, and passed around a projection of the wall. We reached the spot in an instant. It was the place where the mysterious heaps of brick were erected, one of which rose slightly above the sand. She was not there: sea and marsh and beach were utterly vacant.

We went into the house, and, I am bound to confess, we slept little that night.

Captain Holdcomb came early the next morning.

"The widow Perot is dead at last," was his first greeting.

"What time did she die?" asked C——.

"Last night at half-past ten o'clock." C—— rose, and going out beckoned the old man to follow her. "These are graves," she said, pointing to the heap of bricks. "Who were buried here?"

"I didn't keer to tell thee: I was afraid it might make thee oncomfortable. But—as thee knows so much the crew of the Petrel was buried onder them. That one which is part oncovered by the wind is whar Captain John Salterre is laid."

The old man never knew our reason for asking. There is my ghost-story, the only one for which I have never heard a rational explanation.

11

THE WOMAN AT SEVEN BROTHERS

BY WILBUR DANIEL STEELE

A famous author of short stories, plays, and novels, Wilbur Daniel Steele (1886–1970) was raised mainly in Denver, Colorado, where his father was a university professor. Steele was well known for his mastery at creating a dark, foreboding atmosphere in his many ghost stories. "The Woman at Seven Brothers" was published in 1908.

I tell you sir, I was innocent. I didn't know any more about the world at twenty-two than some do at twelve. My uncle and aunt in Duxbury brought me up strict; I studied hard in high school, I worked hard after hours, and I went to church twice on Sundays, and I can't see it's right to put me in a place like this, with crazy people. Oh yes, I know they're crazy—you can't tell *me*. As for what they said in court about finding her with her husband, that's the Inspector's lie, sir, because he's down on me, and wants to make it look like my fault.

No, sir, I can't say as I thought she was handsome—not at first. For one thing, her lips were too thin and white, and her color was bad. I'll tell you a fact, sir; that first day I came off to the Light I was sitting on my cot in the store-room (that's where the assistant keeper sleeps at the Seven Brothers), as lonesome as I could be, away from home for the first time, and the water all around me, and, even though it was a calm day, pounding enough on the ledge to send a kind of a *woom-woom-woom* whining up through all that solid rock of the tower. And when old Fedderson poked his head down from the living-room with the sunshine above making a kind of bright frame around his hair and whiskers, to give me a cheery, "Make yourself to home, son!" I remember I said to myself: "*He's* all right. I'll get along with *him*. But his wife's enough to sour milk." That was queer, because she was so much under him in age—'long about twenty-eight or so, and him nearer fifty. But that's what I said, sir.

Of course that feeling wore off, same as any feeling will wear off sooner or later in a place like the Seven Brothers. Cooped up in a place like that you come to know folks so well that you forget what they *do* look like. There was a long time I never noticed her, any more than you'd notice the cat. We used to sit of an evening around the table, as if you were Fedderson there, and me here, and her somewhere back there, in the rocker, knitting. Fedderson would be working on his Jacob's-ladder, and I'd be reading. He'd been working on that Jacob's-ladder a year, I guess, and every time the Inspector came off with the tender he was so astonished to see how good that ladder was that the old man would go to work and make it better. That's all he lived for.

If I was reading, as I say, I daren't take my eyes off the book, or Fedderson had me. And then he'd begin—what the Inspector said about him. How surprised the member of the board had been, that time, to see everything so clean about the light. What the Inspector had said about Fedderson's being stuck here in a second-class light—best keeper on the coast. And so on and so on, till either he or I had to go aloft and have a look at the wicks.

He'd been there twenty-three years, all told, and he'd got used to the feeling that he was kept down unfair—so used to it, I guess, that he fed on it, and told himself how folks ashore would talk when he was dead and gone—best keeper on the coast—kept down unfair. Not that he said that to me. No, he was far too loyal and humble and respectful, doing his duty without complaint, as anybody could see.

And all that time, night after night, hardly ever a word out of the woman. As I remember it, she seemed more like a piece of furniture than anything else—not even a very good cook, nor over and above tidy. One day, when he and I were trimming the lamp, he passed the remark that his *first* wife used to dust the lens and take a pride in it. Not that he said a word against Anna, though. He never said a word against any living mortal; he was too upright.

I don't know how it came about; or, rather, I *do* know, but it was so sudden, and so far away from my thoughts, that it shocked me, like the world turned over. It was at prayers. That night I remember Fedderson was uncommon long-winded. We'd had a batch of newspapers out by the tender, and at such times the old man always made a long watch of it, getting the world straightened out. For one thing, the United States minister to Turkey was dead. Well, from him and his soul, Fedderson got on to Turkey and the Presbyterian college there, and from that to heathen in general. He rambled on and on, like the surf on the ledge, *woom-woom-woom*, never coming to an end.

You know how you'll be at prayers sometimes. My mind strayed. I counted the canes in the chair-seat where I was kneeling; I plaited a corner of the table-cloth between my fingers for a spell, and by and by my eyes went wandering up the back of the chair.

The woman, sir, was looking at me. Her chair was back to mine, close, and both our heads were down in the shadow under the edge of the table, with Fedderson clear over on the other side by the stove. And there were her two eyes hunting mine between the spindles in the shadow. You won't believe me, sir, but I tell you I felt like jumping to my feet and running out of the room—it was so queer.

I don't know what her husband was praying about after that. His voice didn't mean anything, no more than the seas on the ledge away down there. I went to work to count the canes in the seat again, but all my eyes were in the top of my head. It got so I couldn't stand it. We were at the Lord's prayer, saying it singsong together, when I had to look up again. And there her two eyes were, between the spindles, hunting mine. Just then all of us were saying, "Forgive us our trespasses—" I thought of it afterward.

When we got up she was turned the other way, but I couldn't help seeing her cheeks were red. It was terrible. I wondered if Fedderson would notice, though I might have known he wouldn't—not him. He was in too much of a hurry to get at his Jacob's-ladder, and then he had to tell me for the tenth time what the Inspector'd said that day about getting him another light—Kingdom Come, maybe, he said.

I made some excuse or other and got away. Once in the store-room, I sat down on my cot and stayed there a long time, feeling queerer than anything. I read a chapter in the Bible, I don't know why. After I'd got my boots off I sat with them in my hands for as much as an hour, I guess, staring at the oil-tank and its lopsided shadow on the wall. I tell you, sir, I was shocked. I was only twenty-two remember, and I was shocked and horrified.

And when I did turn in, finally, I didn't sleep at all well. Two or three times I came to, sitting straight up in bed. Once I got up and opened the outer door to have a look. The water was like glass, dim, without a breath of wind, and the moon just going down. Over on the black shore I made out two lights in a village, like a pair of eyes watching. Lonely? My, yes! Lonely and nervous. I had a horror of her, sir. The dinghy-boat hung on its davits just there in front of the door, and for a minute I had an awful hankering to climb into it, lower away, and row off, no matter where. It sounds foolish.

Well, it seemed foolish next morning, with the sun shining and everything as usual—Fedderson sucking his pen and wagging his head over his eternal "log," and his wife down in the rocker with her head in the newspaper, and her breakfast work still waiting. I guess that jarred it out of me more than anything else—sight of her slouched down there, with her stringy, yellow hair and her dusty apron and the pale back of her neck, reading the Society Notes. *Society Notes!* Think of it! For the first time since I came to Seven Brothers I wanted to laugh.

I guess I did laugh when I went aloft to clean the lamp and found everything so free and breezy, gulls flying high and little whitecaps making under a westerly. It was like feeling a big load dropped off your shoulders. Fedderson came up with his dust-rag and cocked his head at me,

"What's the matter, Ray?" said he.

"Nothing," said I. And then I couldn't help it. "Seems kind of out of place for Society Notes," said I, "out here at Seven Brothers."

He was the other side of the lens, and when he looked at me he had a thousand eyes, all sober. For a minute I thought he was going on dusting, but then he came out and sat down on a sill.

"Sometimes," said he, "I get to thinking it may be a mite dull for her out here. She's pretty young, Ray. Not much more'n a girl, hardly."

"Not much more'n a *girl*!" It gave me a turn, sir, as though I'd seen my aunt in short dresses.

"It's a good home for her, though," he went on slow. "I've seen a lot worse ashore, Ray. Of course if I could get a shore light—"

"Kingdom Come's a shore light."

He looked at me out of his deep-set eyes, and then he turned them around the light-room, where he'd been so long.

"No," said he, wagging his head. "It ain't for such as me."

I never saw so humble a man.

"But look here," he went on, more cheerful. "As I was telling her just now, a month from yesterday's our fourth anniversary, and I'm going to take her ashore for the day and give her a holiday—new hat and everything. A girl wants a mite of excitement now and then, Ray."

There it was again, that "girl." It gave me the fidgets, sir. I had to do something about it. It's close quarters for last names in a light, and I'd taken to calling him Uncle Matt soon after I came. Now, when I was at table that noon I spoke over to where she was standing by the stove, getting him another help of chowder.

"I guess I'll have some, too, *Aunt* Anna," said I, matter of fact.

She never said a word nor gave a sign—just stood there kind of round-shouldered, dipping the chowder. And that night at prayers I hitched my chair around the table, with its back the other way.

You get awful lazy in a lighthouse, some ways. No matter how much tinkering you've got, there's still a lot of time and there's such a thing as too much reading. The changes in weather get monotonous, too, by and by; the light burns the same on a thick night as it does on a fair one. Of course there's the ships, north-bound, south-bound—wind-jammers, freighters, passenger-boats full of people. In the watches at night you can see their lights go by, and wonder what they are, how they're laden, where they'll fetch up, and all. I used to do that almost every evening when it was my first watch, sitting out on the walk-around up there with my legs hanging over the edge and my chin propped on the railing—lazy. The Boston boat was the prettiest to see, with her three tiers of port-holes lit, like a string of pearls wrapped round and round a woman's neck—well away, too, for the ledge must have made a couple of hundred fathoms off the Light, like a white dog-tooth of a breaker, even on the darkest night.

Well, I was lolling there one night, as I say, watching the Boston boat go by, not thinking of anything special, when I heard the door on the other side of the tower open and footsteps coming around to me.

By and by I nodded toward the boat and passed the remark that she was fetching in uncommon close to-night. No answer. I made nothing of that, for oftentimes Fedderson wouldn't answer, and after I'd watched the lights crawling on through the dark a spell, just to make conversation I said I guessed there'd be a bit of weather before long.

"I've noticed," said I, "when there's weather coming on, and the wind in the northeast, you can hear the orchestra playing aboard of her just over there. I make it out now. Do you?"

"Yes. Oh—yes—! *I hear it all right!*"

You can imagine I started. It wasn't him, but *her*. And there was something in the way she said that speech, sir—something—well— unnatural. Like a hungry animal snapping at a person's hand.

I turned and looked at her sidewise. She was standing by the railing, leaning a little outward, the top of her from the waist picked out bright by the lens behind her. I didn't know what in the world to say, and yet I had a feeling I ought not to sit there mum.

"I wonder," said I, "what that captain's thinking of, fetching in so handy to-night. It's no way. I tell you, if 'twasn't for this light, she'd go to work and pile up on the ledge some thick night—" She turned at that and stared straight into the lens. I didn't like the look of her face. Somehow, with its edges cut hard all around and its two eyes closed down to slits, like a cat's, it made a kind of mask.

"And then," I went on, uneasy enough—"and then where'd all their music be of a sudden, and their goings-on and their singing—"

"And dancing!" She clipped me off so quick it took my breath.

"D-d-dancing?" said I.

"That's dance-music," said she. She was looking at the boat again.

"How do you know?" I felt I had to keep on talking.

Well, sir—she laughed. I looked at her. She had on a shawl of some stuff or other that shined in the light; she had it pulled tight around her with her two hands in front at her breast, and I saw her shoulders swaying in tune.

"How do I *know*?" she cried. Then she laughed again, the same kind of a laugh. It was queer, sir, to see her, and to hear her. She turned, as quick as that, and leaned toward me. "Don't you know how to dance, Ray?" said she.

"N-no," I managed, and I was going to say *"Aunt Anna,"* but the thing choked in my throat.

I tell you she was looking square at me all the time with her two eyes and moving with the music as if she didn't know it. By heavens, sir, it came over me of a sudden that she wasn't so bad-looking, after all. I guess I must have sounded like a fool.

"You—you see," said I, "she's cleared the rip there now, and the music's gone. You—you hear?"

"Yes," said she, turning back slow. "That's where it stops every night—night after night—it stops just there—at the rip."

When she spoke again her voice was different. I never heard the like of it, thin and taut as a thread. It made me shiver, sir.

"I hate 'em!" That's what she said. "I hate 'em all. I'd like to see 'em dead. I'd love to see 'em torn apart on the rocks, night after night. I could bathe my hands in their blood, night after night."

And do you know, sir, I saw it with my own eyes, her hands moving in each other above the rail. But it was her voice, though. I didn't know what to do, or what to say, so I poked my head through the railing and looked down at the water. I don't think I'm a coward, sir, but it was like a cold—ice-cold—hand, taking hold of my beating heart.

When I looked up finally, she was gone. By and by I went in and had a look at the lamp, hardly knowing what I was about. Then, seeing by my watch it was time for the old man to come on duty, I started to go below. In the Seven Brothers, you understand, the stair goes down in a spiral through a well against the south wall and first there's the door to the keeper's room and then you come to another, and that's the living-room, and then down to the store-room. And at night, if you don't carry a lantern, it's as black as the pit.

Well, down I went, sliding my hand along the rail, and as usual I stopped to give a rap on the keeper's door, in case he was taking a nap after supper. Sometimes he did.

I stood there, blind as a bat, with my mind still up on the walk-around. There was no answer to my knock. I hadn't expected any. Just from habit, and with my right foot already hanging down for the next step, I reached out to give the door one more tap for luck.

Do you know, sir, my hand didn't fetch up on anything. The door had been there a second before, and now the door wasn't there. My hand just went on going through the dark, on and on, and I didn't seem to have sense or power enough to stop it. There didn't seem any air in the well to breathe, and my ears were drumming to the surf—that's how scared I was. And then my hand touched the flesh of a face, and something in the dark said, "Oh!" no louder than a sigh.

Next thing I knew, sir, I was down in the living-room, warm and yellow-lit, with Fedderson cocking his head at me across the table, where he was at that eternal Jacob's-ladder of his.

"What's the matter, Ray?" said he. "Lord's sake, Ray!"

"Nothing," said I. Then I think I told him I was sick. That night I wrote a letter to A.L. Peters, the grain-dealer in Duxbury, asking for a job—even though it wouldn't go ashore for a couple of weeks, just the writing of it made me feel better.

It's hard to tell you how those two weeks went by. I don't know why, but I felt like hiding in a corner all the time. I had to come to meals, but I didn't look at her, though, not once, unless it was by accident. Fedderson thought I was still ailing and nagged me to death with advice and so on. One thing I took care not to do, I can tell you, and that was to knock on his door till I'd made certain he wasn't below in the living-room—though I was tempted to.

Yes, sir; that's a queer thing, and I wouldn't tell you if I hadn't set out to give you the truth. Night after night, stopping there on the landing in that black pit, the air gone out of my lungs and the surf drumming in my ears and sweat standing cold on my neck—and one hand lifting up in the air—God forgive me, sir! Maybe I did wrong not to look at her more, drooping about her work in her gingham apron, with her hair stringing.

When the Inspector came off with the tender, that time, I told him I was through. That's when he took the dislike to me, I guess, for he looked at me kind of sneering and said, soft as I was, I'd have to put up with it till next relief. And then, said he, there'd be a whole house-cleaning at Seven Brothers, because he'd gotten Fedderson the berth at Kingdom Come. And with that he slapped the old man on the back.

I wish you could have seen Fedderson, sir. He sat down on my cot as if his knees had given 'way. Happy? You'd think he'd be happy, with all his dreams come true. Yes, he was happy, beaming all over—for a minute. Then, sir, he began to shrivel up. It was like seeing a man cut down in his prime before your eyes. He began to wag his head.

"No," said he. "No, no; it's not for such as me. I'm good enough for Seven Brothers, and that's all, Mr. Bayliss. That's all."

And for all the Inspector could say, that's what he stuck to. He'd figured himself a martyr so many years, nursed that injustice like a mother with her first-born, sir; and now in his old age, so to speak, they weren't to rob him of it. Fedderson was going to wear out his life in a second-class light, and folks would talk—that was his idea. I heard him hailing down as the tender was casting off:

"See you to-morrow, Mr. Bayliss. Yep. Coming ashore with the wife for a spree. Anniversary. Yep."

But he didn't sound much like a spree. They *had* robbed him, partly, after all. I wondered what *she* thought about it. I didn't know till night. She didn't show up to supper, which Fedderson and I got ourselves— had a headache, he said. It was my early watch. I went and lit up and came back to read a spell. He was finishing off the Jacob's-ladder, and thoughtful, like a man that's lost a treasure. Once or twice I caught him looking about the room on the sly. It was pathetic, sir.

Going up the second time, I stepped out on the walk-around to have a look at things. She was there on the seaward side, wrapped in that silky thing. A fair sea was running across the ledge and it was coming on a little thick—not too thick. Off to the right the Boston boat was blowing, *whroom-whroom!* Creeping up on us, quarter-speed. There was another fellow behind her, and a fisherman's conch farther offshore.

I don't know why, but I stopped beside her and leaned on the rail. She didn't appear to notice me, one way or another. We stood and we stood, listening to the whistles, and the longer we stood the more it got on my nerves, her not noticing me. I suppose she'd been too much on my mind lately. I began to be put out. I scraped my feet. I coughed. By and by I said out loud:

"Look here, I guess I better get out the fog-horn and give those fellows a toot."

"Why?" said she, without moving her head—calm as that.

"*Why?*" It gave me a turn, sir. For a minute I stared at her. "Why? Because if she don't pick up this light before very many minutes she'll be too close in to wear—tide'll have her on the rocks—that's why!"

I couldn't see her face, but I could see one of her silk shoulders lift a little, like a shrug. And there I kept on staring at her, a dumb one, sure enough. I know what brought me to was hearing the Boston boat's three sharp toots as she picked up the light—mad as anything—and swung her helm a-port. I turned away from her, sweat stringing down my face, and walked around to the door. It was just as well, too, for the feed-pipe was plugged in the lamp and the wicks were popping. She'd have been out in another five minutes, sir.

When I'd finished, I saw that woman standing in the doorway. Her eyes were bright. I had a horror of her, sir, a living horror.

"If only the light had been out," said she, low and sweet.

"God forgive you," said I. "You don't know what you're saying." She went down the stair into the well, winding out of sight, and as long as I could see her, her eyes were watching mine. When I went, myself, after a few minutes, she was waiting for me on that first landing, standing still in the dark. She took hold of my hand, though I tried to get it away.

"Good-by," said she in my ear.

"Good-by?" said I. I didn't understand.

"You heard what he said to-day—about Kingdom Come? Be it so— on his own head. I'll never come back here. Once I set foot ashore— I've got friends in Brightonboro, Ray."

I got away from her and started on down. But I stopped. "Brighton-boro?" I whispered back. "Why do you tell *me?*" My throat was raw to the words, like a sore.

"So you'd know," said she.

Well, sir, I saw them off next morning, down that new Jacob's-ladder into the dinghy-boat, her in a dress of blue velvet and him in his best cutaway and derby—rowing away, smaller and smaller, the two of them. And then I went back and sat on my cot, leaving the door open and the ladder still hanging down the wall, along with the boat-falls.

I don't know whether it was relief, or what. I suppose I must have been worked up even more than I'd thought those past weeks, for now it was all over I was like a rag. I got down on my knees, sir, and prayed to God for the salvation of my soul, and when I got up and climbed to the living-room it was half past twelve by the clock. There was rain on the windows and the sea was running blue-black under the sun. I'd sat there all that time not knowing there was a squall.

It was funny; the glass stood high, but those black squalls kept coming and going all afternoon, while I was at work up in the light-room. And I worked hard, to keep myself busy. First thing I knew it was five, and no sign of the boat yet. It began to get dim and kind of purplish-gray over the land. The sun was down. I lit up, made everything snug, and got out the night-glasses to have another look for that boat. He'd said he intended to get back before five. No sign. And then, standing there, it came over me that of course he wouldn't be coming off—he'd be hunting *her*, poor old fool. It looked like I had to stand two men's watches that night.

Never mind. I felt like myself again, even if I hadn't had any dinner or supper. Pride came to me that night on the walk-around, watching the boats go by—little boats, big boats, the Boston boat with all her pearls and her dance-music. They couldn't see me; they didn't know who I was; but to the last of them, they depended on *me*. They say a man must be born again. Well, I was born again. I breathed deep in the wind.

Dawn broke hard and red as a dying coal. I put out the light and started to go below. Born again; yes, sir. I felt so good I whistled in the well, and when I came to the first door on the stair I reached out in the dark to give it a rap for luck. And then, sir, the hair prickled all over my scalp, when I found my hand just going on and on through the air, the same as it had gone once before, and all of a sudden I wanted to yell, because I thought I was going to touch flesh. It's funny what their just forgetting to close their door did to me, isn't it?

Well, I reached for the latch and pulled it to with a bang and ran down as if a ghost was after me. I got up some coffee and bread and bacon for breakfast. I drank the coffee. But somehow I couldn't eat, all along of that open door. The light in the room was blood. I got to thinking. I thought how she'd talked about those men, women, and children on the rocks, and how she'd made to bathe her hands over the rail. I almost jumped out of my chair then; it seemed for a wink she was there beside the stove watching me with that queer half-smile—really, I seemed to see her for a flash across the red table-cloth in the red light of dawn.

"Look here!" said I to myself, sharp enough; and then I gave myself a good laugh and went below. There I took a look out of the door, which was still open, with the ladder hanging down. I made sure to see the poor old fool come pulling around the point before very long now.

My boots were hurting a little, and, taking them off, I lay down on the cot to rest, and somehow I went to sleep. I had horrible dreams. I saw her again standing in that blood-red kitchen, and she seemed to be washing her hands, and the surf on the ledge was whining up the tower, louder and louder all the time, and what it whined was, "Night after night—night after night." What woke me was cold water in my face.

The store-room was in gloom. That scared me at first; I thought night had come, and remembered the light. But then I saw the gloom was of a storm. The floor was shining wet, and the water in my face was spray, flung up through the open door. When I ran to close it, it almost made me dizzy to see the gray-and-white breakers marching past. The land was gone; the sky shut down heavy overhead; there was a piece of wreckage on the back of a swell, and the Jacob's-ladder was carried clean away. How that sea had picked up so quick I can't think. I looked at my watch and it wasn't four in the afternoon yet.

When I closed the door, sir, it was almost dark in the store-room. I'd never been in the Light before in a gale of wind. I wondered why I was shivering so, till I found it was the floor below me shivering, and the walls and stair. Horrible crunchings and grindings ran away up the tower, and now and then there was a great thud somewhere, like a cannon-shot in a cave. I tell you, sir, I was alone, and I was in a mortal fright for a minute or so. And yet I had to get myself together. There was the light up there not tended to, and an early dark coming on and a heavy night and all, and I had to go. And I had to pass that door.

You'll say it's foolish, sir, and maybe it *was* foolish. Maybe it was because I hadn't eaten. But I began thinking of that door up there the minute I set foot on the stair, and all the way up through that howling dark well I dreaded to pass it. I told myself I wouldn't stop. I didn't stop. I felt the landing underfoot and I went on, four steps, five—and then I couldn't. I turned and went back. I put out my hand and it went on into nothing. That door, sir, was open again.

I left it be; I went on up to the light-room and set to work. It was Bedlam there, sir, screeching Bedlam, but I took no notice. I kept my eyes down. I trimmed those seven wicks, sir, as neat as ever they were trimmed; I polished the brass till it shone, and I dusted the lens. It wasn't till that was done that I let myself look back to see who it was standing there, half out of sight in the well. It was her, sir.

"Where'd you come from?" I asked. I remember my voice was sharp.

"Up Jacob's-ladder," said she, and hers was like the syrup of flowers. I shook my head. I was savage, sir. "The ladder's carried away."

"I cast it off," said she, with a smile.

"Then," said I, "you must have come while I was asleep." Another thought came on me heavy as a ton of lead. "And where's *he*?" said I. "Where's the boat?"

"He's drowned," said she, as easy as that. "And I let the boat go adrift. You wouldn't hear me when I called."

"But look here," said I. "If you came through the store-room, why didn't you wake me up? Tell me that!" It sounds foolish enough, me standing like a lawyer in court, trying to prove she *couldn't* be there.

She didn't answer for a moment. I guess she sighed, though I couldn't hear for the gale, and her eyes grew soft, sir, so soft.

"I couldn't," said she. "You looked so peaceful—dear one."

My cheeks and neck went hot, sir, as if a warm iron was laid on them. I didn't know what to say. I began to stammer, "What do you mean—" but she was going back down the stair, out of sight. My God sir, and I used not to think she was good-looking!

I started to follow her. I wanted to know what she meant. Then I said to myself, "If I don't go—if I wait here—she'll come back." And I went to the weather side and stood looking out of the window. Not that there was much to see. It was growing dark, and the Seven Brothers looked like the mane of a running horse, a great, vast, white horse running into the wind. The air was a-welter with it. I caught one peep of a fisherman, lying down flat trying to weather the ledge, and I said,

"God help them all to-night," and then I went hot at sound of that "God."

I was right about her, though. She was back again. I wanted her to speak first, before I turned, but she wouldn't. I didn't hear her go out; I didn't know what she was up to till I saw her coming outside on the walk-around, drenched wet already. I pounded on the glass for her to come in and not be a fool; if she heard she gave no sign of it.

There she stood, and there I stood watching her. Lord, sir—was it just that I'd never had eyes to see? Or are there women who bloom? Her clothes were shining on her, like a carving, and her hair was let down like a golden curtain tossing and streaming in the gale, and there she stood with her lips half open, drinking, and her eyes half closed, gazing straight away over the Seven Brothers, and her shoulders swaying, as if in tune with the wind and water and all the ruin. And when I looked at her hands over the rail, sir, they were moving in each other as if they bathed, and then I remembered, sir.

A cold horror took me. I knew now why she had come back again. She wasn't a woman—she was a devil. I turned my back on her. I said to myself: "It's time to light up. You've got to light up"—like that, over and over, out loud. My hand was shivering so I could hardly find a match; and when I scratched it, it only flared a second and then went out in the back draught from the open door. She was standing in the doorway, looking at me. It's queer, sir, but I felt like a child caught in mischief.

"I—I—was going to light up," I managed to say, finally.

"Why?" said she. No, I can't say it as she did.

"Why?" said I. "My God!"

She came nearer, laughing, as if with pity, low, you know. "Your God? And who is your God? What is God? What is anything on a night like this?"

I drew back from her. All I could say anything about was the light.

"Why not the dark?" said she. "Dark is softer than light—tenderer—dearer than light. From the dark up here, away up here in the wind and storm, we can watch the ships go by, you and I. And you love me so. You've loved me so long, Ray."

"I never have!" I struck out at her. "I don't! I don't!"

Her voice was lower than ever, but there was the same laughing pity in it. "Oh yes, you have." And she was near me again.

"I have?" I yelled. "I'll show you! I'll show you if I have!"

I got another match, sir, and scratched it on the brass. I gave it to the first wick, the little wick that's inside all the others. It bloomed like a yellow flower. "I *have?*" I yelled, and gave it to the next.

Then there was a shadow, and I saw she was leaning beside me, her two elbows on the brass, her two arms stretched out above the wicks, her bare forearms and wrists and hands. I gave a gasp:

"Take care! You'll burn them! For God's sake—"

She didn't move or speak. The match burned my fingers and went out, and all I could do was stare at those arms of hers, helpless. I'd never noticed her arms before. They were rounded and graceful and covered with a soft down, like a breath of gold. Then I heard her speaking close to my ear.

"Pretty arms," she said. "Pretty arms!"

I turned. Her eyes were fixed on mine. They seemed heavy, as if with sleep, and yet between their lids they were two wells, deep and deep, and as if they held all the things I'd ever thought or dreamed in them. I looked away from them, at her lips. Her lips were red as poppies, heavy with redness. They moved, and I heard them speaking:

"Poor boy, you love me so, and you want to kiss me—don't you?"

"No," said I. But I couldn't turn around. I looked at her hair. I'd always thought it was stringy hair. Some hair curls naturally with damp, they say, and perhaps that was it, for there were pearls of wet on it, and it was thick and shimmering around her face, making soft shadows by the temples. There was green in it, queer strands of green like braids.

"What is it?" said I.

"Nothing but weed," said she, with that slow, sleepy smile.

Somehow or other I felt calmer than I had any time. "Look here," said I. "I'm going to light this lamp." I took out a match, scratched it, and touched the third wick. The flame ran around, bigger than the other two together. But still her arms hung there. I bit my lip. "By God, I will!" said I to myself, and I lit the fourth.

It was fierce, sir, fierce! And yet those arms never trembled. I had to look around at her. Her eyes were still looking into mine, so deep and deep, and her red lips were still smiling with that queer, sleepy droop; the only thing was that tears were raining down her cheeks—big, glowing round, jewel tears. It wasn't human, sir. It was like a dream.

"Pretty arms," she sighed, and then, as if those words had broken something in her heart, there came a great sob bursting from her lips. To hear it drove me mad. I reached to drag her away, but she was too quick, sir; she cringed from me and slipped out from between my hands. It was like she faded away, sir, and went down in a bundle, nursing her poor arms and mourning over them with those terrible, broken sobs.

The sound of them took the manhood out of me—you'd have been the same, sir. I knelt down beside her on the floor and covered my face.

"Please!" I moaned. "Please! Please!" That's all I could say. I wanted her to forgive me. I reached out a hand, blind, for forgiveness, and I couldn't find her anywhere. I had hurt her so, and she was afraid of me, of *me*, sir, who loved her so deep it drove me crazy.

I could see her down the stair, though it was dim and my eyes were filled with tears. I stumbled after her, crying, "Please! Please!" The little wicks I'd lit were blowing in the wind from the door and smoking the glass beside them black. One went out. I pleaded with them, the same as I would plead with a human being. I said I'd be back in a second. I promised. And I went on down the stair, crying like a baby because I'd hurt her, and she was afraid of me—of *me*, sir.

She had gone into her room. The door was closed against me and I could hear her sobbing beyond it, broken-hearted. My heart was broken too. I beat on the door with my palms. I begged her to forgive me. I told her I loved her. And all the answer was that sobbing in the dark.

And then I lifted the latch and went in, groping, pleading. "Dearest—please! Because I love you!"

I heard her speak down near the floor. There wasn't any anger in her voice; nothing but sadness and despair.

"No," said she. "You don't love me, Ray. You never have."

"I do! I have!"

"No, no," said she, as if she was tired out.

"Where are you?" I was groping for her. I thought, and lit a match. She had got to the door and was standing there as if ready to fly. I went toward her, and she made me stop. She took my breath away. "I hurt your arms," said I, in a dream.

"No," said she, hardly moving her lips. She held them out to the match's light for me to look and there was never a scar on them—not even that soft, golden down was singed, sir. "You can't hurt my body," said she, sad as anything. "Only my heart, Ray; my poor heart."

I tell you again, she took my breath away. I lit another match. "How can you be so beautiful?" I wondered.

She answered in riddles—but oh, the sadness of her, sir. "Because," said she, "I've always so wanted to be."

"How come your eyes so heavy?" said I.

"Because I've seen so many things I never dreamed of," said she.

"How come your hair so thick?"

"It's the seaweed makes it thick," said she smiling queer, queer.

"How come seaweed there?"

"Out of the bottom of the sea."

She talked in riddles, but it was like poetry to hear her, or a song.

"How come your lips so red?" said I.

"Because they've wanted so long to be kissed."

Fire was on me, sir. I reached out to catch her, but she was gone, out of the door and down the stair. I followed, stumbling. I must have tripped on the turn, for I remember going through the air and fetching up with a crash, and I didn't know anything for a spell—how long I can't say. When I came to, she was there, somewhere, bending over me, crooning, "My love—my love—" under her breath like, a song.

But then when I got up, she was not where my arms went; she was down the stair again, just ahead of me. I followed her. I was tottering and dizzy and full of pain. I tried to catch up with her in the dark of the store-room, but she was too quick for me, sir, always a little too quick for me. Oh, she was cruel to me, sir. I kept bumping against things, hurting myself still worse, and it was cold and wet and a horrible noise all the while, sir; and then, sir, I found the door was open, and a sea had parted the hinges.

I don't know how it all went, sir. I'd tell you if I could, but it's all so blurred—sometimes it seems more like a dream. I couldn't find her any more; I couldn't hear her; I went all over, everywhere. Once, I remember, I found myself hanging out of that door between the davits, looking down into those big black seas and crying like a baby. It's all riddles and blur. I can't seem to tell you much, sir. It was all—all—I don't know.

I was talking to somebody else—not her. It was the Inspector. I hardly knew it was the Inspector. His face was as gray as a blanket, and his eyes were bloodshot, and his lips were twisted. His left wrist hung down, awkward. It was broken coming aboard the Light in that sea. Yes, we were in the living-room. Yes, sir, it was daylight—gray daylight. I tell you, sir, the man looked crazy to me. He was waving his good arm toward the weather windows, and what he was saying, over and over, was this:

"*Look what you done, damn you! Look what you done!*"

And what I was saying was this:

"*I've lost her!*"

I didn't pay any attention to him, nor him to me. By and by he did, though. He stopped his talking all of a sudden, and his eyes looked like the devil's eyes. He put them up close to mine. He grabbed my arm with his good hand, and I cried, I was so weak.

"Johnson," said he, "is that it? By the living God—if you got a woman out here, Johnson!"

"No," said I. "I've lost her."

"What do you mean—lost her?"

"It was dark," said I—and it's funny how my head was clearing up—"and the door was open—the store-room door—and I was after her—and I guess she stumbled, maybe—and I lost her."

"Johnson," said he, "what do you mean? You sound crazy—downright crazy. Who?"

"Her," said I. "Fedderson's wife."

"*Who?*"

"Her," said I. And with that he gave my arm another jerk.

"Listen," said he, like a tiger. "Don't try that on me. It won't do any good—that kind of lies—not where *you're* going to. Fedderson and his wife, too—the both of 'em's drowned deader 'n a door-nail."

"I know," said I, nodding my head. I was so calm it made him wild.

"You're crazy! Crazy as a loon, Johnson!" And he was chewing his lip red. "I know, because it was me that found the old man laying on Back Water Flats yesterday morning—*me*! And she'd been with him in the boat, too, because he had a piece of her jacket tore off, tangled in his arm."

"I know," said I, nodding again, like that.

"You know *what*, you *crazy, murdering fool*?" Those were his words to me, sir.

"I know," said I, "what I know."

"And *I* know," said he, "what *I* know."

And there you are, sir. He's Inspector. I'm—nobody.

12

THE FURNISHED ROOM

BY O. HENRY

*O. Henry was the pen name of William Sydney Porter (1862–1910),
born in North Carolina. Porter worked as a pharmacist and book-
keeper, then moved to Texas at age twenty, where he began writing.
He also worked as a bank teller, but was arrested for embezzlement.
After jumping bail, Porter fled to Honduras, where he coined the term
"banana republic." Eventually he returned to the United States and
was convicted and served three years in prison, where he continued
to write. A popular author, he published about four hundred stories
before dying of cirrhosis of the liver at age forty-seven. "The Furnished
Room" appeared in 1904.*

Restless, shifting, fugacious as time itself is a certain vast bulk of
the population of the red brick district of the lower West Side. Homeless, they have a hundred homes. They flit from furnished room to
furnished room, transients forever—transients in abode, transients in

heart and mind. They sing "Home, Sweet Home" in ragtime; they carry their lares et penates in a bandbox; their vine is entwined about a picture hat; a rubber plant is their fig tree.

Hence the houses of this district, having had a thousand dwellers, should have a thousand tales to tell, mostly dull ones, no doubt; but it would be strange if there could not be found a ghost or two in the wake of all these vagrant guests.

One evening after dark a young man prowled among these crumbling red mansions, ringing their bells. At the twelfth he rested his lean hand baggage upon the step and wiped the dust from his hatband and forehead. The bell sounded faint and far away in some remote, hollow depths.

To the door of this, the twelfth house whose bell he had rung, came a housekeeper who made him think of an unwholesome, surfeited worm that had eaten its nut to a hollow shell and now sought to fill the vacancy with edible lodgers.

He asked if there was a room to let.

"Come in," said the housekeeper. Her voice came from her throat; her throat seemed lined with fur. "I have the third-floor-back, vacant since a week back. Should you wish to look at it?"

The young man followed her up the stairs. A faint light from no particular source mitigated the shadows of the halls. They trod noiselessly upon a stair carpet that its own loom would have forsworn. It seemed to have become vegetable; to have degenerated in that rank, sunless air to lush lichen or spreading moss that grew in patches to the staircase and was viscid under the foot like organic matter. At each turn of the stairs were vacant niches in the wall. Perhaps plants had once been set within them. If so, they had died in that foul and tainted air. It may be that statues of the saints had stood there, but it was not difficult to conceive that imps and devils had dragged them forth in the darkness and down to the unholy depths of some furnished pit below.

"This is the room," said the housekeeper, from her furry throat. "It's a nice room. It ain't often vacant. I had some most elegant people in it last summer—no trouble at all, and paid in advance to the minute. The water's at the end of the hall. Sprowls and Mooney kept it three months. They done a vaudeville sketch. Miss B'retta Sprowls—you may have heard of her—oh, that was just the stage names—right there over the dresser is where the marriage certificate hung, framed. The gas is here, and you see there is plenty of closet room. It's a room everybody likes. It never stays idle long."

"Do you have many theatrical people rooming here?" asked the young man.

"They comes and goes. A good proportion of my lodgers is connected with the theaters. Yes, sir, this is the theatrical district. Actor people never stays long anywhere. I get my share. Yes, they comes and they goes."

He engaged the room, paying for a week in advance. He was tired, he said, and would take possession at once. He counted out the money. The room had been made ready, she said, even to towels and water. As the housekeeper moved away he put, for the thousandth time, the question that he carried at the end of his tongue.

"A young girl—Miss Vashner—Miss Eloise Vashner—do you remember such a one among your lodgers? She would be singing on the stage, most likely. A fair girl, of medium height and slender, with reddish gold hair and a dark mole near her left eyebrow."

"No, I don't remember the name. Them stage people has names they change as often as their rooms. No, I don't call that one to mind."

No. Always no. Five months of ceaseless interrogation and the inevitable negative. So much time spent by day in questioning managers, agents, schools and choruses; by night among the audiences of theaters from all-star casts down to music halls so low that he dreaded to find what he most hoped for. He who had loved her best had tried to find her. He was sure that since her disappearance from home this great, water-girt city held her somewhere, but it was like a monstrous quicksand, shifting its particles constantly, with no foundation, its upper granules of today buried tomorrow in ooze and slime.

The furnished room received its latest guest with a first glow of pseudo hospitality, a hectic, haggard, perfunctory welcome like the specious smile of a demirep. The sophistical comfort came in reflected gleams from the decayed furniture, the ragged brocade upholstery of a couch and two chairs, a foot-wide cheap pier glass between the two windows, from one or two gilt picture frames and a brass bedstead in a corner.

The guest reclined, inert, upon a chair, while the room, confused in speech as though it were an apartment in Babel, tried to discourse to him of its divers tenantry.

A polychromatic rug like some brilliant-flowered, rectangular, tropical islet lay surrounded by a billowy sea of soiled matting. Upon the gay-papered wall were those pictures that pursue the homeless one from house to house—The Huguenot Lovers, The First Quarrel, The Wedding Breakfast, Psyche at the Fountain. The mantel's chastely severe outline was ingloriously veiled behind some pert drapery drawn rakishly askew like the sashes of the Amazonian ballet. Upon it was some desolate flotsam cast aside by the room's marooned when a lucky sail had borne them to a fresh port—a trifling vase or two, pictures of actresses, a medicine bottle, some stray cards out of a deck. One by one, as the characters of a cryptograph became explicit, the little signs left by the furnished room's procession of guests developed a significance. The threadbare space in the rug in front of the dresser told that lovely women had marched in the throng. The tiny fingerprints on the wall spoke of little prisoners trying to feel their way to sun and air. A splattered stain, raying like the shadow of a bursting bomb, witnessed where a hurled glass or bottle had splintered with its contents against the wall. Across the pier glass had been scrawled with a diamond in staggering letters the name Marie. It seemed that the succession of dwellers in the furnished room had turned in fury—perhaps tempted beyond forbearance by its garish coldness—and wreaked upon it their passions. The furniture was chipped and bruised; the couch, distorted by bursting springs, seemed a horrible monster that had been slain during the stress of some grotesque convulsion. Some more potent upheaval had cloven a great slice from the marble mantel. Each plank in the floor owned its particular cant and shriek as from a separate and individual agony. It seemed incredible that all this malice and injury had been wrought upon the room by those who had called it for a time their home; and yet it may have been the cheated home instinct surviving blindly, the resentful rage at false household gods that had kindled their wrath. A hut that is our own we can sweep and adorn and cherish.

The young tenant in the chair allowed these thoughts to file, soft-shod, through his mind, while there drifted into the room furnished sounds and furnished scents. He heard in one room a tittering and incontinent, slack laughter; in others the monologue of a scold, the rattling of dice, a lullaby, and one crying dully; above him a banjo tinkled with spirit. Doors banged somewhere; the elevated trains roared intermittently; a cat yowled miserably upon a back fence. And he breathed the breath of the house—a dank savor rather than a smell—a cold, musty effluvium as from underground vaults mingled with the reeking exhalations of linoleum and mildewed and rotten woodwork.

Then suddenly, as he rested there, the room was filled with the strong, sweet odor of mignonette. It came as upon a single buffet of wind with such sureness and fragrance and emphasis that it almost seemed a living visitant. And the man cried aloud, "What, dear?" as if he had been called, and sprang up and faced about. The rich odor clung to him and wrapped him around. He reached out his arms for it, all his senses for the time confused and commingled. How could one be peremptorily called by an odor? Surely it must have been a sound. But was it not the sound that had touched, that had caressed him?

"She has been in this room," he cried, and he sprang to wrest from it a token, for he knew he would recognize the smallest thing that had belonged to her or that she had touched. This enveloping scent of mignonette, the odor that she had loved and made her own—whence came it?

The room had been but carelessly set in order. Scattered upon the flimsy dresser scarf were half a dozen hairpins—those discreet, indistinguishable friends of womankind, feminine of gender, infinite of mood and uncommunicative of tense. These he ignored, conscious of their triumphant lack of identity. Ransacking the drawers of the dresser he came upon a discarded, tiny, ragged handkerchief. He pressed it to his face. It was racy and insolent with heliotrope; he hurled it to the floor. In another drawer he found odd buttons, a theater program, a pawnbroker's card, two lost marshmallows, a book on the divination of dreams. In the last was a woman's black satin hair bow, which halted him, poised between ice and fire. But the black satin hair bow also is femininity's demure, impersonal common ornament and tells no tales.

And then he traversed the room like a hound on the scent, skimming the walls, considering the corners of the bulging matting on his hands and knees, rummaging mantel and tables, the curtains and hangings, the drunken cabinet in the corner, for a visible sign, unable to perceive that she was there beside, around, against, within, above him, clinging to him, wooing him, calling him so poignantly through the finer senses that even his grosser ones became cognizant of the call. Once again he answered loudly, "Yes, dear!" and turned, wild-eyed, to gaze on vacancy, for he could not yet discern form and color and love and outstretched arms in the odor of mignonette. Oh, God! Whence that odor, and since when have odors had a voice to call! Thus he groped.

He burrowed in crevices and corners, and found corks and ciga-rettes. These he passed in passive contempt. But once he found in a fold of the matting a half-smoked cigar, and this he ground beneath his heel with a green and trenchant oath. He sifted the room, from end to end. He found dreary and ignoble small records of many a peripatetic tenant; but of her whom he sought, and who may have lodged there, and whose spirit seemed to hover there, he found no trace.

And then he thought of the housekeeper.

He ran from the haunted room downstairs and to a door that showed a crack of light. She came out to his knock. He smothered his excitement as best he could.

"Will you tell me, madam," he besought her, "who occupied the room I have before I came?"

"Yes, sir. I can tell you again. Twas Sprowls and Mooney, as I said. Miss B'retta Sprowls it was in the theaters, but Missis Mooney she was. My house is well known for respectability. The marriage certificate hung, framed, on a nail over—"

"What kind of a lady was Miss Sprowls—in looks, I mean?"

"Why, black-haired, sir, short, and stout, with a comical face. They left a week ago Tuesday."

"And before they occupied it?"

"Why, there was a single gentleman connected with the draying business. He left owing me a week. Before him was Missis Crowder and her two children, that stayed four months; and back of them was old Mr. Doyle, whose sons paid for him. He kept the room six months. That goes back a year, sir, and further I do not remember."

He thanked her and crept back to his room. The room was dead. The essence that had vivified it was gone. The perfume of mignonette had departed. In its place was the old, stale odor of moldy house furniture, of atmosphere in storage.

The ebbing of his hope drained his faith. He sat staring at the yellow, singing gaslight. Soon he walked to the bed and began to tear the sheets into strips. With the blade of his knife he drove them tightly into every crevice around windows and door. When all was snug and taut he turned out the light, turned the gas full on again and laid himself gratefully upon the bed.

It was Mrs. McCool's night to go with the can for beer. So she fetched it and sat with Mrs. Purdy in one of those subterranean retreats where housekeepers forgather and the worm dieth seldom.

"I rented out my third-floor-back this evening," said Mrs. Purdy, across a fine circle of foam. "A young man took it. He went up to bed two hours ago."

"Now, did ye, Mrs. Purdy, ma'am?" said Mrs. McCool, with intense admiration. "You do be a wonder for rentin' rooms of that kind. And did ye tell him, then?" she concluded in a husky whisper laden with mystery.

"Rooms," said Mrs. Purdy, in her furriest tones, "are furnished for to rent. I did not tell him, Mrs. McCool."

"'Tis right ye are, ma'am; 'tis by renting rooms we kape alive. Ye have the rale sense for business, ma'am. There be many people will rayjict the rentin' of a room if they be tould a suicide has been after dyin' in the bed of it."

"As you say, we has our living to be making," remarked Mrs. Purdy.

"Yis, ma'am; 'tis true. 'Tis just one wake ago this day I helped ye lay out the third-floor-back. A pretty slip of a colleen she was to be killin' herself wid the gas—a swate little face she had, Mrs. Purdy, ma'am."

"She'd a-been called handsome, as you say," said Mrs. Purdy, assenting but critical, "but for that mole she had a-growin' by her left eyebrow. Do fill up your glass again, Mrs. McCool."

13

THE CROSS-ROADS

BY AMY LOWELL

Born in Brookline, Massachusetts, to the wealthy Lowell family of Boston Brahmins, Amy Lowell (1874–1925) was known primarily as a poet. In 1926, she was posthumously awarded the Pulitzer Prize for Poetry. Despite the fact that her brother (Abbott Lawrence Lowell) became president of Harvard University, she received limited formal education, as her family felt that education was not necessary for women. She was an avid reader, lived as a socialite and traveled widely, and was also well known as a heavy smoker of cigars. Largely forgotten at the time of her death, her work was rediscovered in the 1970s. "The Cross-Roads" was published in 1916.

A bullet through his heart at dawn. On the table a letter signed with a woman's name. A wind that goes howling round the house, and weeping as in shame. Cold November dawn peeping through the windows, cold dawn creeping over the floor, creeping up his cold legs, creeping over his cold body, creeping across his cold face. A glaze of thin yellow sunlight on the staring eyes. Wind howling through bent branches. A wind which never dies down. Howling, wailing. The gazing eyes glitter in the sunlight. The lids are frozen open and the eyes glitter.

The thudding of a pick on hard earth. A spade grinding and crunching. Overhead, branches writhing, winding, interlacing, unwinding, scattering; tortured twinings, tossings, creakings. Wind flinging branches apart, drawing them together, whispering and whining among them. A waning, lobsided moon cutting through black clouds. A stream of pebbles and earth and the empty spade gleams clear in the moonlight, then is rammed again into the black earth. Tramping of feet. Men and horses. Squeaking of wheels.

"Whoa! Ready, Jim?"

"All ready."

Something falls, settles, is still. Suicides have no coffin.

"Give us the stake, Jim. Now."

Pound! Pound!

"He'll never walk. Nailed to the ground."

An ash stick pierces his heart, if it buds the roots will hold him. He is a part of the earth now, clay to clay. Overhead the branches sway, and writhe, and twist in the wind. He'll never walk with a bullet in his heart, and an ash stick nailing him to the cold, black ground.

Six months he lay still. Six months. And the water welled up in his body, and soft blue spots chequered it. He lay still, for the ash stick held him in place. Six months! Then her face came out of a mist of green. Pink and white and frail like Dresden china, lilies-of-the-valley at her breast, puce-coloured silk sheening about her. Under the young green leaves, the horse at a foot-pace, the high yellow wheels of the chaise scarcely turning, her face, rippling like grain a-blowing, under her puce-coloured bonnet; and burning beside her, flaming within his correct blue coat and brass buttons, is someone. What has dimmed the sun? The horse steps on a rolling stone; a wind in the branches makes a moan. The little leaves tremble and shake, turn and quake, over and over, tearing their stems. There is a shower of young leaves, and a sudden-sprung gale wails in the trees.

The yellow-wheeled chaise is rocking—rocking, and all the branches are knocking—knocking. The sun in the sky is a flat, red plate, the branches creak and grate. She screams and cowers, for the green foliage is a lowering wave surging to smother her. But she sees nothing. The stake holds firm. The body writhes, the body squirms. The blue spots widen, the flesh tears, but the stake wears well in the deep, black ground. It holds the body in the still, black ground.

Two years! The body has been in the ground two years. It is worn away; it is clay to clay. Where the heart moulders, a greenish dust, the stake is thrust. Late August it is, and night; a night flauntingly jewelled with stars, a night of shooting stars and loud insect noises. Down the road to Tilbury, silence—and the slow flapping of large leaves. Down the road to Sutton, silence—and the darkness of heavy-foliaged trees. Down the road to Wayfleet, silence—and the whirring scrape of insects in the branches. Down the road to Edgarstown, silence—and stars like stepping-stones in a pathway overhead. It is very quiet at the cross-roads, and the sign-board points the way down the four roads, endlessly points the way where nobody wishes to go.

A horse is galloping, galloping up from Sutton. Shaking the wide, still leaves as he goes under them. Striking sparks with his iron shoes; silencing the katydids. Dr. Morgan riding to a child-birth over Tilbury way; riding to deliver a woman of her first-born son. One o'clock from Wayfleet bell tower, what a shower of shooting stars! And a breeze all of a sudden, jarring the big leaves and making them jerk up and down. Dr. Morgan's hat is blown from his head, the horse swerves, and curves away from the sign-post. An oath—spurs—a blurring of grey mist. A quick left twist, and the gelding is snorting and racing down the Tilbury road with the wind dropping away behind him.

The stake has wrenched, the stake has started, the body, flesh from flesh, has parted. But the bones hold tight, socket and ball, and clamping them down in the hard, black ground is the stake, wedged through ribs and spine. The bones may twist, and heave, and twine, but the stake holds them still in line. The breeze goes down, and the round stars shine, for the stake holds the fleshless bones in line.

Twenty years now! Twenty long years! The body has powdered itself away; it is clay to clay. It is brown earth mingled with brown earth. Only flaky bones remain, lain together so long they fit, although not one bone is knit to another. The stake is there too, rotted through, but upright still, and still piercing down between ribs and spine in a straight line.

Yellow stillness is on the cross-roads, yellow stillness is on the trees. The leaves hang drooping, wan. The four roads point four yellow ways, saffron and gamboge ribbons to the gaze. A little swirl of dust blows up Tilbury road, the wind which fans it has not strength to do more; it ceases, and the dust settles down. A little whirl of wind comes up Tilbury road. It brings a sound of wheels and feet. The wind reels a moment and faints to nothing under the sign-post. Wind again, wheels and feet louder. Wind again—again—again. A drop of rain, flat into the dust. Drop!—Drop! Thick heavy raindrops, and a shrieking wind bending the great trees and wrenching off their leaves.

Under the black sky, bowed and dripping with rain, up Tilbury road, comes the procession. A funeral procession, bound for the graveyard at Wayfleet. Feet and wheels—feet and wheels. And among them one who is carried.

The bones in the deep, still earth shiver and pull. There is a quiver through the rotted stake. Then stake and bones fall together in a little puffing of dust.

Like meshes of linked steel the rain shuts down behind the procession, now well along the Wayfleet road.

He wavers like smoke in the buffeting wind. His fingers blow out like smoke, his head ripples in the gale. Under the sign-post, in the pouring rain, he stands, and watches another quavering figure drifting down the Wayfleet road. Then swiftly he streams after it. It flickers among the trees. He licks out and winds about them. Over, under, blown, contorted. Spindrift after spindrift; smoke following smoke. There is a wailing through the trees, a wailing of fear, and after it laughter—laughter—laughter, skirling up to the black sky. Lightning jags over the funeral procession. A heavy clap of thunder. Then darkness and rain, and the sound of feet and wheels.

14

JEAN-AH POQUELIN

BY GEORGE WASHINGTON CABLE

Born to a wealthy, slave-owning family in New Orleans, Louisiana, George Washington Cable (1844–1925) volunteered as a young man to fight for the Confederacy in the American Civil War. He later became famous for his realistic novels depicting Creole life and the interplay of American, French, Caribbean, and African cultures in antebellum Louisiana. "Jean-ah Poquelin" first appeared in 1879.

In the first decade of the present century, when the newly established American Government was the most hateful thing in Louisiana—when the Creoles were still kicking at such vile innovations as the trial by jury, American dances, anti-smuggling laws, and the printing of the Governor's proclamation in English—when the Anglo-American flood that was presently to burst in a crevasse of immigration upon the delta had thus far been felt only as slippery seepage which made the Creole tremble for his footing—there stood, a short distance above what is now

Canal Street, and considerably back from the line of villas which fringed the river-bank on Tchoupitoulas Road, an old colonial plantation-house half in ruin.

It stood aloof from civilization, the tracts that had once been its indigo fields given over to their first noxious wildness, and grown up into one of the horridest marshes within a circuit of fifty miles.

The house was of heavy cypress, lifted up on pillars, grim, solid, and spiritless, its massive build a strong reminder of days still earlier, when every man had been his own peace officer and the insurrection of the blacks a daily contingency. Its dark, weatherbeaten roof and sides were hoisted up above the jungly plain in a distracted way, like a gigantic ammunition-wagon stuck in the mud and abandoned by some retreating army. Around it was a dense growth of low water willows, with half a hundred sorts of thorny or fetid bushes, savage strangers alike to the "language of flowers" and to the botanist's Greek. They were hung with countless strands of discolored and prickly smilax, and the impassable mud below bristled with *chevaux de frise* of the dwarf palmetto. Two lone forest-trees, dead cypresses, stood in the centre of the marsh, dotted with roosting vultures. The shallow strips of water were hid by myriads of aquatic plants, under whose coarse and spiritless flowers, could one have seen it, was a harbor of reptiles, great and small, to make one shudder to the end of his days.

The house was on a slightly raised spot, the levee of a draining canal. The waters of this canal did not run; they crawled, and were full of big, ravening fish and alligators, that held it against all comers.

Such was the home of old Jean Marie Poquelin, once an opulent indigo planter, standing high in the esteem of his small, proud circle of exclusively male acquaintances in the old city; now a hermit, alike shunned by and shunning all who had ever known him. "The last of his line," said the gossips. His father lies under the floor of the St.

Louis Cathedral, with the wife of his youth on one side, and the wife of his old age on the other. Old Jean visits the spot daily. His half-brother—alas! there was a mystery; no one knew what had become of the gentle, young half brother, more than thirty years his junior, whom once he seemed so fondly to love, but who, seven years ago, had disappeared suddenly, once for all, and left no clew of his fate.

They had seemed to live so happily in each other's love. No father, mother, wife to either, no kindred upon earth. The elder a bold, frank, impetuous, chivalric adventurer; the younger a gentle, studious, book-loving recluse; they lived upon the ancestral estate like mated birds, one always on the wing, the other always in the nest.

There was no trait in Jean Marie Poquelin, said the old gossips, for which he was so well known among his few friends as his apparent fondness for his "little brother."

"Jacques said this," and "Jacques said that;" he "would leave this or that, or any thing to Jacques," for "Jacques was a scholar," and "Jacques was good," or "wise," or "just," or "far-sighted," as the nature of the case required; and "he should ask Jacques as soon as he got home," since Jacques was never elsewhere to be seen.

It was between the roving character of the one brother, and the bookishness of the other, that the estate fell into decay. Jean Marie, generous gentleman, gambled the slaves away one by one, until none was left, man or woman, but one old African mute.

The indigo-fields and vats of Louisiana had been generally abandoned as unremunerative. Certain enterprising men had substituted the culture of sugar; but while the recluse was too apathetic to take so active a course, the other saw larger, and, at time, equally respectable profits, first in smuggling, and later in the African slave-trade. What harm could he see in it? The whole people said it was vitally necessary, and to minister to a vital public necessity,—good enough, certainly, and so he laid up many a doubloon, that made him none the worse in the public regard.

One day old Jean Marie was about to start upon a voyage that was to be longer, much longer, than any that he had yet made. Jacques had begged him hard for many days not to go, but he laughed him off, and finally said, kissing him:

"*Adieu, 'tit frère.*"

"No," said Jacques, "I shall go with you."

They left the old hulk of a house in the sole care of the African mute, and went away to the Guinea coast together.

Two years after, old Poquelin came home without his vessel. He must have arrived at his house by night. No one saw him come. No one saw "his little brother;" rumor whispered that he, too, had returned, but he had never been seen again.

A dark suspicion fell upon the old slave-trader. No matter that the few kept the many reminded of the tenderness that had ever marked his bearing to the missing man. The many shook their heads. "You know he has a quick and fearful temper;" and "why does he cover his loss with mystery?" "Grief would out with the truth." "But," said the charitable few, "look in his face; see that expression of true humanity." The many did look in his face, and, as he looked in theirs, he read the silent question: "Where is thy brother Abel?" The few were silenced, his former friends died off, and the name of Jean Marie Poquelin became a symbol of witchery, devilish crime, and hideous nursery fictions.

The man and his house were alike shunned. The snipe and duck hunters forsook the marsh, and the wood-cutters abandoned the canal. Sometimes the hardier boys who ventured out there snake-shooting heard a slow thumping of oar-locks on the canal. They would look at each other for a moment half in consternation, half in glee, then rush from their sport in wanton haste to assail with their gibes the unoffending, withered old man who, in rusty attire, sat in the stern of a skiff, rowed homeward by his white-headed African mute.

"O Jean-ah Poquelin! O Jean-ah! Jean-ah Poquelin!"

It was not necessary to utter more than that. No hint of wickedness, deformity, or any physical or moral demerit; merely the name and tone of mockery: "Oh, Jean-ah Poquelin!" and while they tumbled one over another in their needless haste to fly, he would rise carefully from his seat, while the aged mute, with downcast face, went on rowing, and rolling up his brown fist and extending it toward the urchins, would pour forth such an unholy broadside of French imprecation and invective as would all but craze them with delight.

Among both blacks and whites the house was the object of a thousand superstitions. Every midnight they affirmed, the *feu follet* came out of the marsh and ran in and out of the rooms, flashing from window to window. The story of some lads, whose words in ordinary statements were worthless, was generally credited, that the night they camped in the woods, rather than pass the place after dark, they saw, about sunset, every window blood-red, and on each of the four chimneys an owl sitting, which turned his head three times round, and moaned and laughed with a human voice. There was a bottomless well, everybody professed to know, beneath the sill of the big front door under the rotten veranda; whoever set his foot upon that threshold disappeared forever in the depth below.

What wonder the marsh grew as wild as Africa! Take all the Faubourg Ste. Marie, and half the ancient city, you would not find one graceless dare-devil reckless enough to pass within a hundred yards of the house after nightfall.

The alien races pouring into old New Orleans began to find the few streets named for the Bourbon princes too strait for them. The wheel of fortune, beginning to whirl, threw them off beyond the ancient corporation lines, and sowed civilization and even trade upon the lands of the Graviers and Girods. Fields became roads, roads streets. Everywhere the leveller was peering through his glass, rodsmen were whacking their way through willow-brakes and rose-hedges, and the sweating Irishmen tossed the blue clay up with their long-handled shovels.

"Ha! that is all very well," quoth the Jean-Baptistes, fueling the reproach of an enterprise that asked neither co-operation nor advice of them, "but wait till they come yonder to Jean Poquelin's marsh; ha! ha! ha!" The supposed predicament so delighted them, that they put on a mock terror and whirled about in an assumed stampede, then caught their clasped hands between their knees in excess of mirth, and laughed till the tears ran; for whether the street-makers mired in the marsh, or contrived to cut through old "Jean-ah's" property, either event would be joyful. Meantime a line of tiny rods, with bits of white paper in their split tops, gradually extended its way straight through the haunted ground, and across the canal diagonally.

"We shall fill that ditch," said the men in mud-boots, and brushed close along the chained and padlocked gate of the haunted mansion. Ah, Jean-ah Poquelin, those were not Creole boys, to be stampeded with a little hard swearing.

He went to the Governor. That official scanned the odd figure with no slight interest. Jean Poquelin was of short, broad frame, with a bronzed leonine face. His brow was ample and deeply furrowed. His eye, large and black, was bold and open like that of a war-horse, and his jaws shut together with the firmness of iron. He was dressed in a suit of Attakapas cottonade, and his shirt unbuttoned and thrown back from the throat and bosom, sailor-wise, showed a herculean breast; hard and grizzled. There was no fierceness or defiance in his look, no harsh ungentleness, no symptom of his unlawful life or violent temper; but rather a peaceful and peaceable fearlessness. Across the whole face, not marked in one or another feature, but as it were laid softly upon the countenance like an almost imperceptible veil, was the imprint of some great grief. A careless eye might easily overlook it, but, once seen, there it hung—faint, but unmistakable.

The Governor bowed.

"*Parlez-vous français?*" asked the figure.

"I would rather talk English, if you can do so," said the Governor.

"My name, Jean Poquelin."

"How can I serve you, Mr. Poquelin?"

"My 'ouse is yond'; *dans le marais là-bas.*"

The Governor bowed.

"Dat *marais* billong to me."

"Yes, sir."

"To me; Jean Poquelin; I hown 'im meself."

"Well, sir?"

"He don't billong to you; I get him from me father."

"That is perfectly true, Mr. Poquelin, as far as I am aware."

"You want to make strit pass yond'?"

"I do not know, sir; it is quite probable; but the city will indemnify you for any loss you may suffer—you will get paid, you understand."

"Strit can't pass dare."

"You will have to see the municipal authorities about that, Mr. Poquelin."

A bitter smile came upon the old man's face:

"*Pardon, Monsieur*, you is not *le Gouverneur?*"

"Yes."

"*Mais*, yes. You har *le Gouverneur*—yes. Veh-well. I come to you. I tell you, strit can't pass at me 'ouse."

"But you will have to see—"

"I come to you. You is *le Gouverneur*. I know not the new laws. I ham a Fr-r-rench-a-man! Fr-rench-a-man have something *aller au contraire*—he come at his *Gouverneur*. I come at you. If me not had been bought from me king like *bossals* in the hold time, ze king gof—France would-a-show *Monsieur le Gouverneur* to take care his men to make strit in right places. *Mais*, I know; we billong to *Monsieur le Président*. I want you do somesin for me, eh?"

"What is it?" asked the patient Governor.

"I want you tell *Monsieur le Président*, strit—can't—pass—at—me—'ouse."

"Have a chair, Mr. Poquelin;" but the old man did not stir. The Governor took a quill and wrote a line to a city official, introducing Mr. Poquelin, and asking for him every possible courtesy. He handed it to him, instructing him where to present it.

"Mr. Poquelin," he said with a conciliatory smile, "tell me, is it your house that our Creole citizens tell such odd stories about?"

The old man glared sternly upon the speaker, and with immovable features said:

"You don't see me trade some Guinea nigga'?"

"Oh, no."

"You don't see me make some smuggling."

"No, sir; not at all."

"But, I am Jean Marie Poquelin. I mine me hown bizniss. Dat all right? Adieu."

He put his hat on and withdrew. By and by he stood, letter in hand, before the person to whom it was addressed. This person employed an interpreter.

"He says," said the interpreter to the officer, "he come to make you the fair warning how you muz not make the street pas' at his 'ouse."

The officer remarked that "such impudence was refreshing;" but the experienced interpreter translated freely.

"He says: 'Why you don't want?'" said the interpreter.

The old slave-trader answered at some length.

"He says," said the interpreter, again turning to the officer, "the marass is a too unhealth' for peopl' to live."

"But we expect to drain his old marsh; it's not going to be a marsh."

"*Il dit*—" The interpreter explained in French.

The old man answered tersely.

"He says the canal is a private," said the interpreter.

"Oh! *that* old ditch; that's to be filled up. Tell the old man we're going to fix him up nicely."

Translation being duly made, the man in power was amused to see a thunder-cloud gathering on the old man's face.

"Tell him," he added, "by the time we finish, there'll not be a ghost left in his shanty."

The interpreter began to translate, but—

"*J' comprends, J' comprends*," said the old man, with an impatient gesture, and burst forth, pouring curses upon the United States, the President, the Territory of Orleans, Congress, the Governor and all his subordinates, striding out of the apartment as he cursed, while the object of his maledictions roared with merriment and rammed the floor with his foot.

"Why, it will make his old place worth ten dollars to one," said the official to the interpreter.

"'Tis not for de worse of de property," said the interpreter.

"I should guess not," said the other, whittling his chair,—"seems to me as if some of these old Creoles would liever live in a crawfish hole than to have a neighbor."

"You know what make old Jean Poquelin make like that? I will tell you. You know"—

The interpreter was rolling a cigarette, and paused to light his tinder; then, as the smoke poured in a thick double stream from his nostrils, he said, in a solemn whisper:

"He is a witch."

"Ho, ho, ho!" laughed the other.

"You don't believe it? What you want to bet?" cried the interpreter, jerking himself half up and thrusting out one arm while he bared it of its coat-sleeve with the hand of the other. "What you want to bet?"

"How do you know?" asked the official.

"Dass what I goin' to tell you. You know, one evening I was shooting some *grosbec*. I killed three, but I had trouble to fine them, it was becoming so dark. When I have them I start' to come home; then I got to pas' at Jean Poquelin's house."

"Ho, ho, ho!" laughed the other, throwing his leg over the arm of his chair.

"Wait," said the interpreter. "I come along slow, not making some noises; still, still—"

"And scared," said the smiling one.

"*Mais*, wait. I get all pas' the 'ouse. 'Ah!' I say; 'all right!' Then I see two thing' before! Hah! I get as cold and humide, and shake like a leaf. You think it was nothing? There I see, so plain as can be (though it was making nearly dark), I see Jean—Marie—Po-que-lin walkin' right in front, and right there beside of him was something like a man—but not a man—white like paint!—I dropp' on the grass from scared—they pass'; so sure as I live 'twas the ghos' of Jacques Poquelin, his brother!"

"Pooh!" said the listener.

"I'll put my han' in the fire," said the interpreter.

"But did you never think," asked the other, "that that might be Jack Poquelin, as you call him, alive and well, and for some cause hid away by his brother?"

"But there har' no cause!" said the other, and the entrance of third parties changed the subject.

Some months passed and the street was opened. A canal was first dug through the marsh, the small one which passed so close to Jean Poquelin's house was filled, and the street, or rather a sunny road, just touched a corner of the old mansion's dooryard. The morass ran dry. Its venomous denizens slipped away through the bulrushes; the cattle roaming freely upon its hardened surface trampled the superabundant undergrowth. The bellowing frogs croaked to westward. Lilies and the flower-de-luce sprang up in the place of reeds; smilax and poison-oak gave way to the purple-plumed iron-weed and pink spiderwort; the bindweeds ran everywhere blooming as they ran, and on one of the dead cypresses a giant creeper hung its green burden of foliage and lifted its scarlet trumpets. Sparrows and red-birds flitted through the bushes, and dewberries grew ripe beneath. Over all these came a sweet, dry smell of salubrity which the place had not known since the sediments of the Mississippi first lifted it from the sea.

But its owner did not build. Over the willow-brakes, and down the vista of the open street, bright new houses, some singly, some by ranks, were prying in upon the old man's privacy. They even settled down toward his southern side. First a wood-cutter's hut or two, then a market gardener's shanty, then a painted cottage, and all at once the faubourg had flanked and half surrounded him and his dried-up marsh.

Ah! then the common people began to hate him. "The old tyrant!"

"You don't mean an old *tyrant?*"

"Well, then, why don't he build when the public need demands it? What does he live in that unneighborly way for?"

"The old pirate!"

"The old kidnapper!" How easily even the most ultra Louisianians put on the imported virtues of the North when they could be brought to bear against the hermit. "There he goes, with the boys after him! Ah! ha! ha! Jean-ah Poquelin! Ah! Jean-ah! Aha! aha! Jean-ah Marie! Jean-ah Poquelin! The old villain!" How merrily the swarming Américains echo the spirit of persecution! "The old fraud," they say—"pretends to live in a haunted house, does he? We'll tar and feather him some day. Guess we can fix him."

He cannot be rowed home along the old canal now; he walks. He has broken sadly of late, and the street urchins are ever at his heels. It is like the days when they cried: "Go up, thou bald-head," and the old man now and then turns and delivers ineffectual curses.

To the Creoles—to the incoming lower class of superstitious Germans, Irish, Sicilians, and others—he became an omen and embodiment of public and private ill-fortune. Upon him all the vagaries of their superstitions gathered and grew. If a house caught fire, it was imputed to his machinations. Did a woman go off in a fit, he had bewitched her. Did a child stray off for an hour, the mother shivered with the apprehension that Jean Poquelin had offered him to strange gods. The house was the subject of every bad boy's invention who loved to contrive ghostly lies. "As long as that house stands we shall have bad luck. Do you not see our peas and beans dying, our cabbages and lettuce going to seed and our gardens turning to dust, while every day you can see it raining in the woods? The rain will never pass old Poquelin's house. He keeps a fetich. He has conjured the whole Faubourg St. Marie. And why, the old wretch? Simply because our playful and innocent children call after him as he passes."

A "Building and Improvement Company," which had not yet got its charter, "but was going to," and which had not, indeed, any tangible capital yet, but "was going to have some," joined the "Jean-ah Poquelin" war. The haunted property would be such a capital site for a market-house! They sent a deputation to the old mansion to ask its occupant to sell. The deputation never got beyond the chained gate and a very barren interview with the African mute. The President of the Board was then empowered (for he had studied French in Pennsylvania and was considered qualified) to call and persuade M. Poquelin to subscribe to the company's stock; but—

"Fact is, gentlemen," he said at the next meeting, "it would take us at least twelve months to make Mr. Pokaleen understand the rather original features of our system, and he wouldn't subscribe when we'd done; besides, the only way to see him is to stop him on the street."

There was a great laugh from the Board; they couldn't help it. "Better meet a bear robbed of her whelps," said one.

"You're mistaken as to that," said the President. "I did meet him, and stopped him, and found him quite polite. But I could get no satisfaction from him; the fellow wouldn't talk in French, and when I spoke in English he hoisted his old shoulders up, and gave the same answer to every thing I said."

"And that was—?" asked one or two, impatient of the pause.

"That it 'don't worse w'ile?'"

One of the Board said: "Mr. President, this market-house project, as I take it, is not altogether a selfish one; the community is to be benefited by it. We may feel that we are working in the public interest [the Board smiled knowingly], if we employ all possible means to oust this old nuisance from among us. You may know that at the time the street was cut through, this old Poquelann did all he could to prevent it. It was owing to a certain connection which I had with that affair that I

heard a ghost story [smiles, followed by a sudden dignified check]—
ghost story, which, of course, I am not going to relate; but I *may* say
that my profound conviction, arising from a prolonged study of that
story, is, that this old villain, John Poquelann, has his brother locked up
in that old house. Now, if this is so, and we can fix it on him, I merely
suggest that we can make the matter highly useful. I don't know," he
added, beginning to sit down, "but that it is an action we owe to the
community—hem!"

"How do you propose to handle the subject?" asked the President.

"I was thinking," said the speaker, "that, as a Board of Directors, it
would be unadvisable for us to authorize any action involving trespass;
but if you, for instance, Mr. President, should, as it were, for mere curiosity, *request* some one, as, for instance, our excellent Secretary, simply
as a personal favor, to look into the matter—this is merely a suggestion."

The Secretary smiled sufficiently to be understood that, while
he certainly did not consider such preposterous service a part of his
duties as secretary, he might, notwithstanding, accede to the President's request; and the Board adjourned.

Little White, as the Secretary was called, was a mild, kind-hearted
little man, who, nevertheless, had no fear of any thing, unless it was
the fear of being unkind.

"I tell you frankly," he privately said to the President, "I go into this
purely for reasons of my own."

The next day, a little after nightfall, one might have descried this
little man slipping along the rear fence of the Poquelin place, prepa-
ratory to vaulting over into the rank, grass-grown yard, and bearing
himself altogether more after the manner of a collector of rare chick-
ens than according to the usage of secretaries.

The picture presented to his eye was not calculated to enliven his
mind. The old mansion stood out against the western sky, black and

silent. One long, lurid pencil-stroke along a sky of slate was all that was left of daylight. No sign of life was apparent; no light at any window, unless it might have been on the side of the house hidden from view. No owls were on the chimneys, no dogs were in the yard.

He entered the place, and ventured up behind a small cabin which stood apart from the house. Through one of its many crannies he easily detected the African mute crouched before a flickering pine-knot, his head on his knees, fast asleep.

He concluded to enter the mansion, and, with that view, stood and scanned it. The broad rear steps of the veranda would not serve him; he might meet some one midway. He was measuring, with his eye, the proportions of one of the pillars which supported it, and estimating the practicability of climbing it, when he heard a footstep. Some one dragged a chair out toward the railing, then seemed to change his mind and began to pace the veranda, his footfalls resounding on the dry boards with singular loudness. Little White drew a step backward, got the figure between himself and the sky, and at once recognized the short, broad-shouldered form of old Jean Poquelin.

He sat down upon a billet of wood, and, to escape the stings of a whining cloud of mosquitoes, shrouded his face and neck in his handkerchief, leaving his eyes uncovered.

He had sat there but a moment when he noticed a strange, sickening odor, faint, as if coming from a distance, but loathsome and horrid.

Whence could it come? Not from the cabin; not from the marsh, for it was as dry as powder. It was not in the air; it seemed to come from the ground.

Rising up, he noticed, for the first time, a few steps before him a narrow footpath leading toward the house. He glanced down it—ha! right there was some one coming—ghostly white!

Quick as thought, and as noiselessly, he lay down at full length against the cabin. It was bold strategy, and yet, there was no denying it, little White felt that he was frightened. "It is not a ghost," he said to himself. "I *know* it cannot be a ghost;" but the perspiration burst out at every pore, and the air seemed to thicken with heat. "It is a living man," he said in his thoughts. "I hear his footstep, and I hear old Poquelin's footsteps, too, separately, over on the veranda. I am not discovered; the thing has passed; there is that odor again; what a smell of death! Is it coming back? Yes. It stops at the door of the cabin. Is it peering in at the sleeping mute? It moves away. It is in the path again. Now it is gone." He shuddered. "Now, if I dare venture, the mystery is solved." He rose cautiously, close against the cabin, and peered along the path.

The figure of a man, a presence if not a body—but whether clad in some white stuff or naked the darkness would not allow him to determine—had turned, and now, with a seeming painful gait, moved slowly from him. "Great Heaven! can it be that the dead do walk?" He withdrew again the hands which had gone to his eyes. The dreadful object passed between two pillars and under the house. He listened. There was a faint sound as of feet upon a staircase; then all was still except the measured tread of Jean Poquelin walking on the veranda, and the heavy respirations of the mute slumbering in the cabin.

The little Secretary was about to retreat; but as he looked once more toward the haunted house a dim light appeared in the crack of a closed window, and presently old Jean Poquelin came, dragging his chair, and sat down close against the shining cranny. He spoke in a low, tender tone in the French tongue, making some inquiry. An answer came from within. Was it the voice of a human? So unnatural was it—so hollow, so discordant, so unearthly—that the stealthy listener shuddered again from head to foot, and when something stirred in some bushes near by—though it may have been nothing more than a rat—and came scuttling through the grass, the little Secretary actually turned and fled. As he left the enclosure he moved with bolder leisure through the bushes; yet now and then he spoke aloud: "Oh, oh! I see, I understand!" and shut his eyes in his hands.

How strange that henceforth little White was the champion of Jean Poquelin! In season and out of season—wherever a word was uttered against him—the Secretary, with a quiet, aggressive force that instantly arrested gossip, demanded upon what authority the statement or conjecture was made; but as he did not condescend to explain his own remarkable attitude, it was not long before the disrelish and suspicion which had followed Jean Poquelin so many years fell also upon him.

It was only the next evening but one after his adventure that he made himself a source of sullen amazement to one hundred and fifty boys, by ordering them to desist from their wanton hallooing. Old Jean Poquelin, standing and shaking his cane, rolling out his long-drawn maledictions, paused and stared, then gave the Secretary a courteous bow and started on. The boys, save one, from pure astonishment, ceased but a ruffianly little Irish lad, more daring than any had yet been, threw a big hurtling clod, that struck old Poquelin between the shoulders and burst like a shell. The enraged old man wheeled with uplifted staff to give chase to the scampering vagabond; and—he may have tripped, or he may not, but he fell full length. Little White hastened to help him up, but he waved him off with a fierce imprecation and staggering to his feet resumed his way homeward. His lips were reddened with blood.

Little White was on his way to the meeting of the Board. He would have given all he dared spend to have staid away, for he felt both too fierce and too tremulous to brook the criticisms that were likely to be made.

"I can't help it, gentlemen; I can't help you to make a case against the old man, and I'm not going to."

"We did not expect this disappointment, Mr. White."

"I can't help that, sir. No, sir; you had better not appoint any more investigations. Somebody'll investigate himself into trouble. No, sir; it isn't a threat, it is only my advice, but I warn you that whoever takes the task in hand will rue it to his dying day—which may be hastened, too."

The President expressed himself "surprised."

"I don't care a rush," answered little White, wildly and foolishly. "I don't care a rush if you are, sir. No, my nerves are not disordered; my head's as clear as a bell. No, I'm *not* excited." A Director remarked that the Secretary looked as though he had waked from a nightmare.

"Well, sir, if you want to know the fact, I have; and if you choose to cultivate old Poquelin's society you can have one, too."

"White," called a facetious member, but White did not notice. "White," he called again.

"What?" demanded White, with a scowl.

"Did you see the ghost?"

"Yes, sir; I did," cried White, hitting the table, and handing the President a paper which brought the Board to other business.

The story got among the gossips that somebody (they were afraid to say little White) had been to the Poquelin mansion by night and beheld something appalling. The rumor was but a shadow of the truth, magnified and distorted as is the manner of shadows. He had seen skeletons walking, and had barely escaped the clutches of one by making the sign of the cross.

Some madcap boys with an appetite for the horrible plucked up courage to venture through the dried marsh by the cattle-path, and come before the house at a spectral hour when the air was full of bats.

Something which they but half saw—half a sight was enough—sent them tearing back through the willow-brakes and acacia bushes to their homes, where they fairly dropped down, and cried:

"Was it White?"

"No—yes—nearly so—we can't tell—but we saw it." And one could hardly doubt, to look at their ashen faces, that they had, whatever it was.

"If that old rascal lived in the country we come from," said certain Américains, "he'd have been tarred and feathered before now, wouldn't he, Sanders?"

"Well, now he just would."

"And we'd have rid him on a rail, wouldn't we?"

"That's what I allow."

"Tell you what you *could* do." They were talking to some rollicking Creoles who had assumed an absolute necessity for doing *something*. "What is it you call this thing where an old man marries a young girl, and you come out with horns and"—

"*Charivari?*" asked the Creoles.

"Yes, that's it. Why don't you shivaree him?" Felicitous suggestion.

Little White, with his wife beside him, was sitting on their doorsteps on the sidewalk, as Creole custom had taught them, looking toward the sunset. They had moved into the lately-opened street. The view was not attractive on the score of beauty. The houses were small and scattered, and across the flat commons, spite of the lofty tangle of weeds and bushes, and spite of the thickets of acacia, they needs must see the dismal old Poquelin mansion, tilted awry and shutting out the declining sun. The moon, white and slender, was hanging the tip of its horn over one of the chimneys.

"And you say," said the Secretary, "the old black man has been going by here alone? Patty, suppose old Poquelin should be concocting some mischief; he don't lack provocation; the way that clod hit him the other day was enough to have killed him. Why, Patty, he dropped as quick as *that*! No wonder you haven't seen him. I wonder if they haven't heard something about him up at the drug-store. Suppose I go and see."

"Do," said his wife.

She sat alone for half an hour, watching that sudden going out of the day peculiar to the latitude.

"That moon is ghost enough for one house," she said, as her husband returned. "It has gone right down the chimney."

"Patty," said little White, "the drug-clerk says the boys are going to shivaree old Poquelin to-night. I'm going to try to stop it."

"Why, White," said his wife, "you'd better not. You'll get hurt."

"No, I'll not."

"Yes, you will."

"I'm going to sit out here until they come along. They're compelled to pass right by here."

"Why, White, it may be midnight before they start; you're not going to sit out here till then."

"Yes, I am."

"Well, you're very foolish," said Mrs. White in an undertone, looking anxious, and tapping one of the steps with her foot.

They sat a very long time talking over little family matters.

"What's that?" at last said Mrs. White.

"That's the nine-o'clock gun," said White, and they relapsed into a long-sustained, drowsy silence.

"Patty, you'd better go in and go to bed," said he at last.

"I'm not sleepy."

"Well, you're very foolish," quietly remarked little White, and again silence fell upon them.

"Patty, suppose I walk out to the old house and see if I can find out any thing."

"Suppose," said she, "you don't do any such—listen!"

Down the street arose a great hubbub. Dogs and boys were howling and barking; men were laughing, shouting, groaning, and blowing horns, whooping, and clanking cow-bells, whinnying, and howling, and rattling pots and pans.

"They are coming this way," said little White. "You had better go into the house, Patty."

"So had you."

"No. I'm going to see if I can't stop them."

"Why, White!"

"I'll be back in a minute," said White, and went toward the noise.

In a few moments the little Secretary met the mob. The pen hesitates on the word, for there is a respectable difference, measurable only on the scale of the half century, between a mob and a *charivari*. Little White lifted his ineffectual voice. He faced the head of the disorderly column, and cast himself about as if he were made of wood and moved by the jerk of a string. He rushed to one who seemed, from the size and clatter of his tin pan, to be a leader. *"Stop these fellows, Bienvenu, stop them just a minute, till I tell them something."* Bienvenu turned and brandished his instruments of discord in an imploring way to the crowd. They slackened their pace, two or three hushed their horns and joined the prayer of little White and Bienvenu for silence. The throng halted. The hush was delicious.

"Bienvenu," said little White, "don't shivaree old Poquelin to-night; he's—"

"My fwang," said the swaying Bienvenu, "who tail you I goin' to chahivahi somebody, eh? Yon sink bickause I make a little playfool wiz zis tin pan zat I am *dhonk?*"

"Oh, no, Bienvenu, old fellow, you're all right. I was afraid you might not know that old Poquelin was sick, you know, but you're not going there, are you?"

"My fwang, I vay soy to tail you zat you ah dhonk as de dev'. I am *shem* of you. I ham ze servan' of ze *publique*. Zese *citoyens* goin' to wickwest Jean Poquelin to give to the Ursuline' two hondred fifty dolla'—"

"*Hé quoi!*" cried a listener, "*Cinq cent piastres, oui!*"

"*Oui!*" said Bienvenu, "and if he wiffuse we make him some lit' *musique*; ta-ra ta!" He hoisted a merry hand and foot, then frowning, added: "Old Poquelin got no bizniz dhink s'much w'isky."

"But, gentlemen," said little White, around whom a circle had gathered, "the old man is very sick."

"My faith!" cried a tiny Creole, "we did not make him to be sick. W'en we have say we going make *le charivari*, do you want that we hall tell a lie? My faith! 'sfools!"

"But you can shivaree somebody else," said desperate little White.

"*Oui*" cried Bienvenu, "*et chahivahi* Jean-ah Poquelin tomo'w!"

"Let us go to Madame Schneider!" cried two or three, and amid huzzas and confused cries, among which was heard a stentorian Celtic call for drinks, the crowd again began to move.

"*Cent piastres pour l'hôpital de charité!*"

"Hurrah!"

"One hongred dolla' for Charity Hospital!"

"Hurrah!"

"Whang!" went a tin pan, the crowd yelled, and Pandemonium gaped again.

They were off at a right angle.

Nodding, Mrs. White looked at the mantle-clock.

"Well, if it isn't away after midnight."

The hideous noise down street was passing beyond earshot. She raised a sash and listened. For a moment there was silence. Some one came to the door.

"Is that you, White?"

"Yes." He entered. "I succeeded, Patty."

"Did you?" said Patty, joyfully.

"Yes. They've gone down to shivaree the old Dutchwoman who married her step-daughter's sweetheart. They say she has got to pay a hundred dollars to the hospital before they stop."

The couple retired, and Mrs. White slumbered. She was awakened by her husband snapping the lid of his watch.

"What time?" she asked.

"Half-past three. Patty, I haven't slept a wink. Those fellows are out yet. Don't you hear them?"

"Why, White, they're coming this way!"

"I know they are," said White, sliding out of bed and drawing on his clothes, "and they're coming fast. You'd better go away from that window, Patty. My! what a clatter!"

"Here they are," said Mrs. White, but her husband was gone. Two or three hundred men and boys pass the place at a rapid walk straight down the broad, new street, toward the hated house of ghosts. The din was terrific. She saw little White at the head of the rabble brandishing his arms and trying in vain to make himself heard; but they only shook their heads laughing and hooting the louder, and so passed, bearing him on before them.

Swiftly they pass out from among the houses, away from the dim oil lamps of the street, out into the broad starlit commons, and enter the willowy jungles of the haunted ground. Some hearts fail and their owners lag behind and turn back, suddenly remembering how near morning it is. But the most part push on, tearing the air with their clamor.

Down ahead of them in the long, thicket-darkened way there is—singularly enough—a faint, dancing light. It must be very near the old house; it is. It has stopped now. It is a lantern, and is under a well-known sapling which has grown up on the wayside since the canal was filled. Now it swings mysteriously to and fro. A goodly number of the more ghost-fearing give up the sport; but a full hundred move forward at a run, doubling their devilish howling and banging.

Yes; it is a lantern, and there are two persons under the tree. The crowd draws near—drops into a walk; one of the two is the old African mute; he lifts the lantern up so that it shines on the other; the crowd recoils; there is a hush of all clangor, and all at once, with a cry of mingled fright and horror from every throat, the whole throng rushes back, dropping every thing, sweeping past little White and hurrying on, never stopping until the jungle is left behind, and then to find that not one in ten has seen the cause of the stampede, and not one of the tenth is certain what it was.

There is one huge fellow among them who looks capable of any villany. He finds something to mount on, and, in the Creole *patois*, calls a general halt. Bienvenu sinks down, and, vainly trying to recline gracefully, resigns the leadership. The herd gather round the speaker; he assures them that they have been outraged. Their right peaceably to traverse the public streets has been trampled upon. Shall such encroachments be endured? It is now daybreak. Let them go now by the open light of day and force a free passage of the public highway!

A scattering consent was the response, and the crowd, thinned now and drowsy, straggled quietly down toward the old house. Some drifted ahead, others sauntered behind, but every one, as he again neared the tree, came to a stand-still. Little White sat upon a bank of turf on the opposite side of the way looking very stern and sad. To each new-comer he put the same question:

"Did you come here to go to old Poquelin's?"

"Yes."

"He's dead." And if the shocked hearer started away he would say: "Don't go away."

"Why not?"

"I want you to go to the funeral presently."

If some Louisianian, too loyal to dear France or Spain to understand English, looked bewildered, some one would interpret for him; and presently they went. Little White led the van, the crowd trooping after him down the middle of the way. The gate, that had never been seen before unchained, was open. Stern little White stopped a short distance from it; the rabble stopped behind him. Something was moving out from under the veranda. The many whisperers stretched upward to see. The African mute came very slowly toward the gate, leading by a cord in the nose a small brown bull, which was harnessed to a rude cart. On the flat body of the cart, under a black cloth, were seen the outlines of a long box.

"Hats off, gentlemen," said little White, as the box came in view, and the crowd silently uncovered.

"Gentlemen," said little White, "here come the last remains of Jean Marie Poquelin, a better man, I'm afraid, with all his sins,—yes a better—a kinder man to his blood—a man of more self-forgetful goodness—than all of you put together will ever dare to be."

There was a profound hush as the vehicle came creaking through the gate; but when it turned away from them toward the forest, those in front started suddenly. There was a backward rush, then all stood still again staring one way; for there, behind the bier, with eyes cast down and labored step, walked the living remains—all that was left— of little Jacques Poquelin, the long-hidden brother—a leper, as white as snow.

Dumb with horror, the cringing crowd gazed upon the walking death. They watched, in silent awe, the slow *cortège* creep down the long, straight road and lessen on the view, until by and by it stopped where a wild, unfrequented path branched off into the undergrowth toward the rear of the ancient city.

"They are going to the *Terre aux Lépreux*," said one in the crowd. The rest watched them in silence.

The little bull was set free; the mute, with the strength of an ape, lifted the long box to his shoulder. For a moment more the mute and the leper stood in sight, while the former adjusted his heavy burden; then, without one backward glance upon the unkind human world, turning their faces toward the ridge in the depths of the swamp known as the Leper's Land, they stepped into the jungle, disappeared, and were never seen again.

15

MISTRESS MARIAN'S LIGHT

BY GERTRUDE MORTON

So far as is known, "Mistress Marian's Light," published in The New England Magazine *in 1889, when she resided in Aurora, Maine, is Gertrude Morton's (?–?) only published work. This seems surprising, given the author's evident talent and skill. It is also possible that "Gertrude Morton" is a pseudonym.*

Far down the Maine coast, in one of the many harbors of that good old State, is a picturesque little island inhabited by simple fisher folk. Generation after generation has been born, lived, and died in this same island village, yet all the people seem to retain the customs and quaint ways of fifty years ago; from the old, weather-worn sailor, to the youngest child among them, they seem, to an unusual degree, guileless and simple and kindly, while to the stranger within their gates their goodness is unlimited. It is like a reminiscence of bygone days to partake of their generous hospitality.

At a late hour one soft, sweet night in early summer, while sojourning for a time among these people, I noticed, far down on a point of land, that rocky and waveworn, makes out into the sea, a strange light, that seemed to be suspended a few feet from the earth. Soft and wavering it was, sometimes dim; but so unmistakably a light, that I was somewhat perplexed, and the next morning I asked my hostess the cause of the strange phenomenon.

The woman's countenance changed in an instant, and she assumed a sympathetic, pitying look as she replied, with a wise, uncanny shake of her head, "Why, that is Mistress Marian's light." And so she went on and told me this story.

Away down on the point, where the brown soil of the interior of the island begins to mingle with the white sand along the sea, there was, many years ago, a small cottage, built by a seafaring man, who, with his family, occupied it for a short time. They then removed to a neighboring shore, and the house remained untenanted many months.

In the course of time two strangers came to the island,—an old man and his little daughter. Venerable indeed was the father, and with his snow-white hair and beard, and his dignified, scholarly bearing, he might have been a king among men. No one seemed to know just when or how they came; they appeared suddenly and unexpectedly, and seemed to find relief in the quietness of the place. As a wandering meteor, travelling through limitless space, finds rest somewhere in God's great universe, so did these two strangers find a dwelling-place in this secluded spot.

To the little uninhabited cottage on the point they went, and the simple life of the islanders became their life. They became a part, and still not a part, of the fisher folk. The dignified old man was so unlike any one whom they had ever seen before that they were shy of him; and long though he lived among them, quietly assisting the needy, and lending a helping hand to all, they were never quite at ease with him, though they worshipped him from afar. It was as though he breathed a rarer atmosphere than they, and dwelt above them; and they were content to accept his kindness and to marvel at his greatness.

Not so the child, with her soft brown eyes and her gentle, winning manner. "A lady born and bred, she is," the good dames said, one to another, many times. But she was a child, strangely alone, so the motherly arms were opened to her, and the children made this little Marian their playmate.

They seemed to be people of means,—this father and daughter. The cottage was furnished comfortably, even luxuriously, and many books, some of them in quaint and curious bindings, were about. On the low walls hung several pictures, the like of which the islanders had never seen before; rich rugs covered the bare floors; a piece of rare Eastern embroidery was flung over a low couch; upon an oddly carved shelf were some bits of china, delicate and fragile, as though fashioned from rose leaves; while everywhere in the tiny house were evidences of refinement. From what faraway land the strangers came, or why they sought refuge on the little island, they themselves never said, nor were they ever questioned. The people, with their simple faith and childlike credulity, accepted the fact of their coming as they did all the good things that befell them,—thankful, asking naught.

So these two lived on in an alien land, their lives replete with the satisfaction that comes from helping others, their desire to do good satisfied by the appreciation with which their efforts were met. Thus the little girl, the dainty Marian, grew to maidenhood, learning much from her father and his books, but more from Nature: of the sea with its wonderful treasures; of the rocks that she loved, gaunt and gray though they were; of flowers and fishes and birds. She learned, too, much of human nature—the kindly side—from the people about her; and their interests she made hers. Every mother on the island felt a deep affection for her, and her young mates were proud to be called her friends. She was a constant surprise to them. The dainty gowns that she fashioned for herself, out of strange fabrics, were marvels; even her language seemed somehow different from theirs; and when a stranger chanced to visit the little building where they gathered on Sundays for worship, "our young lady," brown-eyed "Mistress Marian," was always pointed out with secret pride. So she grew to pure and noble womanhood, winning respect and admiration from all.

The lads of the village were filled with unspeakable delight when she spoke to them in her sweet, low voice. Not one of them but that would have risked his limbs, almost his life, for anything that she wanted,—a wild-flower, a stone, or a bright bit of seaweed. Yet for none of them had she more than a word or a smile, except for tall, manly Phil Anderson. From her childhood she had seemed to set him apart from all others as a hero; and when he came to her out on the rocks one sweet summer night, when the moon was softly shining and the sea was bright with the phosphorescent gleam, and told her of his love for her, she accepted it quietly and trustfully.

It was a happy summer for the two, passing all too quickly. When autumn came, Phil was to sail with his father on one more voyage—to make his fortune, he said; then he was coming back to marry Marian and to take her away into the great world of which they were never tired of talking.

So the weeks slipped by. October came. The trees donned their gayest colors; each bush took its own particular, matchless tint, and the breakers dashed high in the cool breeze, as though to speed the parting, which was even then at hand. One bright, cool morning Phil went down to the little house to say good-by. Tremblingly the old man bade the brave young sailor farewell, then sent him out to the rocks—the place of their betrothal—where Marian was waiting. Silently he took her in his strong arms, kissed her soft hair, her forehead and her sweet red lips, then turned and strode quickly away, as though he could not trust his courage longer.

A year passed, bringing two letters to Marian from her lover, telling her of such success as even his fondest hopes had failed to picture. At the end of the third year, just after another letter had come, telling her that the *Watersprite* was homeward bound, and happiness seemed in store for her, her father died. For months the old man had been slowly failing, living only in his daughter's happiness. Now that she did not need him longer, he seemed to lose all power of holding on to his life, and one evening passed quietly away with the setting of the sun.

The grief of the young girl was well-nigh unbearable. The only bright thing that life seemed to hold for her was the fact that her lover was on his way to her. So she waited anxiously, longingly, expecting tidings every day. But after the third letter no news came.

As the days lengthened to weeks, and the weeks to months, the islanders were filled with apprehension and forebodings. A gloom settled over the people, which even the lingering Indian summer failed to brighten; and when, one bleak November day, beneath a darkening sky, a strange vessel came into the harbor with tidings that the gallant *Watersprite* had sunk and every soul on board had perished, it was almost a relief to the anxious watchers. Certainty, though hard to bear, was better than hope deferred.

Gently did sympathetic friends tell the mournful news to the lonely girl at the point; but dazed and bewildered, she did not seem to comprehend their meaning. For days she lay in a kind of stupor, unheeding everything, even the presence of the kind old dame who watched by her side night and day with tear-dimmed eyes. Only when the waves dashed loudest would the girl stir uneasily, raising her head as though listening for some one's coming.

At last she awoke from her long sleep, coming back once more to life and to her senses; but the beautiful hair was as white as the foam that dashed against the rocks she used to love, and the dark eyes looked large and mournful beneath the snowy wealth. As strength slowly came back to her, so also came the firm conviction that her lover was not dead, but would one day return to her. So firm was her faith that she grew cheerful, almost happy. Once more she assumed her duties,—clothing little children, ministering to the sick and aged, helping weary housewives. There was not a person on the island who had not at one time or another felt her kindly influence or her strong, stimulating presence.

Every night at dusk, after her day's work was done, she would place a large bright light in the window of the little sitting-room that looked toward the harbor, leaving the curtain drawn aside, so that should he for whom she watched come at night, he would find her still waiting for him. Not a night did she fail in this most important of all her duties. Her light was a bright beacon. Sailors soon learned to know it and look for it, and they never looked in vain; it was always there, steady, clear, unwavering.

Thus passed several years, when suddenly, mysteriously, without a shadow of warning, Mistress Marian disappeared. As silently as years ago she had entered the life of the fisher folk, so now did she leave it; and as they knew not then whence she came, neither did they know now whither she went.

There were many conjectures as to her strange disappearance. One old sailor affirmed that one night when he was out fishing he saw a little boat come from the point, bearing a solitary passenger with snow-white hair, who rowed out toward a large ship that could be dimly seen, as through a fog, and was taken on board; then the huge ship quickly vanished. But as this old man was well known to take his black bottle with him on his fishing expeditions, and as no other person could be found who saw the wonderful ship, his story did not gain the credence that its ingenuity deserved. The most of the people inclined to the belief that she had gone back to her father's relatives; but how, when, or where, not even the old woman who lived with her could tell.

A decade or two passed, and the old house in its exposed locality grew more and more weatherworn and dilapidated; and finally, one winter, doubtless feeling that its time of usefulness had passed, it succumbed to fate and, during a heavy gale, fell to the ground. Some of the timbers were washed away, others were used for fire-wood by campers and fishermen; so that after a time nothing remained to mark the spot where the cottage had been, save a few damp, moss-covered logs.

But still in this same place on quiet summer nights during the hot sultry time of July and August,—the time when the *Watersprite* was said to have perished,—this weird, white, uncertain, trembling light, a few feet from the ground, is at times plainly seen. Not all the scientific explanations of wiser heads can convince the simple villagers that this strange light is any other than Marian's beacon for her sailor lover, or shake their faith in the plausibility of a story handed down from successive generations.

The merriest sailing party, rounding the point of a sweet summer night, will become subdued at the sight of the light, while the timid maiden will nestle closer to the skipper at the helm, as she says in awe-struck tones, "See! Mistress Marian's light is still burning."

16

CONSEQUENCES

BY WILLA CATHER

Born in Virginia, Willa Cather (1873–1947) became a highly successful novelist and short story writer. Her childhood on the Nebraska frontier inspired some of her best-known works, especially O Pioneers! *She also worked as an English and Latin teacher in Pittsburgh, Pennsylvania. Beginning in 1906 she was an editor, in New York City, at* McClure's Magazine, *which published many of her stories. In 1922, her novel* One of Ours *won the Pulitzer Prize. "Consequences" first appeared in* McClure's *in 1915.*

Henry Eastman, a lawyer, aged forty, was standing beside the Flatiron building in a driving November rainstorm, signaling frantically for a taxi. It was six-thirty, and everything on wheels was engaged. The streets were in confusion about him, the sky was in turmoil above him, and the Flatiron building, which seemed about to blow down, threw water like a mill-shoot. Suddenly, out of the brutal struggle of men and cars and machines and people tilting at each other with umbrellas, a quiet, well-mannered limousine paused before him, at the curb, and an agreeable, ruddy countenance confronted him through the open window of the car.

"Don't you want me to pick you up, Mr. Eastman? I'm running directly home now."

Eastman recognized Kier Cavenaugh, a young man of pleasure, who lived in the house on Central Park South, where he himself had an apartment.

"Don't I?" he exclaimed, bolting into the car. "I'll risk getting your cushions wet without compunction. I came up in a taxi, but I didn't hold it. Bad economy. I thought I saw your car down on Fourteenth Street about half an hour ago."

The owner of the car smiled. He had a pleasant, round face and round eyes, and a fringe of smooth, yellow hair showed under the rim of his soft felt hat. "With a lot of little broilers fluttering into it? You did. I know some girls who work in the cheap shops down there. I happened to be down-town and I stopped and took a load of them home. I do sometimes. Saves their poor little clothes, you know. Their shoes are never any good."

Eastman looked at his rescuer. "Aren't they notoriously afraid of cars and smooth young men?" he inquired.

Cavenaugh shook his head. "They know which cars are safe and which are chancy. They put each other wise. You have to take a bunch at a time, of course. The Italian girls can never come along; their men shoot. The girls understand, all right; but their fathers don't. One gets to see queer places, sometimes, taking them home."

Eastman laughed drily. "Every time I touch the circle of your acquaintance, Cavenaugh, it's a little wider. You must know New York pretty well by this time."

"Yes, but I'm on my good behavior below Twenty-third Street," the young man replied with simplicity. "My little friends down there would give me a good character. They're wise little girls. They have grand ways with each other, a romantic code of loyalty. You can find a good many of the lost virtues among them."

The car was standing still in a traffic block at Fortieth Street, when Cavenaugh suddenly drew his face away from the window and touched Eastman's arm. "Look, please. You see that hansom with the bony gray horse—driver has a broken hat and red flannel around his throat. Can you see who is inside?"

Eastman peered out. The hansom was just cutting across the line, and the driver was making a great fuss about it, bobbing his head and waving his whip. He jerked his dripping old horse into Fortieth Street and clattered off past the Public Library grounds toward Sixth Avenue. "No, I couldn't see the passenger. Someone you know?"

"Could you see whether there was a passenger?" Cavenaugh asked.

"Why, yes. A man, I think. I saw his elbow on the apron. No driver ever behaves like that unless he has a passenger."

"Yes, I may have been mistaken," Cavenaugh murmured absent-mindedly. Ten minutes or so later, after Cavenaugh's car had turned off Fifth Avenue into Fifty-eighth Street, Eastman exclaimed, "There's your same cabby, and his cart's empty. He's headed for a drink now, I suppose." The driver in the broken hat and the red flannel neck cloth was still brandishing the whip over his old gray. He was coming from the west now, and turned down Sixth Avenue, under the elevated.

Cavenaugh's car stopped at the bachelor apartment house between Sixth and Seventh Avenues where he and Eastman lived, and they went up in the elevator together. They were still talking when the lift stopped at Cavenaugh's floor, and Eastman stepped out with him and walked down the hall, finishing his sentence while Cavenaugh found his latch-key. When he opened the door, a wave of fresh cigarette smoke greeted them. Cavenaugh stopped short and stared into his hallway. "Now how in the devil—!" he exclaimed angrily.

"Someone waiting for you? Oh, no, thanks. I wasn't coming in. I have to work to-night. Thank you, but I couldn't." Eastman nodded and went up the two flights to his own rooms.

Though Eastman did not customarily keep a servant he had this winter a man who had been lent to him by a friend who was abroad. Rollins met him at the door and took his coat and hat.

"Put out my dinner clothes, Rollins, and then get out of here until ten o'clock. I've promised to go to a supper to-night. I shan't be dining. I've had a late tea and I'm going to work until ten. You may put out some kumiss and biscuit for me."

Rollins took himself off, and Eastman settled down at the big table in his sitting-room. He had to read a lot of letters submitted as evidence in a breach of contract case, and before he got very far he found that long paragraphs in some of the letters were written in German. He had a German dictionary at his office, but none here. Rollins had gone, and anyhow, the bookstores would be closed. He remembered having seen a row of dictionaries on the lower shelf of one of Cavenaugh's bookcases. Cavenaugh had a lot of books, though he never read anything but new stuff. Eastman prudently turned down his student's lamp very low—the thing had an evil habit of smoking—and went down two flights to Cavenaugh's door.

The young man himself answered Eastman's ring. He was freshly dressed for the evening, except for a brown smoking jacket, and his yellow hair had been brushed until it shone. He hesitated as he confronted his caller, still holding the door knob, and his round eyes and smooth forehead made their best imitation of a frown. When Eastman began to apologize, Cavenaugh's manner suddenly changed.

He caught his arm and jerked him into the narrow hall. "Come in, come in. Right along!" he said excitedly. "Right along," he repeated as he pushed Eastman before him into his sitting-room. "Well I'll—" he stopped short at the door and looked about his own room with an air of complete mystification. The back window was wide open and a strong wind was blowing in. Cavenaugh walked over to the window and stuck out his head, looking up and down the fire escape. When he pulled his head in, he drew down the sash.

"I had a visitor I wanted you to see," he explained with a nervous smile. "At least I thought I had. He must have gone out that way," nodding toward the window.

"Call him back. I only came to borrow a German dictionary, if you have one. Can't stay. Call him back."

Cavenaugh shook his head despondently. "No use. He's beat it. Nowhere in sight."

"He must be active. Has he left something?" Eastman pointed to a very dirty white glove that lay on the floor under the window.

"Yes, that's his." Cavenaugh reached for his tongs, picked up the glove, and tossed it into the grate, where it quickly shriveled on the coals. Eastman felt that he had happened in upon something disagreeable, possibly something shady, and he wanted to get away at once. Cavenaugh stood staring at the fire and seemed stupid and dazed; so he repeated his request rather sternly, "I think I've seen a German dictionary down there among your books. May I have it?"

Cavenaugh blinked at him. "A German dictionary? Oh, possibly! Those were my father's. I scarcely know what there is." He put down the tongs and began to wipe his hands nervously with his handkerchief.

Eastman went over to the bookcase behind the Chesterfield, opened the door, swooped upon the book he wanted and stuck it under his arm. He felt perfectly certain now that something shady had been going on in Cavenaugh's rooms, and he saw no reason why he should come in for any hang-over. "Thanks. I'll send it back tomorrow," he said curtly as he made for the door.

Cavenaugh followed him. "Wait a moment. I wanted you to see him. You did see his glove," glancing at the grate.

Eastman laughed disagreeably. "I saw a glove. That's not evidence. Do your friends often use that means of exit? Somewhat inconvenient."

Cavenaugh gave him a startled glance. "Wouldn't you think so? For an old man, a very rickety old party? The ladders are steep, you know, and rusty." He approached the window again and put it up softly. In a moment he drew his head back with a jerk. He caught Eastman's arm and shoved him toward the window. "Hurry, please. Look! Down there." He pointed to the little patch of paved court four flights down.

The square of pavement was so small and the walls about it were so high, that it was a good deal like looking down a well. Four tall buildings backed upon the same court and made a kind of shaft, with flagstones at the bottom, and at the top a square of dark blue with some stars in it. At the bottom of the shaft Eastman saw a black figure, a man in a caped coat and a tall hat stealing cautiously around, not across the square of pavement, keeping close to the dark wall and avoiding the streak of light that fell on the flagstones from a window in the opposite house. Seen from that height he was of course fore-shortened and probably looked more shambling and decrepit than he was. He picked his way along with exaggerated care and looked like a silly old cat crossing a wet street. When he reached the gate that led into an alley way between two buildings, he felt about for the latch, opened the door a mere crack, and then shot out under the feeble lamp that burned in the brick arch over the gateway. The door closed after him.

"He'll get run in," Eastman remarked curtly, turning away from the window. "That door shouldn't be left unlocked. Any crook could come in. I'll speak to the janitor about it, if you don't mind," he added sarcastically.

"Wish you would." Cavenaugh stood brushing down the front of his jacket, first with his right hand and then with his left. "You saw him, didn't you?"

"Enough of him. Seems eccentric. I have to see a lot of buggy people. They don't take me in any more. But I'm keeping you and I'm in a hurry myself. Good night."

Cavenaugh put out his hand detainingly and started to say something; but Eastman rudely turned his back and went down the hall and out of the door. He had never felt anything shady about Cavenaugh before, and he was sorry he had gone down for the dictionary. In five minutes he was deep in his papers; but in the half hour when he was loafing before he dressed to go out, the young man's curious behavior came into his mind again.

Eastman had merely a neighborly acquaintance with Cavenaugh. He had been to a supper at the young man's rooms once, but he didn't particularly like Cavenaugh's friends; so the next time he was asked, he had another engagement. He liked Cavenaugh himself, if for nothing else than because he was so cheerful and trim and ruddy. A good complexion is always at a premium in New York, especially when it shines reassuringly on a man who does everything in the world to lose it. It encourages fellow mortals as to the inherent vigor of the human organism and the amount of bad treatment it will stand for. "Footprints that perhaps another," etc.

Cavenaugh, he knew, had plenty of money. He was the son of a Pennsylvania preacher, who died soon after he discovered that his ancestral acres were full of petroleum, and Kier had come to New

York to burn some of the oil. He was thirty-two and was still at it; spent his life, literally, among the breakers. His motor hit the Park every morning as if it were the first time ever. He took people out to supper every night. He went from restaurant to restaurant, sometimes to half-a-dozen in an evening. The head waiters were his hosts and their cordiality made him happy. They made a life-line for him up Broadway and down Fifth Avenue. Cavenaugh was still fresh and smooth, round and plump, with a lustre to his hair and white teeth and a clear look in his round eyes. He seemed absolutely unwearied and unimpaired; never bored and never carried away.

Eastman always smiled when he met Cavenaugh in the entrance hall, serenely going forth to or returning from gladiatorial combats with joy, or when he saw him rolling smoothly up to the door in his car in the morning after a restful night in one of the remarkable new roadhouses he was always finding. Eastman had seen a good many young men disappear on Cavenaugh's route, and he admired this young man's endurance.

To-night, for the first time, he had got a whiff of something unwholesome about the fellow—bad nerves, bad company, something on hand that he was ashamed of, a visitor old and vicious, who must have had a key to Cavenaugh's apartment, for he was evidently there when Cavenaugh returned at seven o'clock. Probably it was the same man Cavenaugh had seen in the hansom. He must have been able to let himself in, for Cavenaugh kept no man but his chauffeur; or perhaps the janitor had been instructed to let him in. In either case, and whoever he was, it was clear enough that Cavenaugh was ashamed of him and was mixing up in questionable business of some kind.

Eastman sent Cavenaugh's book back by Rollins, and for the next few weeks he had no word with him beyond a casual greeting when they happened to meet in the hall or the elevator. One Sunday morning Cavenaugh telephoned up to him to ask if he could motor out to a roadhouse in Connecticut that afternoon and have supper; but when Eastman found there were to be other guests he declined.

On New Year's eve Eastman dined at the University Club at six o'clock and hurried home before the usual manifestations of insanity had begun in the streets. When Rollins brought his smoking coat, he asked him whether he wouldn't like to get off early.

"Yes, sir. But won't you be dressing, Mr. Eastman?" he inquired.

"Not to-night." Eastman handed him a bill. "Bring some change in the morning. There'll be fees."

Rollins lost no time in putting everything to rights for the night, and Eastman couldn't help wishing that he were in such a hurry to be off somewhere himself. When he heard the hall door close softly, he wondered if there were any place, after all, that he wanted to go. From his window he looked down at the long lines of motors and taxis waiting for a signal to cross Broadway. He thought of some of their probable destinations and decided that none of those places pulled him very hard. The night was warm and wet, the air was drizzly. Vapor hung in clouds about the *Times* Building, half hid the top of it, and made a luminous haze along Broadway. While he was looking down at the army of wet, black carriage-tops and their reflected headlights and tail-lights, Eastman heard a ring at his door. He deliberated. If it were a caller, the hall porter would have telephoned up. It must be the janitor. When he opened the door, there stood a rosy young man in a tuxedo, without a coat or hat.

"Pardon. Should I have telephoned? I half thought you wouldn't be in."

Eastman laughed. "Come in, Cavenaugh. You weren't sure whether you wanted company or not, eh, and you were trying to let chance decide it? That was exactly my state of mind. Let's accept the verdict."

When they emerged from the narrow hall into his sitting-room, he pointed out a seat by the fire to his guest. He brought a tray of decanters and soda bottles and placed it on his writing table.

Cavenaugh hesitated, standing by the fire. "Sure you weren't starting for somewhere?"

"Do I look it? No, I was just making up my mind to stick it out alone when you rang. Have one?" he picked up a tall tumbler.

"Yes, thank you. I always do."

Eastman chuckled. "Lucky boy! So will I. I had a very early dinner. New York is the most arid place on holidays," he continued as he rattled the ice in the glasses. "When one gets too old to hit the rapids down there, and tired of gobbling food to heathenish dance music, there is absolutely no place where you can get a chop and some milk toast in peace, unless you have strong ties of blood brotherhood on upper Fifth Avenue. But you, why aren't you starting for somewhere?"

The young man sipped his soda and shook his head as he replied:

"Oh, I couldn't get a chop, either. I know only flashy people, of course." He looked up at his host with such a grave and candid expression that Eastman decided there couldn't be anything very crooked about the fellow. His smooth cheeks were positively cherubic.

"Well, what's the matter with them? Aren't they flashing to-night?"

"Only the very new ones seem to flash on New Year's eve. The older ones fade away. Maybe they are hunting a chop, too."

"Well"—Eastman sat down—"holidays do dash one. I was just about to write a letter to a pair of maiden aunts in my old home town, up-state; old coasting hill, snow-covered pines, lights in the church windows. That's what you've saved me from."

Cavenaugh shook himself. "Oh, I'm sure that wouldn't have been good for you. Pardon me," he rose and took a photograph from the bookcase, a handsome man in shooting clothes. "Dudley, isn't it? Did you know him well?"

"Yes. An old friend. Terrible thing, wasn't it? I haven't got over the jolt yet."

"His suicide? Yes, terrible! Did you know his wife?"

"Slightly. Well enough to admire her very much. She must be terribly broken up. I wonder Dudley didn't think of that."

Cavenaugh replaced the photograph carefully, lit a cigarette, and standing before the fire began to smoke. "Would you mind telling me about him? I never met him, but of course I'd read a lot about him, and I can't help feeling interested. It was a queer thing."

Eastman took out his cigar case and leaned back in his deep chair. "In the days when I knew him best he hadn't any story, like the happy nations. Everything was properly arranged for him before he was born. He came into the world happy, healthy, clever, straight, with the right sort of connections and the right kind of fortune, neither too large nor too small. He helped to make the world an agreeable place to live in until he was twenty-six. Then he married as he should have married. His wife was a Californian, educated abroad. Beautiful. You have seen her picture?"

Cavenaugh nodded. "Oh, many of them."

"She was interesting, too. Though she was distinctly a person of the world, she had retained something, just enough of the large Western manner. She had the habit of authority, of calling out a special train if she needed it, of using all our ingenious mechanical contrivances lightly and easily, without over-rating them. She and Dudley knew how to live better than most people. Their house was the most charming one I have ever known in New York. You felt freedom there, and a zest of life, and safety—absolute sanctuary—from everything sordid or petty. A whole society like that would justify the creation of man and would make our planet shine with a soft, peculiar radiance among the constellations. You think I'm putting it on thick?"

The young man sighed gently. "Oh, no! One has always felt there must be people like that. I've never known any."

"They had two children, beautiful ones. After they had been married for eight years, Rosina met this Spaniard. He must have amounted to something. She wasn't a flighty woman. She came home and told Dudley how matters stood. He persuaded her to stay at home for six months and try to pull up. They were both fair-minded people, and I'm as sure as if I were the Almighty, that she did try. But at the end of the time, Rosina went quietly off to Spain, and Dudley went to hunt in the Canadian Rockies. I met his party out there. I didn't know his wife had left him and talked about her a good deal. I noticed that he never drank anything, and his light used to shine through the log chinks of his room until all hours, even after a hard day's hunting. When I got back to New York, rumors were creeping about. Dudley did not come back. He bought a ranch in Wyoming, built a big log house and kept splendid dogs and horses. One of his sisters went out to keep house for him, and the children were there when they were not in school. He had a great many visitors, and everyone who came back talked about how well Dudley kept things going.

"He put in two years out there. Then, last month, he had to come back on business. A trust fund had to be settled up, and he was administrator. I saw him at the club; same light, quick step, same gracious handshake. He was getting gray, and there was something softer in his manner; but he had a fine red tan on his face and said he found it delightful to be here in the season when everything is going hard. The Madison Avenue house had been closed since Rosina left it. He went there to get some things his sister wanted. That, of course, was the mistake. He went alone, in the afternoon, and didn't go out for dinner—found some sherry and tins of biscuit in the sideboard. He shot himself sometime that night. There were pistols in his smoking-room. They found burnt out candles beside him in the morning. The gas and electricity were shut off. I suppose there, in his own house, among his own things, it was too much for him. He left no letters."

Cavenaugh blinked and brushed the lapel of his coat. "I suppose," he said slowly, "that every suicide is logical and reasonable, if one knew all the facts."

Eastman roused himself. "No, I don't think so. I've known too many fellows who went off like that—more than I deserve, I think—and some of them were absolutely inexplicable. I can understand Dudley; but I can't see why healthy bachelors, with money enough, like ourselves, need such a device. It reminds me of what Dr. Johnson said, that the most discouraging thing about life is the number of fads and hobbies and fake religions it takes to put people through a few years of it."

"Dr. Johnson? The specialist? Oh, the old fellow!" said Cavenaugh imperturbably. "Yes, that's interesting. Still, I fancy if one knew the facts—Did you know about Wyatt?"

"I don't think so."

"You wouldn't, probably. He was just a fellow about town who spent money. He wasn't one of the *forestieri*, though. Had connections here and owned a fine old place over on Staten Island. He went in for botany, and had been all over, hunting things; rusts, I believe. He had a yacht and used to take a gay crowd down about the South Seas, botanizing. He really did botanize, I believe. I never knew such a spender— only not flashy. He helped a lot of fellows and he was awfully good to girls, the kind who come down here to get a little fun, who don't like to work and still aren't really tough, the kind you see talking hard for their dinner. Nobody knows what becomes of them, or what they get out of it, and there are hundreds of new ones every year. He helped dozens of 'em; it was he who got me curious about the little shop girls. Well, one afternoon when his tea was brought, he took prussic acid instead. He didn't leave any letters, either; people of any taste don't. They wouldn't leave any material reminder if they could help it. His lawyers found that he had just $314.72 above his debts when he died. He had planned to spend all his money, and then take his tea; he had worked it out carefully."

Eastman reached for his pipe and pushed his chair away from the fire. "That looks like a considered case, but I don't think philosophical suicides like that are common. I think they usually come from stress of feeling and are really, as the newspapers call them, desperate acts; done without a motive. You remember when Anna Karenina was under the wheels, she kept saying, 'Why am I here?'"

Cavenaugh rubbed his upper lip with his pink finger and made an effort to wrinkle his brows. "May I, please?" reaching for the whiskey. "But have you," he asked, blinking as the soda flew at him, "have you ever known, yourself, cases that were really inexplicable?"

"A few too many. I was in Washington just before Captain Jack Purden was married and I saw a good deal of him. Popular army man, fine record in the Philippines, married a charming girl with lots of money; mutual devotion. It was the gayest wedding of the winter, and they started for Japan. They stopped in San Francisco for a week and missed their boat because, as the bride wrote back to Washington, they were too happy to move. They took the next boat, were both good sailors, had exceptional weather. After they had been out for two weeks, Jack got up from his deck chair one afternoon, yawned, put down his book, and stood before his wife. 'Stop reading for a moment and look at me.' She laughed and asked him why. 'Because you happen to be good to look at.' He nodded to her, went back to the stern and was never seen again. Must have gone down to the lower deck and slipped overboard, behind the machinery. It was the luncheon hour, not many people about; steamer cutting through a soft green sea. That's one of the most baffling cases I know. His friends raked up his past, and it was as trim as a cottage garden. If he'd so much as dropped an ink spot on his fatigue uniform, they'd have found it. He wasn't emotional or moody; wasn't, indeed, very interesting; simply a good soldier, fond of all the pompous little formalities that make up a military man's life. What do you make of that, my boy?"

Cavenaugh stroked his chin. "It's very puzzling, I admit. Still, if one knew everything—"

"But we do know everything. His friends wanted to find something to help them out, to help the girl out, to help the case of the human creature."

"Oh, I don't mean things that people could unearth," said Cavenaugh uneasily. "But possibly there were things that couldn't be found out."

Eastman shrugged his shoulders. "It's my experience that when there are 'things' as you call them, they're very apt to be found. There is no such thing as a secret. To make any move at all one has to employ human agencies, employ at least one human agent. Even when the pirates killed the men who buried their gold for them, the bones told the story."

Cavenaugh rubbed his hands together and smiled his sunny smile.

"I like that idea. It's reassuring. If we can have no secrets, it means that we can't, after all, go so far afield as we might," he hesitated, "yes, as we might."

Eastman looked at him sourly. "Cavenaugh, when you've practised law in New York for twelve years, you find that people can't go far in any direction, except—" He thrust his forefinger sharply at the floor.

"Even in that direction, few people can do anything out of the ordinary. Our range is limited. Skip a few baths, and we become personally objectionable. The slightest carelessness can rot a man's integrity or give him ptomaine poisoning. We keep up only by incessant cleansing operations, of mind and body. What we call character, is held together by all sorts of tacks and strings and glue."

Cavenaugh looked startled. "Come now, it's not so bad as that, is it? I've always thought that a serious man, like you, must know a lot of Launcelots." When Eastman only laughed, the younger man squirmed about in his chair. He spoke again hastily, as if he were embarrassed. "Your military friend may have had personal experiences, however, that his friends couldn't possibly get a line on. He may accidentally have come to a place where he saw himself in too unpleasant a light. I believe people can be chilled by a draft from outside, somewhere."

"Outside?" Eastman echoed. "Ah, you mean the far outside! Ghosts, delusions, eh?"

Cavenaugh winced. "That's putting it strong. Why not say tips from the outside? Delusions belong to a diseased mind, don't they? There are some of us who have no minds to speak of, who yet have had experiences. I've had a little something in that line myself and I don't look it, do I?"

Eastman looked at the bland countenance turned toward him. "Not exactly. What's your delusion?"

"It's not a delusion. It's a haunt."

The lawyer chuckled. "Soul of a lost Casino girl?"

"No; an old gentleman. A most unattractive old gentleman, who follows me about."

"Does he want money?"

Cavenaugh sat up straight. "No. I wish to God he wanted any-thing—but the pleasure of my society! I'd let him clean me out to be rid of him. He's a real article. You saw him yourself that night when you came to my rooms to borrow a dictionary, and he went down the fire-escape. You saw him down in the court."

"Well, I saw somebody down in the court, but I'm too cautious to take it for granted that I saw what you saw. Why, anyhow, should I see your haunt? If it was your friend I saw, he impressed me disagreeably. How did you pick him up?"

Cavenaugh looked gloomy. "That was queer, too. Charley Burke and I had motored out to Long Beach, about a year ago, sometime in October, I think. We had supper and stayed until late. When we were coming home, my car broke down. We had a lot of girls along who had to get back for morning rehearsals and things; so I sent them all into town in Charley's car, and he was to send a man back to tow me home. I was driving myself, and didn't want to leave my machine. We had not taken a direct road back; so I was stuck in a lonesome, woody place, no houses about. I got chilly and made a fire, and was putting in the time comfortably enough, when this old party steps up. He was in shabby evening clothes and a top hat, and had on his usual white gloves. How he got there, at three o'clock in the morning, miles from any town or railway, I'll leave it to you to figure out. *He* surely had no car. When I saw him coming up to the fire, I disliked him. He had a silly, apologetic walk. His teeth were chattering, and I asked him to sit down. He got down like a clothes-horse folding up. I offered him a cigarette, and when he took off his gloves I couldn't help noticing how knotted and spotty his hands were. He was asthmatic, and took his breath with a wheeze. 'Haven't you got anything—refreshing in there?' he asked, nodding at the car. When I told him I hadn't, he sighed. 'Ah, you young fellows are greedy. You drink it all up. You drink it all up, all up—up!' he kept chewing it over."

Cavenaugh paused and looked embarrassed again. "The thing that was most unpleasant is difficult to explain. The old man sat there by the fire and leered at me with a silly sort of admiration that was— well, more than humiliating. 'Gay boy, gay dog!' he would mutter, and when he grinned he showed his teeth, worn and yellow—shells. I remembered that it was better to talk casually to insane people; so I remarked carelessly that I had been out with a party and got stuck.

"'Oh yes, I remember,' he said, 'Flora and Lottie and Maybelle and Marcelline, and poor Kate.'

"He had named them correctly; so I began to think I had been hitting the bright waters too hard.

"Things I drank never had seemed to make me woody; but you can never tell when trouble is going to hit you. I pulled my hat down and tried to look as uncommunicative as possible; but he kept croaking on from time to time, like this: 'Poor Kate! Splendid arms, but dope got her. She took up with Eastern religions after she had her hair dyed. Got to going to a Swami's joint, and smoking opium. Temple of the Lotus, it was called, and the police raided it.'

"This was nonsense, of course; the young woman was in the pink of condition. I let him rave, but I decided that if something didn't come out for me pretty soon, I'd foot it across Long Island. There wasn't room enough for the two of us. I got up and took another try at my car. He hopped right after me.

"'Good car,' he wheezed, 'better than the little Ford.'

"I'd had a Ford before, but so has everybody; that was a safe guess.

"'Still,' he went on, 'that run in from Huntington Bay in the rain wasn't bad. Arrested for speeding, he-he.'

"It was true I had made such a run, under rather unusual circumstances, and had been arrested. When at last I heard my life-boat snorting up the road, my visitor got up, sighed, and stepped back into the shadow of the trees. I didn't wait to see what became of him, you may believe. That was visitation number one. What do you think of it?"

Cavenaugh looked at his host defiantly. Eastman smiled.

"I think you'd better change your mode of life, Cavenaugh. Had many returns?" he inquired.

"Too many, by far." The young man took a turn about the room and came back to the fire. Standing by the mantel he lit another cigarette before going on with his story:

"The second visitation happened in the street, early in the evening, about eight o'clock. I was held up in a traffic block before the Plaza. My chauffeur was driving. Old Nibbs steps up out of the crowd, opens the door of my car, gets in and sits down beside me. He had on wilted evening clothes, same as before, and there was some sort of heavy scent about him. Such an unpleasant old party! A thorough-going rotter; you knew it at once. This time he wasn't talkative, as he had been when I first saw him. He leaned back in the car as if he owned it, crossed his hands on his stick and looked out at the crowd—sort of hungrily.

"I own I really felt a loathing compassion for him. We got down the avenue slowly. I kept looking out at the mounted police. But what could I do? Have him pulled? I was afraid to. I was awfully afraid of getting him into the papers.

"'I'm going to the New Astor,' I said at last. 'Can I take you anywhere?'

"'No, thank you,' says he. 'I get out when you do. I'm due on West 44th. I'm dining to-night with Marcelline—all that is left of her!'

"He put his hand to his hat brim with a grewsome salute. Such a scandalous, foolish old face as he had! When we pulled up at the Astor, I stuck my hand in my pocket and asked him if he'd like a little loan.

"'No, thank you, but'—he leaned over and whispered, ugh!—'but save a little, save a little. Forty years from now—a little—comes in handy. Save a little.'

"His eyes fairly glittered as he made his remark. I jumped out. I'd have jumped into the North River. When he tripped off, I asked my chauffeur if he'd noticed the man who got into the car with me. He said he knew someone was with me, but he hadn't noticed just when he got in. Want to hear any more?"

Cavenaugh dropped into his chair again. His plump cheeks were a trifle more flushed than usual, but he was perfectly calm. Eastman felt that the young man believed what he was telling him.

"Of course I do. It's very interesting. I don't see quite where you are coming out though."

Cavenaugh sniffed. "No more do I. I really feel that I've been put upon. I haven't deserved it any more than any other fellow of my kind. Doesn't it impress you disagreeably?"

"Well, rather so. Has anyone else seen your friend?"

"You saw him."

"We won't count that. As I said, there's no certainty that you and I saw the same person in the court that night. Has anyone else had a look in?"

"People sense him rather than see him. He usually crops up when I'm alone or in a crowd on the street. He never approaches me when I'm with people I know, though I've seen him hanging about the doors of theatres when I come out with a party; loafing around the stage exit, under a wall; or across the street, in a doorway. To be frank, I'm not anxious to introduce him. The third time, it was I who came upon him. In November my driver, Harry, had a sudden attack of appendicitis. I took him to the Presbyterian Hospital in the car, early in the evening. When I came home, I found the old villain in my rooms. I offered him a drink, and he sat down. It was the first time I had seen him in a steady light, with his hat off.

"His face is lined like a railway map, and as to color—Lord, what a liver! His scalp grows tight to his skull, and his hair is dyed until it's perfectly dead, like a piece of black cloth."

Cavenaugh ran his fingers through his own neatly trimmed thatch, and seemed to forget where he was for a moment.

"I had a twin brother, Brian, who died when we were sixteen. I have a photograph of him on my wall, an enlargement from a kodak of him, doing a high jump, rather good thing, full of action. It seemed to annoy the old gentleman. He kept looking at it and lifting his eyebrows, and finally he got up, tip-toed across the room, and turned the picture to the wall.

"'Poor Brian! Fine fellow, but died young,' says he.

"Next morning, there was the picture, still reversed."

"Did he stay long?" Eastman asked interestedly.

"Half an hour, by the clock."

"Did he talk?"

"Well, he rambled."

"What about?"

Cavenaugh rubbed his pale eyebrows before answering.

"About things that an old man ought to want to forget. His conversation is highly objectionable. Of course he knows me like a book; everything I've ever done or thought. But when he recalls them, he throws a bad light on them, somehow. Things that weren't much off color, look rotten. He doesn't leave one a shred of self-respect, he really doesn't. That's the amount of it." The young man whipped out his handkerchief and wiped his face.

"You mean he really talks about things that none of your friends know?"

"Oh, dear, yes! Recalls things that happened in school. Anything disagreeable. Funny thing, he always turns Brian's picture to the wall."

"Does he come often?"

"Yes, oftener, now. Of course I don't know how he gets in downstairs. The hall boys never see him. But he has a key to my door. I don't know how he got it, but I can hear him turn it in the lock."

"Why don't you keep your driver with you, or telephone for me to come down?"

"He'd only grin and go down the fire escape as he did before. He's often done it when Harry's come in suddenly. Everybody has to be alone sometimes, you know. Besides, I don't want anybody to see him. He has me there."

"But why not? Why do you feel responsible for him?"

Cavenaugh smiled wearily. "That's rather the point, isn't it? Why do I? But I absolutely do. That identifies him, more than his knowing all about my life and my affairs."

Eastman looked at Cavenaugh thoughtfully. "Well, I should advise you to go in for something altogether different and new, and go in for it hard; business, engineering, metallurgy, something this old fellow wouldn't be interested in. See if you can make him remember logarithms."

Cavenaugh sighed. "No, he has me there, too. People never really change; they go on being themselves. But I would never make much trouble. Why can't they let me alone, damn it! I'd never hurt anybody, except, perhaps—"

"Except your old gentleman, eh?" Eastman laughed. "Seriously, Cavenaugh, if you want to shake him, I think a year on a ranch would do it. He would never be coaxed far from his favorite haunts. He would dread Montana."

Cavenaugh pursed up his lips. "So do I!"

"Oh, you think you do. Try it, and you'll find out. A gun and a horse beats all this sort of thing. Besides losing your haunt, you'd be putting ten years in the bank for yourself. I know a good ranch where they take people, if you want to try it."

"Thank you. I'll consider. Do you think I'm batty?"

"No, but I think you've been doing one sort of thing too long. You need big horizons. Get out of this."

Cavenaugh smiled meekly. He rose lazily and yawned behind his hand. "It's late, and I've taken your whole evening." He strolled over to the window and looked out. "Queer place, New York; rough on the little fellows. Don't you feel sorry for them, the girls especially? I do. What a fight they put up for a little fun! Why, even that old goat is sorry for them, the only decent thing he kept."

Eastman followed him to the door and stood in the hall, while Cavenaugh waited for the elevator. When the car came up Cavenaugh extended his pink, warm hand. "Good night."

The cage sank and his rosy countenance disappeared, his round-eyed smile being the last thing to go.

Weeks passed before Eastman saw Cavenaugh again. One morning, just as he was starting for Washington to argue a case before the Supreme Court, Cavenaugh telephoned him at his office to ask him about the Montana ranch he had recommended; said he meant to take his advice and go out there for the spring and summer.

When Eastman got back from Washington, he saw dusty trunks, just up from the trunk room, before Cavenaugh's door. Next morning, when he stopped to see what the young man was about, he found Cavenaugh in his shirt sleeves, packing.

"I'm really going; off to-morrow night. You didn't think it of me, did you?" he asked gaily.

"Oh, I've always had hopes of you!" Eastman declared. "But you are in a hurry, it seems to me."

"Yes, I am in a hurry." Cavenaugh shot a pair of leggings into one of the open trunks. "I telegraphed your ranch people, used your name, and they said it would be all right. By the way, some of my crowd are giving a little dinner for me at Rector's to-night. Couldn't you be persuaded, as it's a farewell occasion?" Cavenaugh looked at him hopefully.

Eastman laughed and shook his head. "Sorry, Cavenaugh, but that's too gay a world for me. I've got too much work lined up before me. I wish I had time to stop and look at your guns, though. You seem to know something about guns. You've more than you'll need, but nobody can have too many good ones." He put down one of the revolvers regretfully. "I'll drop in to see you in the morning, if you're up."

"I shall be up, all right. I've warned my crowd that I'll cut away before midnight."

"You won't, though," Eastman called back over his shoulder as he hurried down-stairs.

The next morning, while Eastman was dressing, Rollins came in greatly excited.

"I'm a little late, sir. I was stopped by Harry, Mr. Cavenaugh's driver. Mr. Cavenaugh shot himself last night, sir."

Eastman dropped his vest and sat down on his shoe-box. "You're drunk, Rollins," he shouted. "He's going away to-day!"

"Yes, sir. Harry found him this morning. Ah, he's quite dead, sir. Harry's telephoned for the coroner. Harry don't know what to do with the ticket."

Eastman pulled on his coat and ran down the stairway. Cavenaugh's trunks were strapped and piled before the door. Harry was walking up and down the hall with a long green railroad ticket in his hand and a look of complete stupidity on his face.

"What shall I do about this ticket, Mr. Eastman?" he whispered. "And what about his trunks? He had me tell the transfer people to come early. They may be here any minute. Yes, sir. I brought him home in the car last night, before twelve, as cheerful as could be."

"Be quiet, Harry. Where is he?"

"In his bed, sir."

Eastman went into Cavenaugh's sleeping-room. When he came back to the sitting-room, he looked over the writing table; railway folders, time-tables, receipted bills, nothing else. He looked up for the photograph of Cavenaugh's twin brother. There it was, turned to the wall. Eastman took it down and looked at it; a boy in track clothes, half lying in the air, going over the string shoulders first, above the heads of a crowd of lads who were running and cheering. The face was somewhat blurred by the motion and the bright sunlight. Eastman put the picture back, as he found it. Had Cavenaugh entertained his visitor last night, and had the old man been more convincing than usual? "Well, at any rate, he's seen to it that the old man can't establish identity. What a soft lot they are, fellows like poor Cavenaugh!" Eastman thought of his office as a delightful place.

17

THE TELL-TALE HEART

BY EDGAR ALLAN POE

One of America's preeminent poets and authors, Edgar Allan Poe (1809–1849) was born in Boston, Massachusetts. He lived a troubled and tumultuous life plagued by depression, alcoholism, and drug use. Orphaned at age two, he was raised by the wealthy John and Frances Allan of Richmond, Virginia. From 1815 to 1820, Poe and the Allans lived in Scotland and England. Appointed to the U.S. Military Academy at West Point, New York, he deliberately broke multiple rules and was court-martialed and expelled. Thereafter Poe made a tenuous living as a magazine editor and critic, though the 1845 publication of his poem "The Raven," along with multiple macabre short stories, made him a household name. Poe's fiction is part of the literary movement known as Gothic Romanticism, of which "The Tell-Tale Heart" (1843) is considered a masterpiece. He died at age forty, under mysterious circumstances, in Baltimore, Maryland.

Art is long, and Time is fleeting,
And our hearts, though stout and brave,
Still, like muffled drums, are beating
Funeral marches to the grave.

—Longfellow

TRUE!—nervous—very, very dreadfully nervous I had—been and am; but why *will* you say that I am mad? The disease had sharpened my senses—not destroyed—not dulled them. Above all was the sense of hearing acute. I heard all things in the heaven and in the earth. I heard many things in hell. How, then, am I mad? Hearken! and observe how healthily—how calmly I can tell you the whole story.

It is impossible to say how first the idea entered my brain; but once conceived, it haunted me day and night. Object there was none. Passion there was none. I loved the old man. He had never wronged me. He had never given me insult. For his gold I had no desire. I think it was his eye! yes, it was this! He had the eye of a vulture—a pale blue eye, with a film over it. Whenever it fell upon me, my blood ran cold; and so by degrees—very gradually—I made up my mind to take the life of the old man, and thus rid myself of the eye forever.

Now this is the point. You fancy me mad. Madmen know nothing. But you should have seen me. You should have seen how wisely I proceeded—with what caution—with what foresight—with what dissimulation I went to work! I was never kinder to the old man than during the whole week before I killed him. And every night, about midnight, I turned the latch of his door and opened it—oh so gently! And then, when I had made an opening sufficient for my head, I put in a dark lantern, all closed, closed, so that no light shone out, and then I thrust in my head. Oh, you would have laughed to see how cunningly I thrust it in! I moved it slowly—very, very slowly, so that

I might not disturb the old man's sleep. It took me an hour to place my whole head within the opening so far that I could see him as he lay upon his bed. Ha!—would a madman have been so wise as this? And then, when my head was well in the room, I undid the lantern cautiously—oh, so cautiously—cautiously (for the hinges creaked)—I undid it just so much that a single thin ray fell upon the vulture eye. And this I did for seven long nights—every night just at midnight—but I found the eye always closed; and so it was impossible to do the work; for it was not the old man who vexed me, but his Evil Eye. And every morning, when the day broke, I went boldly into the chamber, and spoke courageously to him, calling him by name in a hearty tone, and inquiring how he has passed the night. So you see he would have been a very profound old man, indeed, to suspect that every night, just at twelve, I looked in upon him while he slept. Upon the eighth night I was more than usually cautious in opening the door. A watch's minute hand moves more quickly than did mine. Never before that night had I *felt* the extent of my own powers—of my sagacity. I could scarcely contain my feelings of triumph. To think that there I was, opening the door, little by little, and he not even to dream of my secret deeds or thoughts. I fairly chuckled at the idea; and perhaps he heard me; for he moved on the bed suddenly, as if startled. Now you may think that I drew back—but no. His room was as black as pitch with the thick darkness, (for the shutters were close fastened, through fear of robbers,) and so I knew that he could not see the opening of the door, and I kept pushing it on steadily, steadily. I had my head in, and was about to open the lantern, when my thumb slipped upon the tin fastening, and the old man sprang up in bed, crying out—"Who's there?"

I kept quite still and said nothing. For a whole hour I did not move a muscle, and in the meantime I did not hear him lie down. He was still sitting up in the bed listening;—just as I have done, night after night, hearkening to the death watches in the wall.

Presently I heard a slight groan, and I knew it was the groan of mortal terror. It was not a groan of pain or of grief—oh, no!—it was the low stifled sound that arises from the bottom of the soul when overcharged with awe. I knew the sound well. Many a night, just at midnight, when all the world slept, it has welled up from my own bosom, deepening, with its dreadful echo, the terrors that distracted me. I say I knew it well. I knew what the old man felt, and pitied him, although I chuckled at heart. I knew that he had been lying awake ever since the first slight noise, when he had turned in the bed. His fears had been ever since growing upon him. He had been trying to fancy them causeless, but could not. He had been saying to himself—"It is nothing but the wind in the chimney—it is only a mouse crossing the floor," or "It is merely a cricket which has made a single chirp." Yes, he had been trying to comfort himself with these suppositions: but he had found all in vain. *All in vain*; because Death, in approaching him had stalked with his black shadow before him, and enveloped the victim. And it was the mournful influence of the unperceived shadow that caused him to feel—although he neither saw nor heard—to *feel* the presence of my head within the room.

When I had waited a long time, very patiently, without hearing him lie down, I resolved to open a little—a very, very little crevice in the lantern. So I opened it—you cannot imagine how stealthily, stealthily—until, at length a single dim ray, like the thread of the spider, shot from out the crevice and fell full upon the vulture eye.

It was open—wide, wide open—and I grew furious as I gazed upon it. I saw it with perfect distinctness—all a dull blue, with a hideous veil over it that chilled the very marrow in my bones; but I could see nothing else of the old man's face or person: for I had directed the ray as if by instinct, precisely upon the damned spot.

And have I not told you that what you mistake for madness is but over acuteness of the senses?—now, I say, there came to my ears a low, dull, quick sound, such as a watch makes when enveloped in cotton. I knew that sound well, too. It was the beating of the old man's heart. It increased my fury, as the beating of a drum stimulates the soldier into courage. But even yet I refrained and kept still. I scarcely breathed. I held the lantern motionless. I tried how steadily I could maintain the ray upon the eye. Meantime the hellish tattoo of the heart increased. It grew quicker and quicker, and louder and louder every instant. The old man's terror *must* have been extreme! It grew louder, I say, louder every moment!—do you mark me well? I have told you that I am nervous: so I am. And now at the dead hour of the night, amid the dreadful silence of that old house, so strange a noise as this excited me to uncontrollable terror. Yet, for some minutes longer I refrained and stood still. But the beating grew louder, louder! I thought the heart must burst. And now a new anxiety seized me—the sound would be heard by a neighbor! The old man's hour had come! With a loud yell, I threw open the lantern and leaped into the room. He shrieked once—once only. In an instant I dragged him to the floor, and pulled the heavy bed over him. I then smiled gaily, to find the deed so far done. But, for many minutes, the heart beat on with a muffled sound. This, however, did not vex me; it would not be heard through the wall. At length it ceased. The old man was dead. I removed the bed and examined the corpse. Yes, he was stone, stone dead. I placed my hand upon the heart and held it there many minutes. There was no pulsation. He was stone dead. His eye would trouble me no more.

If still you think me mad, you will think so no longer when I describe the wise precautions I took for the concealment of the body.

The night waned, and I worked hastily, but in silence. First of all I dismembered the corpse. I cut off the head and the arms and the legs.

I then took up three planks from the flooring of the chamber, and deposited all between the scantlings. I then replaced the boards so cleverly, so cunningly, that no human eye—not even *his*—could have detected any thing wrong. There was nothing to wash out—no stain of any kind—no blood-spot whatever. I had been too wary for that. A tub had caught all—ha! ha!

When I had made an end of these labors, it was four o'clock—still dark as midnight. As the bell sounded the hour, there came a knocking at the street door. I went down to open it with a light heart,—for what had I now to fear? There entered three men, who introduced themselves, with perfect suavity, as officers of the police. A shriek had been heard by a neighbor during the night; suspicion of foul play had been aroused; information had been lodged at the police office, and they (the officers) had been deputed to search the premises.

I smiled,—for what had I to fear? I bade the gentlemen welcome. The shriek, I said, was my own in a dream. The old man, I mentioned, was absent in the country. I took my visitors all over the house. I bade them search—search well. I led them, at length, to his chamber. I showed them his treasures, secure, undisturbed. In the enthusiasm of my confidence, I brought chairs into the room, and desired them here to rest from their fatigues, while I myself, in the wild audacity of my perfect triumph, placed my own seat upon the very spot beneath which reposed the corpse of the victim.

The officers were satisfied. My manner had convinced them. I was singularly at ease. They sat, and while I answered cheerily, they chatted of familiar things. But, ere long, I felt myself getting pale and wished them gone. My head ached, and I fancied a ringing in my ears: but still they sat and still they chatted. The ringing became more distinct:—it continued and became more distinct: I talked more freely to get rid of the feeling: but it continued and gained definiteness—until, at length, I found that the noise was not within my ears.

No doubt I now grew very pale;—but I talked more fluently, and with a heightened voice. Yet the sound increased—and what could I do? It was a low, dull, quick sound—much such a sound as a watch makes when enveloped in cotton. I gasped for breath—and yet the officers heard it not. I talked more quickly—more vehemently; but the noise steadily increased. I arose and argued about trifles, in a high key and with violent gesticulations; but the noise steadily increased. Why would they not be gone? I paced the floor to and fro with heavy strides, as if excited to fury by the observations of the men—but the noise steadily increased. Oh God! what could I do? I foamed—I raved—I swore! I swung the chair upon which I had been sitting, and grated it upon the boards, but the noise arose over all and continually increased. It grew louder—louder—louder! And still the men chatted pleasantly, and smiled. Was it possible they heard not? Almighty God!—no, no! They heard!—they suspected!—they *knew!*—they were making a mockery of my horror!—this I thought, and this I think. But anything was better than this agony! Anything was more tolerable than this derision! I could bear those hypocritical smiles no longer! I felt that I must scream or die!—and now—again!—hark! louder! louder! louder! *louder!*—

"Villains!" I shrieked, "dissemble no more! I admit the deed!—tear up the planks!—here, here!—it is the beating of his hideous heart!"

18

THE WIND IN
THE ROSE-BUSH

BY MARY E. WILKINS FREEMAN

*Known especially for her many stories of the macabre and the super-
natural, Mary E. Wilkins Freeman (1852–1930) was born—appropri-
ately enough—on Halloween, October 31, 1852, in Randolph, Massachusetts. A versatile author who began writing poems and stories for
children while still a teenager, she also wrote novels as an adult. Many
of her short stories are set in New England. "The Wind in the Rose-
Bush" was first published in 1902.*

Ford Village has no railroad station, being on the other side of the
river from Porter's Falls, and accessible only by the ford which gives it
its name, and a ferry line.

The ferry-boat was waiting when Rebecca Flint got off the train
with her bag and lunch basket. When she and her small trunk were

safely embarked she sat stiff and straight and calm in the ferry-boat as it shot swiftly and smoothly across stream. There was a horse attached to a light country wagon on board, and he pawed the deck uneasily. His owner stood near, with a wary eye upon him, although he was chewing, with as dully reflective an expression as a cow. Beside Rebecca sat a woman of about her own age, who kept looking at her with furtive curiosity; her husband, short and stout and saturnine, stood near her. Rebecca paid no attention to either of them. She was tall and spare and pale, the type of a spinster, yet with rudimentary lines and expressions of matronhood. She all unconsciously held her shawl, rolled up in a canvas bag, on her left hip, as if it had been a child. She wore a settled frown of dissent at life, but it was the frown of a mother who regarded life as a forward child, rather than as an overwhelming fate.

The other woman continued staring at her; she was mildly stupid, except for an over-developed curiosity which made her at times sharp beyond belief. Her eyes glittered, red spots came on her flaccid cheeks; she kept opening her mouth to speak, making little abortive motions. Finally she could endure it no longer; she nudged Rebecca boldly.

"A pleasant day," said she.

Rebecca looked at her and nodded coldly.

"Yes, very," she assented.

"Have you come far?"

"I have come from Michigan."

"Oh!" said the woman, with awe. "It's a long way," she remarked presently.

"Yes, it is," replied Rebecca, conclusively.

Still the other woman was not daunted; there was something which she determined to know, possibly roused thereto by a vague sense of incongruity in the other's appearance. "It's a long ways to come and leave a family," she remarked with painful slyness.

"I ain't got any family to leave," returned Rebecca shortly.

"Then you ain't—"

"No, I ain't."

"Oh!" said the woman.

Rebecca looked straight ahead at the race of the river.

It was a long ferry. Finally Rebecca herself waxed unexpectedly loquacious. She turned to the other woman and inquired if she knew John Dent's widow who lived in Ford Village. "Her husband died about three years ago," said she, by way of detail.

The woman started violently. She turned pale, then she flushed; she cast a strange glance at her husband, who was regarding both women with a sort of stolid keenness.

"Yes, I guess I do," faltered the woman finally.

"Well, his first wife was my sister," said Rebecca with the air of one imparting important intelligence.

"Was she?" responded the other woman feebly. She glanced at her husband with an expression of doubt and terror, and he shook his head forbiddingly.

"I'm going to see her, and take my niece Agnes home with me," said Rebecca.

Then the woman gave such a violent start that she noticed it.

"What is the matter?" she asked.

"Nothin', I guess," replied the woman, with eyes on her husband, who was slowly shaking his head, like a Chinese toy.

"Is my niece sick?" asked Rebecca with quick suspicion.

"No, she ain't sick," replied the woman with alacrity, then she caught her breath with a gasp.

"When did you see her?"

"Let me see; I ain't seen her for some little time," replied the woman. Then she caught her breath again.

"She ought to have grown up real pretty, if she takes after my sister. She was a real pretty woman," Rebecca said wistfully.

"Yes, I guess she did grow up pretty," replied the woman in a trembling voice.

"What kind of a woman is the second wife?"

The woman glanced at her husband's warning face. She continued to gaze at him while she replied in a choking voice to Rebecca:

"I—guess she's a nice woman," she replied. "I—don't know, I—guess so. I—don't see much of her."

"I felt kind of hurt that John married again so quick," said Rebecca; "but I suppose he wanted his house kept, and Agnes wanted care. I wasn't so situated that I could take her when her mother died. I had my own mother to care for, and I was school-teaching. Now mother has gone, and my uncle died six months ago and left me quite a little property, and I've given up my school, and I've come for Agnes. I guess she'll be glad to go with me, though I suppose her stepmother is a good woman, and has always done for her."

The man's warning shake at his wife was fairly portentous.

"I guess so," said she.

"John always wrote that she was a beautiful woman," said Rebecca.

Then the ferry-boat grated on the shore.

John Dent's widow had sent a horse and wagon to meet her sister-in-law. When the woman and her husband went down the road, on which Rebecca in the wagon with her trunk soon passed them, she said reproachfully:

"Seems as if I'd ought to have told her, Thomas."

"Let her find it out herself," replied the man. "Don't you go to burnin' your fingers in other folks' puddin', Maria."

"Do you s'pose she'll see anything?" asked the woman with a spasmodic shudder and a terrified roll of her eyes.

"See!" returned her husband with stolid scorn. "Better be sure there's anything to see."

"Oh, Thomas, they say—"

"Lord, ain't you found out that what they say is mostly lies?"

"But if it should be true, and she's a nervous woman, she might be scared enough to lose her wits," said his wife, staring uneasily after Rebecca's erect figure in the wagon disappearing over the crest of the hilly road.

"Wits that so easy upset ain't worth much," declared the man. "You keep out of it, Maria."

Rebecca in the meantime rode on in the wagon, beside a flaxen-headed boy, who looked, to her understanding, not very bright. She asked him a question, and he paid no attention. She repeated it, and he responded with a bewildered and incoherent grunt. Then she let him alone, after making sure that he knew how to drive straight.

They had traveled about half a mile, passed the village square, and gone a short distance beyond, when the boy drew up with a sudden Whoa! before a very prosperous-looking house. It had been one of the aboriginal cottages of the vicinity, small and white, with a roof extending on one side over a piazza, and a tiny "L" jutting out in the rear, on the right hand. Now the cottage was transformed by dormer windows, a bay window on the piazzaless side, a carved railing down the front steps, and a modern hard-wood door.

"Is this John Dent's house?" asked Rebecca.

The boy was as sparing of speech as a philosopher. His only response was in flinging the reins over the horse's back, stretching out one foot to the shaft, and leaping out of the wagon, then going around to the rear for the trunk. Rebecca got out and went toward the house. Its white paint had a new gloss; its blinds were an immaculate apple green; the lawn was trimmed as smooth as velvet, and it was dotted with scrupulous groups of hydrangeas and cannas.

"I always understood that John Dent was well-to-do," Rebecca reflected comfortably. "I guess Agnes will have considerable. I've got enough, but it will come in handy for her schooling. She can have advantages."

The boy dragged the trunk up the fine gravel-walk, but before he reached the steps leading up to the piazza, for the house stood on a terrace, the front door opened and a fair, frizzled head of a very large and handsome woman appeared. She held up her black silk skirt, disclosing voluminous ruffles of starched embroidery, and waited for Rebecca. She smiled placidly, her pink, double-chinned face widened and dimpled, but her blue eyes were wary and calculating. She extended her hand as Rebecca climbed the steps.

"This is Miss Flint, I suppose," said she.

"Yes, ma'am," replied Rebecca, noticing with bewilderment a curious expression compounded of fear and defiance on the other's face.

"Your letter only arrived this morning," said Mrs. Dent, in a steady voice. Her great face was a uniform pink, and her china-blue eyes were at once aggressive and veiled with secrecy.

"Yes, I hardly thought you'd get my letter," replied Rebecca. "I felt as if I could not wait to hear from you before I came. I supposed you would be so situated that you could have me a little while without putting you out too much, from what John used to write me about his circumstances, and when I had that money so unexpected I felt as if I must come for Agnes. I suppose you will be willing to give her up. You know she's my own blood, and of course she's no relation to you, though you must have got attached to her. I know from her picture what a sweet girl she must be, and John always said she looked like her own mother, and Grace was a beautiful woman, if she was my sister."

Rebecca stopped and stared at the other woman in amazement and alarm. The great handsome blonde creature stood speechless, livid, gasping, with her hand to her heart, her lips parted in a horrible caricature of a smile.

"Are you sick!" cried Rebecca, drawing near. "Don't you want me to get you some water!"

Then Mrs. Dent recovered herself with a great effort. "It is nothing," she said. "I am subject to—spells. I am over it now. Won't you come in, Miss Flint?"

As she spoke, the beautiful deep-rose colour suffused her face, her blue eyes met her visitor's with the opaqueness of turquoise—with a revelation of blue, but a concealment of all behind.

Rebecca followed her hostess in, and the boy, who had waited quiescently, climbed the steps with the trunk. But before they entered the door a strange thing happened. On the upper terrace close to the piazza-post, grew a great rose-bush, and on it, late in the season though it was, one small red, perfect rose.

Rebecca looked at it, and the other woman extended her hand with a quick gesture. "Don't you pick that rose!" she brusquely cried.

Rebecca drew herself up with stiff dignity.

"I ain't in the habit of picking other folks' roses without leave," said she.

As Rebecca spoke she started violently, and lost sight of her resentment, for something singular happened. Suddenly the rose-bush was agitated violently as if by a gust of wind, yet it was a remarkably still day. Not a leaf of the hydrangea standing on the terrace close to the rose trembled.

"What on earth—" began Rebecca, then she stopped with a gasp at the sight of the other woman's face. Although a face, it gave somehow the impression of a desperately clutched hand of secrecy.

"Come in!" said she in a harsh voice, which seemed to come forth from her chest with no intervention of the organs of speech. "Come into the house. I'm getting cold out here."

"What makes that rose-bush blow so when there isn't any wind?" asked Rebecca, trembling with vague horror, yet resolute.

"I don't see as it is blowing," returned the woman calmly. And as she spoke, indeed, the bush was quiet.

"It was blowing," declared Rebecca.

"It isn't now," said Mrs. Dent. "I can't try to account for everything that blows out-of-doors. I have too much to do."

She spoke scornfully and confidently, with defiant, unflinching eyes, first on the bush, then on Rebecca, and led the way into the house.

"It looked queer," persisted Rebecca, but she followed, and also the boy with the trunk.

Rebecca entered an interior, prosperous, even elegant, according to her simple ideas. There were Brussels carpets, lace curtains, and plenty of brilliant upholstery and polished wood.

"You're real nicely situated," remarked Rebecca, after she had become a little accustomed to her new surroundings and the two women were seated at the tea-table.

Mrs. Dent stared with a hard complacency from behind her silver-plated service. "Yes, I be," said she.

"You got all the things new?" said Rebecca hesitatingly, with a jealous memory of her dead sister's bridal furnishings.

"Yes," said Mrs. Dent; "I was never one to want dead folks' things, and I had money enough of my own, so I wasn't beholden to John. I had the old duds put up at auction. They didn't bring much."

"I suppose you saved some for Agnes. She'll want some of her poor mother's things when she is grown up," said Rebecca with some indignation.

The defiant stare of Mrs. Dent's blue eyes waxed more intense. "There's a few things up garret," said she.

"She'll be likely to value them," remarked Rebecca. As she spoke she glanced at the window. "Isn't it most time for her to be coming home?" she asked.

"Most time," answered Mrs. Dent carelessly; "but when she gets over to Addie Slocum's she never knows when to come home."

"Is Addie Slocum her intimate friend?"

"Intimate as any."

"Maybe we can have her come out to see Agnes when she's living with me," said Rebecca wistfully. "I suppose she'll be likely to be homesick at first."

"Most likely," answered Mrs. Dent.

"Does she call you mother?" Rebecca asked.

"No, she calls me Aunt Emeline," replied the other woman shortly. "When did you say you were going home?"

"In about a week, I thought, if she can be ready to go so soon," answered Rebecca with a surprised look.

She reflected that she would not remain a day longer than she could help after such an inhospitable look and question.

"Oh, as far as that goes," said Mrs. Dent, "it wouldn't make any difference about her being ready. You could go home whenever you felt that you must, and she could come afterward."

"Alone?"

"Why not? She's a big girl now, and you don't have to change cars."

"My niece will go home when I do, and not travel alone; and if I can't wait here for her, in the house that used to be her mother's and my sister's home, I'll go and board somewhere," returned Rebecca with warmth.

"Oh, you can stay here as long as you want to. You're welcome," said Mrs. Dent.

Then Rebecca started. "There she is!" she declared in a trembling, exultant voice. Nobody knew how she longed to see the girl.

"She isn't as late as I thought she'd be," said Mrs. Dent, and again that curious, subtle change passed over her face, and again it settled into that stony impassiveness.

Rebecca stared at the door, waiting for it to open. "Where is she?" she asked presently.

"I guess she's stopped to take off her hat in the entry," suggested Mrs. Dent.

Rebecca waited. "Why don't she come? It can't take her all this time to take off her hat."

For answer Mrs. Dent rose with a stiff jerk and threw open the door.

"Agnes!" she called. "Agnes!" Then she turned and eyed Rebecca. "She ain't there."

"I saw her pass the window," said Rebecca in bewilderment.

"You must have been mistaken."

"I know I did," persisted Rebecca.

"You couldn't have."

"I did. I saw first a shadow go over the ceiling, then I saw her in the glass there"—she pointed to a mirror over the sideboard opposite—"and then the shadow passed the window."

"How did she look in the glass?"

"Little and light-haired, with the light hair kind of tossing over her forehead."

"You couldn't have seen her."

"Was that like Agnes?"

"Like enough; but of course you didn't see her. You've been thinking so much about her that you thought you did."

"You thought *you* did."

"I thought I saw a shadow pass the window, but I must have been mistaken. She didn't come in, or we would have seen her before now. I knew it was too early for her to get home from Addie Slocum's, anyhow."

When Rebecca went to bed Agnes had not returned. Rebecca had resolved that she would not retire until the girl came, but she was very tired, and she reasoned with herself that she was foolish. Besides, Mrs. Dent suggested that Agnes might go to the church social with Addie Slocum. When Rebecca suggested that she be sent for and told that her aunt had come, Mrs. Dent laughed meaningly.

"I guess you'll find out that a young girl ain't so ready to leave a sociable, where there's boys, to see her aunt," said she.

"She's too young," said Rebecca incredulously and indignantly.

"She's sixteen," replied Mrs. Dent; "and she's always been great for the boys."

"She's going to school four years after I get her before she thinks of boys," declared Rebecca.

"We'll see," laughed the other woman.

After Rebecca went to bed, she lay awake a long time listening for the sound of girlish laughter and a boy's voice under her window; then she fell asleep.

The next morning she was down early. Mrs. Dent, who kept no servants, was busily preparing breakfast.

"Don't Agnes help you about breakfast?" asked Rebecca.

"No, I let her lay," replied Mrs. Dent shortly.

"What time did she get home last night?"

"She didn't get home."

"What?"

"She didn't get home. She stayed with Addie. She often does."

"Without sending you word?"

"Oh, she knew I wouldn't worry."

"When will she be home?"

"Oh, I guess she'll be along pretty soon."

Rebecca was uneasy, but she tried to conceal it, for she knew of no good reason for uneasiness. What was there to occasion alarm in the fact of one young girl staying overnight with another? She could not eat much breakfast. Afterward she went out on the little piazza, although her hostess strove furtively to stop her.

"Why don't you go out back of the house? It's real pretty—a view over the river," she said.

"I guess I'll go out here," replied Rebecca. She had a purpose: to watch for the absent girl.

Presently Rebecca came hustling into the house through the sitting-room, into the kitchen where Mrs. Dent was cooking.

"That rose-bush!" she gasped.

Mrs. Dent turned and faced her.

"What of it?"

"It's a-blowing."

"What of it?"

"There isn't a mite of wind this morning."

Mrs. Dent turned with an inimitable toss of her fair head. "If you think I can spend my time puzzling over such nonsense as—" she began, but Rebecca interrupted her with a cry and a rush to the door.

"There she is now!" she cried. She flung the door wide open, and curiously enough a breeze came in and her own gray hair tossed, and a paper blew off the table to the floor with a loud rustle, but there was nobody in sight.

"There's nobody here," Rebecca said.

She looked blankly at the other woman, who brought her rolling-pin down on a slab of pie-crust with a thud.

"I didn't hear anybody," she said calmly.

"*I saw somebody pass that window!*"

"You were mistaken again."

"I *know* I saw somebody."

"You couldn't have. Please shut that door."

Rebecca shut the door. She sat down beside the window and looked out on the autumnal yard, with its little curve of footpath to the kitchen door.

"What smells so strong of roses in this room?" she said presently. She sniffed hard.

"I don't smell anything but these nutmegs."

"It is not nutmeg."

"I don't smell anything else."

"Where do you suppose Agnes is?"

"Oh, perhaps she has gone over the ferry to Porter's Falls with Addie. She often does. Addie's got an aunt over there, and Addie's got a cousin, a real pretty boy."

"You suppose she's gone over there?"

"Mebbe. I shouldn't wonder."

"When should she be home?"

"Oh, not before afternoon."

Rebecca waited with all the patience she could muster. She kept reassuring herself, telling herself that it was all natural, that the other woman could not help it, but she made up her mind that if Agnes did not return that afternoon she should be sent for.

When it was four o'clock she started up with resolution. She had been furtively watching the onyx clock on the sitting-room mantel;

she had timed herself. She had said that if Agnes was not home by that time she should demand that she be sent for. She rose and stood before Mrs. Dent, who looked up coolly from her embroidery.

"I've waited just as long as I'm going to," she said. "I've come 'way from Michigan to see my own sister's daughter and take her home with me. I've been here ever since yesterday—twenty-four hours—and I haven't seen her. Now I'm going to. I want her sent for."

Mrs. Dent folded her embroidery and rose.

"Well, I don't blame you," she said. "It is high time she came home. I'll go right over and get her myself."

Rebecca heaved a sigh of relief. She hardly knew what she had suspected or feared, but she knew that her position had been one of antagonism if not accusation, and she was sensible of relief.

"I wish you would," she said gratefully, and went back to her chair, while Mrs. Dent got her shawl and her little white head-tie. "I wouldn't trouble you, but I do feel as if I couldn't wait any longer to see her," she remarked apologetically.

"Oh, it ain't any trouble at all," said Mrs. Dent as she went out. "I don't blame you; you have waited long enough."

Rebecca sat at the window watching breathlessly until Mrs. Dent came stepping through the yard alone. She ran to the door and saw, hardly noticing it this time, that the rose-bush was again violently agitated, yet with no wind evident elsewhere.

"Where is she?" she cried.

Mrs. Dent laughed with stiff lips as she came up the steps over the terrace. "Girls will be girls," said she. "She's gone with Addie to Lincoln. Addie's got an uncle who's conductor on the train, and lives there, and he got 'em passes, and they're goin' to stay to Addie's Aunt Margaret's a few days. Mrs. Slocum said Agnes didn't have time to come over and ask me before the train went, but she took it on herself to say it would be all right, and—"

"Why hadn't she been over to tell you?" Rebecca was angry, though not suspicious. She even saw no reason for her anger.

"Oh, she was putting up grapes. She was coming over just as soon as she got the black off her hands. She heard I had company, and her hands were a sight. She was holding them over sulphur matches."

"You say she's going to stay a few days?" repeated Rebecca dazedly.

"Yes; till Thursday, Mrs. Slocum said."

"How far is Lincoln from here?"

"About fifty miles. It'll be a real treat to her. Mrs. Slocum's sister is a real nice woman."

"It is goin' to make it pretty late about my goin' home."

"If you don't feel as if you could wait, I'll get her ready and send her on just as soon as I can," Mrs. Dent said sweetly.

"I'm going to wait," said Rebecca grimly.

The two women sat down again, and Mrs. Dent took up her embroidery.

"Is there any sewing I can do for her?" Rebecca asked finally in a desperate way. "If I can get her sewing along some—"

Mrs. Dent arose with alacrity and fetched a mass of white from the closet. "Here," she said, "if you want to sew the lace on this night-gown. I was going to put her to it, but she'll be glad enough to get rid of it. She ought to have this and one more before she goes. I don't like to send her away without some good underclothing."

Rebecca snatched at the little white garment and sewed feverishly.

That night she wakened from a deep sleep a little after midnight and lay a minute trying to collect her faculties and explain to herself what she was listening to. At last she discovered that it was the then popular strains of "The Maiden's Prayer" floating up through the floor from the piano in the sitting-room below. She jumped up, threw a shawl over her nightgown, and hurried downstairs trembling. There was nobody in the sitting-room; the piano was silent. She ran to Mrs. Dent's bedroom and called hysterically:

"Emeline! Emeline!"

"What is it?" asked Mrs. Dent's voice from the bed. The voice was stern, but had a note of consciousness in it.

"Who—who was that playing 'The Maiden's Prayer' in the sitting-room, on the piano?"

"I didn't hear anybody."

"There was some one."

"I didn't hear anything."

"I tell you there was some one. But—*there ain't anybody there.*"

"I didn't hear anything."

"I did—somebody playing 'The Maiden's Prayer' on the piano. Has Agnes got home? I want to know."

"Of course Agnes hasn't got home," answered Mrs. Dent with rising inflection. "Be you gone crazy over that girl? The last boat from Porter's Falls was in before we went to bed. Of course she ain't come."

"I heard—"

"You were dreaming."

"I wasn't; I was broad awake."

Rebecca went back to her chamber and kept her lamp burning all night.

The next morning her eyes upon Mrs. Dent were wary and blazing with suppressed excitement. She kept opening her mouth as if to speak, then frowning, and setting her lips hard. After breakfast she went upstairs, and came down presently with her coat and bonnet.

"Now, Emeline," she said, "I want to know where the Slocums live."

Mrs. Dent gave a strange, long, half-lidded glance at her. She was finishing her coffee.

"Why?" she asked.

"I'm going over there and find out if they have heard anything from her daughter and Agnes since they went away. I don't like what I heard last night."

"You must have been dreaming."

"It don't make any odds whether I was or not. Does she play 'The Maiden's Prayer' on the piano? I want to know."

"What if she does? She plays it a little, I believe. I don't know. She don't half play it, anyhow; she ain't got an ear."

"That wasn't half played last night. I don't like such things happening. I ain't superstitious, but I don't like it. I'm going. Where do the Slocums live?"

"You go down the road over the bridge past the old grist mill, then you turn to the left; it's the only house for half a mile. You can't miss it. It has a barn with a ship in full sail on the cupola."

"Well, I'm going. I don't feel easy."

About two hours later Rebecca returned. There were red spots on her cheeks. She looked wild. "I've been there," she said, "and there isn't a soul at home. Something *has* happened."

"What has happened?"

"I don't know. Something. I had a warning last night. There wasn't a soul there. They've been sent for to Lincoln."

"Did you see anybody to ask?" asked Mrs. Dent with thinly concealed anxiety.

"I asked the woman that lives on the turn of the road. She's stone deaf. I suppose you know. She listened while I screamed at her to know where the Slocums were, and then she said, 'Mrs. Smith don't live here.' I didn't see anybody on the road, and that's the only house. What do you suppose it means?"

"I don't suppose it means much of anything," replied Mrs. Dent coolly. "Mr. Slocum is conductor on the railroad, and he'd be away anyway, and Mrs. Slocum often goes early when he does, to spend the day with her sister in Porter's Falls. She'd be more likely to go away than Addie."

"And you don't think anything has happened?" Rebecca asked with diminishing distrust before the reasonableness of it.

"Land, no!"

Rebecca went upstairs to lay aside her coat and bonnet. But she came hurrying back with them still on.

"Who's been in my room?" she gasped. Her face was pale as ashes.

Mrs. Dent also paled as she regarded her.

"What do you mean?" she asked slowly.

"I found when I went upstairs that—little nightgown of—Agnes's on—the bed, laid out. It was—*laid out*. The sleeves were folded across the bosom, and there was that little red rose between them. Emeline, what is it? Emeline, what's the matter? Oh!"

Mrs. Dent was struggling for breath in great, choking gasps. She clung to the back of a chair. Rebecca, trembling herself so she could scarcely keep on her feet, got her some water.

As soon as she recovered herself Mrs. Dent regarded her with eyes full of the strangest mixture of fear and horror and hostility.

"What do you mean talking so?" she said in a hard voice.

"It *is there*."

"Nonsense. You threw it down and it fell that way."

"It was folded in my bureau drawer."

"It couldn't have been."

"Who picked that red rose?"

"Look on the bush," Mrs. Dent replied shortly.

Rebecca looked at her; her mouth gaped. She hurried out of the room. When she came back her eyes seemed to protrude. (She had in the meantime hastened upstairs, and come down with tottering steps, clinging to the banisters.)

"Now I want to know what all this means?" she demanded.

"What *what* means?"

"The rose is on the bush, and it's gone from the bed in my room! Is this house haunted, or what?"

"I don't know anything about a house being haunted. I don't believe in such things. Be you crazy?" Mrs. Dent spoke with gathering force. The colour flashed back to her cheeks.

"No," said Rebecca shortly. "I ain't crazy yet, but I shall be if this keeps on much longer. I'm going to find out where that girl is before night."

Mrs. Dent eyed her.

"What be you going to do?"

"I'm going to Lincoln."

A faint triumphant smile overspread Mrs. Dent's large face.

"You can't," said she; "there ain't any train."

"No train?"

"No; there ain't any afternoon train from the Falls to Lincoln."

"Then I'm going over to the Slocums' again to-night."

However, Rebecca did not go; such a rain came up as deterred even her resolution, and she had only her best dresses with her. Then in the evening came the letter from the Michigan village which she had left nearly a week ago. It was from her cousin, a single woman, who had come to keep her house while she was away. It was a pleasant unexciting letter enough, all the first of it, and related mostly how she missed Rebecca; how she hoped she was having pleasant weather and kept her health; and how her friend, Mrs. Greenaway, had come to stay with her since she had felt lonesome the first night in the house; how she hoped Rebecca would have no objections to this, although nothing had been said about it, since she had not realized that she might be nervous alone. The cousin was painfully conscientious, hence the letter. Rebecca smiled in spite of her disturbed mind as she read it, then her eye caught the postscript. That was in a different hand, purporting to be written by the friend, Mrs. Hannah Greenaway, informing her that the cousin had fallen down the cellar stairs and broken her hip, and was in a dangerous condition, and begging Rebecca to return at once, as she herself was rheumatic and unable to nurse her properly, and no one else could be obtained.

Rebecca looked at Mrs. Dent, who had come to her room with the letter quite late; it was half-past nine, and she had gone upstairs for the night.

"Where did this come from?" she asked.

"Mr. Amblecrom brought it," she replied.

"Who's he?"

"The postmaster. He often brings the letters that come on the late mail. He knows I ain't anybody to send. He brought yours about your coming. He said he and his wife came over on the ferry-boat with you."

"I remember him," Rebecca replied shortly. "There's bad news in this letter."

Mrs. Dent's face took on an expression of serious inquiry.

"Yes, my Cousin Harriet has fallen down the cellar stairs—they were always dangerous—and she's broken her hip, and I've got to take the first train home to-morrow."

"You don't say so. I'm dreadfully sorry."

"No, you ain't sorry!" said Rebecca, with a look as if she leaped. "You're glad. I don't know why, but you're glad. You've wanted to get rid of me for some reason ever since I came. I don't know why. You're a strange woman. Now you've got your way, and I hope you're satisfied."

"How you talk."

Mrs. Dent spoke in a faintly injured voice, but there was a light in her eyes.

"I talk the way it is. Well, I'm going to-morrow morning, and I want you, just as soon as Agnes Dent comes home, to send her out to me. Don't you wait for anything. You pack what clothes she's got, and don't wait even to mend them, and you buy her ticket. I'll leave the money, and you send her along. She don't have to change cars. You start her off, when she gets home, on the next train!"

"Very well," replied the other woman. She had an expression of covert amusement.

"Mind you do it."

"Very well, Rebecca."

Rebecca started on her journey the next morning. When she arrived, two days later, she found her cousin in perfect health. She found, moreover, that the friend had not written the postscript in the cousin's letter. Rebecca would have returned to Ford Village the next morning, but the fatigue and nervous strain had been too much for her. She was not able to move from her bed. She had a species of low fever induced by anxiety and fatigue. But she could write, and she did, to the Slocums, and she received no answer. She also wrote to Mrs. Dent; she even sent numerous telegrams, with no response. Finally she wrote to the postmaster, and an answer arrived by the first possible mail. The letter was short, curt, and to the purpose. Mr. Amblecrom, the postmaster, was a man of few words, and especially wary as to his expressions in a letter.

"Dear madam," he wrote, "your favour rec'ed. No Slocums in Ford's Village. All dead. Addie ten years ago, her mother two years later, her father five. House vacant. Mrs. John Dent said to have neglected stepdaughter. Girl was sick. Medicine not given. Talk of taking action. Not enough evidence. House said to be haunted. Strange sights and sounds. Your niece, Agnes Dent, died a year ago, about this time.

"Yours truly,

"THOMAS AMBLECROM."

SOURCES

"The Crime of Micah Rood" by Elia W. Peattie, originally published in *Cosmopolitan Magazine*, Schlicht & Field, New York, January 1888.

Elia W. Peattie with her son

"The Devil and Tom Walker" by Washington Irving, originally published in *Tales of a Traveller* by Geoffrey Crayon, Gent. (Irving's pseudonym), H. C. Cary & I. Lee, Philadelphia, 1824.

Washington Irving, circa 1855

"An Occurrence at Owl Creek Bridge" by Ambrose Bierce, originally published in the *San Francisco Examiner*, July 13, 1890.

Ambrose Bierce

"The Snow-Image: A Childish Miracle" by Nathaniel Hawthorne, first published in *The Snow-Image, and Other Twice-Told Tales* by Nathaniel Hawthorne, Ticknor, Reed & Fields, Boston, 1852.

Nathaniel Hawthorne, 1851

"A Ghost of the Sierras" by Bret Harte, first published in *The Writings of Bret Harte: Tales of the Argonauts*, Houghton, Mifflin & Company, Boston, 1876.

Bret Harte, 1872

"The Lady's Maid's Bell" by Edith Wharton, first published in *Scribner's Magazine*, New York, November 1902.

Edith Wharton

"A Ghost Story" by Mark Twain, first published in *Mark Twain's Sketches, New and Old*, American Publishing Company, Hartford, CT, 1875.

Mark Twain, 1867

"The Night Call" by Henry van Dyke, first published in *The Unknown Quantity* by Henry van Dyke, Harper & Brothers, New York, 1913.

Henry van Dyke, 1920

"Tom Toothacre's Ghost Story" by Harriet Beecher Stowe, first published in *Sam Lawson's Oldtown Fireside Stories* by Harriet Beecher Stowe, Houghton, Mifflin & Company, Boston, 1871.

Harriet Beecher Stowe, 1880

"A Strange Story from the Coast" by Rebecca Harding Davis, first published in *Lippincott's Monthly Magazine: A Popular Journal of General Literature*, Philadelphia, January 1879.

Rebecca Harding Davis

"The Woman at Seven Brothers" by Wilbur Daniel Steele, first published in *Harper's Magazine*, New York, December 1908.

Wilbur Daniel Steele

"The Furnished Room" by O. Henry, first published in the *New York Sunday World* magazine, August 14, 1904.

William Sydney Porter, pseudonym O. Henry

"The Cross-Roads" by Amy Lowell, first published in *A Dome of Many-Coloured Glass*, MacMillan Company, New York, 1916.

Amy Lowell, 1916

"Jean-ah Poquelin" by George Washington Cable, first published in *Old Creole Days: A Story of Creole Life* by George Washington Cable, Charles Scribner's Sons, New York, 1879.

George Washington Cable, 1898

"Mistress Marian's Light" by Gertrude Morton, first published in *New England Magazine*, Boston, 1889.

The cover of *New England Magazine*

"Consequences" by Willa Cather, first published in *McClure's Magazine*, New York, November 1915.

Willa Cather

"The Tell-Tale Heart" by Edgar Allan Poe, first published in *The Pioneer: A Literary and Critical Magazine*, J. R. Lowell and R. Carter, Editors and Proprietors, Leland & Whiting, Boston, January–March 1843.

Edgar Allan Poe

"The Wind in the Rose-Bush" by Mary E. Wilkins Freeman, first published in *The Wind in the Rose-Bush and Other Stories of the Supernatural*, Doubleday, Page & Company, New York, 1902.

Mary E. Wilkins Freeman

ACKNOWLEDGMENTS

Regardless whose name appears on the cover, every book is a collaborative effort involving many hands, and this little volume is no exception. My heartfelt thanks:

To Keith Wallman at Lyons Press, who has guided this project with professionalism, patience, and good humor.

To production editor Lynn Zelem, whose skill and good humor have made the review process for copy and page proofs smooth and painless.

To my former colleague, longtime friend, and editor and writer par excellence Tom McCarthy, for valuable help and advice.

To Nick Lyons, for first opening the doors into the wonderful world of publishing. If not for Nick, none of this would ever have happened.

And, last but certainly not least, to Eileen, without whom none of this would be possible.

ABOUT THE EDITOR

Bill Bowers is a freelance editor and writer. He lives in rural New England with his wife and longtime collaborator, Eileen Bowers.